D1527305

The Collection of
Jerome Fanger
Treasurer
Board of Library Trustees
2009-2018

DAMON RUNYON
FAVORITES

Damon Runyon
FAVORITES

With a Foreword by

WALTER WINCHELL

The American Reprint Company
MATTITUCK

Copyright © 1929, 1930, 1931, 1932, 1933, 1934, 1935
By Damon Runyon

Reprinted 1976 by Special Arrangement

International Standard Book Number 0-89190-440-9

To order contact
AMERICAN REPRINT COMPANY
Box 1200
Mattituck, New York 11952

Manufactured in the United States of America

CONTENTS

FOREWORD

Ask any of us who jot down notes for the various gazettes in New York our idea of a big-time, first-rate, Grade-A reporter—and eleven times out of ten, the retort will be "Damon Runyon!"

Because, among other things, Runyon is the most exciting and spellbinding of historians—whether his assignment is the Kentucky Derby, the Madison Square Garden farces, the current murder mystery, or the sitchee-ay-shun in the Orient.

Damon, I mean to report, (*oh, get your story in the first paragraph, Winchell!*) possesses all the necessary attributes that go to make the guy the rest of us on the staff wish we were. He has that manner about him, for one thing. He looks like a star newspaperman—not anything like the counterfeiters you've witnessed in the editorial rooms of the newspaper in the kodak amusements. (*I don't mean you, Lee Tracy!*)

He was content, until recently, it appears, to rest on his laurels as a sports chronicler for the more widely read journals throughout the country. When you discussed sports and sports experts—you naturally discussed Damon Runyon. You'd think a fellow who enjoyed that distinction would let it go at that.

Then suddenly like an old Dempsey left hook—he startled his best critics and severest friends with magazine articles. The sort that not only were read and enjoyed, but the sort that tilted circulation. From these delightfully comical stories about Broadway, the prize ring and the banditti—embroidered in a language rich with style—came a book by Damon called "Guys and Dolls."

Yet—with all the grand pieces Damon has done for the editors—I suspect he will never be forgotten for his thrilling document on Sande, the jockey of his time. The one line in it that always "got" me was "Gimme a handy guy like Sande bootin' those winners home!" It has the tempo of the winner in the race. But so has everything he paragraphs.

For the benefit of future historians, Damon Runyon is a coffee fiend. From ten to fifteen cups at a sitting. His one weakness is snappy clothes, and there is a race horse bearing his tag, which, however, isn't as fleet as the one christened for his lovely bride, Patrice.

He actually makes wagers on the ring fighters he picks to win in his columns. (No wonder, he has so many sidelines. Probably to pay off!) He once observed: "If you have two friends—on Broadway—consider yourself a success!" From that manner of figuring—then Runyon is a millionaire.

The outlaws on both coasts, who respect his opinions on sports, also respect his articles on crime. The lethal sock he packs in his pillars of pithy patter for the paper—has driven mobsters out of New York faster than an extra girl in Hollywood says "Yes."

His initial screen achievement was an incessantly robust

laugh-provoker named "Lady for a Day." * But this is the lustiest of the laughs about that grand flicker. An Academy in Hollywood awards prizes annually for the best this and that. "Lady for a Day" copped three of them. One prize went to the director—another to the adapters—and the third to the star. Damon Runyon, the author, didn't rate a nod! Haw!!!!!

Then came his "Little Miss Marker" which the critics acclaimed. Don't tell anybody you missed it. Because you'll be listed among the clunks.

And now, frankly, I think I've been on too long. The next act is much better.

WALTER WINCHELL

* "Lady for a Day" the picture mentioned by Mr. Winchell, and one of the most popular in history, was founded on the story "Madame La Gimp."

DAMON RUNYON
FAVORITES

BUTCH MINDS THE BABY

ONE evening along about seven o'clock I am sitting in Mindy's restaurant putting on the gefillte fish, which is a dish I am very fond of, when in comes three parties from Brooklyn wearing caps as follows: Harry the Horse, Little Isadore and Spanish John.

Now these parties are not such parties as I will care to have much truck with, because I often hear rumors about them that are very discreditable, even if the rumors are not true. In fact, I hear that many citizens of Brooklyn will be very glad indeed to see Harry the Horse, Little Isadore and Spanish John move away from there, as they are always doing something that is considered a knock to the community, such as robbing people, or maybe shooting or stabbing them, and throwing pineapples, and carrying on generally.

I am really much surprised to see these parties on Broadway, as it is well known that the Broadway coppers just naturally love to shove such parties around, but here they are in Mindy's, and there I am, so of course I give them a very large hello, as I never wish to seem inhospitable, even to Brooklyn parties. Right away they come over to my table and sit down, and Little Isadore reaches out and spears himself a big hunk of my gefillte fish with his fingers, but I overlook this, as I am using the only knife on the table.

Then they all sit there looking at me without saying anything, and the way they look at me makes me very nervous indeed. Finally I figure that maybe they are a little embarrassed being in a high-class spot such as Mindy's, with legitimate people around and about, so I say to them, very polite:

"It is a nice night."

"What is nice about it?" asks Harry the Horse, who is a thin man with a sharp face and sharp eyes.

Well, now that it is put up to me in this way, I can see there is nothing so nice about the night, at that, so I try to think of something else jolly to say, while Little Isadore keeps spearing at my gefillte fish with his fingers, and Spanish John nabs one of my potatoes.

"Where does Big Butch live?" Harry the Horse asks.

"Big Butch?" I say, as if I never hear the name before in my life, because in this man's town it is never a good idea to answer any question without thinking it over, as some time you may give the right answer to the wrong guy, or the wrong answer to the right guy. "Where does Big Butch live?" I ask them again.

"Yes, where does he live?" Harry the Horse says, very impatient. "We wish you to take us to him."

"Now wait a minute, Harry," I say, and I am now more nervous than somewhat. "I am not sure I remember the exact house Big Butch lives in, and furthermore I am not sure Big Butch will care to have me bringing people to see him, especially three at a time, and especially from Brooklyn. You know Big Butch has a very bad disposition, and there is no telling what he may say to me if he does not like the idea of me taking you to him."

"Everything is very kosher," Harry the Horse says. "You

need not be afraid of anything whatever. We have a business proposition for Big Butch. It means a nice score for him, so you take us to him at once, or the chances are I will have to put the arm on somebody around here."

Well, as the only one around there for him to put the arm on at this time seems to be me, I can see where it will be good policy for me to take these parties to Big Butch, especially as the last of my gefillte fish is just going down Little Isadore's gullet, and Spanish John is finishing up my potatoes, and is donking a piece of rye bread in my coffee, so there is nothing more for me to eat.

So I lead them over into West Forty-ninth Street, near Tenth Avenue, where Big Butch lives on the ground floor of an old brownstone-front house, and who is sitting out on the stoop but Big Butch himself. In fact, everybody in the neighborhood is sitting out on the front stoops over there, including women and children, because sitting out on the front stoops is quite a custom in this section.

Big Butch is peeled down to his undershirt and pants, and he has no shoes on his feet, as Big Butch is a guy who likes his comfort. Furthermore, he is smoking a cigar, and laid out on the stoop beside him on a blanket is a little baby with not much clothes on. This baby seems to be asleep, and every now and then Big Butch fans it with a folded newspaper to shoo away the mosquitoes that wish to nibble on the baby. These mosquitoes come across the river from the Jersey side on hot nights and they seem to be very fond of babies.

"Hello, Butch," I say, as we stop in front of the stoop.

"Sh-h-h-h!" Butch says, pointing at the baby, and making more noise with his shush than an engine blowing off steam. Then he gets up and tiptoes down to the sidewalk where we are standing, and I am hoping that Butch feels all right, because when Butch does not feel so good he is apt to be very short with one and all. He is a guy of maybe six foot two and a couple of feet wide, and he has big hairy hands and a mean look.

In fact, Big Butch is known all over this man's town as a guy you must not monkey with in any respect, so it takes plenty of weight off of me when I see that he seems to know the parties from Brooklyn, and nods at them very friendly, especially at Harry the Horse. And right away Harry states a most surprising proposition to Big Butch.

It seems that there is a big coal company which has an office in an old building down in West Eighteenth Street, and in this office is a safe, and in this safe is the company pay-roll of twenty thousand dollars cash money. Harry the Horse knows the money is there because a personal friend of his who is the paymaster for the company puts it there late this very afternoon.

It seems that the paymaster enters into a dicker with Harry the Horse and Litte Isadore and Spanish John for them to slug him while is carrying the pay roll from the bank to the office in the afternoon, but something happens that they miss connections on the exact spot, so the pay-master has to carry the sugar on to the office without being slugged, and there it is now in two fat bundles.

Personally it seems to me as I listen to Harry's story that the paymaster must be a very dishonest character to be making deals to hold still while he is being slugged and the company's sugar taken away from him, but of course it is none of my business, so I take no part in the conversation.

Well, it seems that Harry the Horse and Little Isadore and Spanish John wish to get the money out of the safe, but none of them knows anything about opening safes, and while they are standing around over in Brooklyn talking over what is to be done in this emergency Harry suddenly remembers that Big Butch is once in the business of opening safes for a living.

In fact, I hear afterwards that Big Butch is considered the best safe opener east of the Mississippi River in his day, but the law finally takes to sending him to Sing Sing for opening these safes, and after he is in and out of Sing Sing three different times for opening safes Butch gets sick and tired of the place, especially as they pass what is called the Baumes Law in New York, which is a law that says if a guy is sent to Sing Sing four times hand running, he must stay there the rest of his life, without any argument about it.

So Big Butch gives up opening safes for a living, and goes into business in a small way, such as running beer, and handling a little Scotch now and then, and becomes an honest citizen. Furthermore, he marries one of the neighbor's children over on the West Side by the name of Mary Murphy, and I judge the baby on this stoop comes of this marriage between Big Butch and Mary because I can see that it is a very homely baby, indeed. Still, I never see many babies that I consider rose geraniums for looks, anyway.

Well, it finally comes out that the idea of Harry the Horse and Little Isadore and Spanish John is to get Big Butch to open the coal company's safe and take the pay-roll money out, and they are willing to give him fifty per cent of the money for his bother, taking fifty per cent for themselves for finding the plant, and paying all the overhead,

such as the paymaster, out of their bit, which strikes me
as a pretty fair sort of deal for Big Butch. But Butch only
shakes his head.

"It is old-fashioned stuff," Butch says. "Nobody opens
pete boxes for a living any more. They make the boxes too
good, and they are all wired up with alarms and are a lot
of trouble generally. I am in a legitimate business now and
going along. You boys know I cannot stand another fall,
what with being away three times already, and in addition
to this I must mind the baby. My old lady goes to Mrs.
Clancy's wake tonight up in the Bronx, and the chances are
she will be there all night, as she is very fond of wakes,
so I must mind little John Ignatius Junior."

"Listen, Butch," Harry the Horse says, "this is a very soft
pete. It is old-fashioned, and you can open it with a tooth-
pick. There are no wires on it, because they never put more
than a dime in it before in years. It just happens they have
to put the twenty G's in it tonight because my pal the paymaster makes it a point not to get back from the jug with
the scratch in time to pay off today, especially after he sees
we miss out on him. It is the softest touch you will ever
know, and where can a guy pick up ten G's like this?"

I can see that Big Butch is thinking the ten G's over very
seriously, at that, because in these times nobody can afford
to pass up ten G's, especially a guy in the beer business,
which is very, very tough just now. But finally he shakes
his head again and says like this:

"No," he says, "I must let it go, because I must mind
the baby. My old lady is very, very particular about this,
and I dast not leave little John Ignatius Junior for a minute.
If Mary comes home and finds I am not minding the baby

she will put the blast on me plenty. I like to turn a few honest bobs now and then as well as anybody, but," Butch says, "John Ignatius Junior comes first with me."

Then he turns away and goes back to the stoop as much as to say he is through arguing, and sits down beside John Ignatius Junior again just in time to keep a mosquito from carrying off one of John's legs. Anybody can see that Big Butch is very fond of this baby, though personally I will not give you a dime a dozen for babies, male and female.

Well, Harry the Horse and Little Isadore and Spanish John are very much disappointed, and stand around talking among themselves, and paying no attention to me, when all of a sudden Spanish John, who never has much to say up to this time, seems to have a bright idea. He talks to Harry and Isadore, and they get all pleasured up over what he has to say, and finally Harry goes to Big Butch.

"Sh-h-h-h!" Big Butch says, pointing to the baby as Harry opens his mouth.

"Listen, Butch," Harry says in a whisper, "we can take the baby with us, and you can mind it and work, too."

"Why," Big Butch whispers back, "this is quite an idea indeed. Let us go into the house and talk things over."

So he picks up the baby and leads us into his joint, and gets out some pretty fair beer, though it is needled a little, at that, and we sit around the kitchen chewing the fat in whispers. There is a crib in the kitchen, and Butch puts the baby in this crib, and it keeps on snoozing away first rate while we are talking. In fact, it is sleeping so sound that I am commencing to figure that Butch must give it some of the needled beer he is feeding us, because I am feeling a little dopey myself.

Finally Butch says that as long as he can take John Ignatius Junior with him he sees no reason why he shall not go and open the safe for them, only he says he must have five per cent more to put in the baby's bank when he gets back, so as to round himself up with his ever-loving wife in case of a beef from her over keeping the baby out in the night air. Harry the Horse says he considers this extra five per cent a little strong, but Spanish John, who seems to be a very square guy, says that after all it is only fair to cut the baby in if it is to be with them when they are making the score, and Little Isadore seems to think this is all right, too. So Harry the Horse gives in, and says five per cent it is.

Well, as they do not wish to start out until after midnight, and as there is plenty of time, Big Butch gets out some more needled beer, and then he goes looking for the tools with which he opens safes, and which he says he does not see since the day John Ignatius Junior is born and he gets them out to build the crib.

Now this is a good time for me to bid one and all farewell, and what keeps me there is something I cannot tell you to this day, because personally I never before have any idea of taking part in a safe opening, especially with a baby, as I consider such actions very dishonorable. When I come to think things over afterwards, the only thing I can figure is the needled beer, but I wish to say I am really very much surprised at myself when I find myself in a taxicab along about one o'clock in the morning with these Brooklyn parties and Big Butch and the baby.

Butch has John Ignatius Junior rolled up in a blanket, and John is still pounding his ear. Butch has a satchel of tools, and what looks to me like a big flat book, and just before we leave the house Butch hands me a package and tells me to be very careful with it. He gives Little Isadore a smaller package, which Isadore shoves into his pistol pocket, and when Isadore sits down in the taxi something goes wa-wa, like a sheep, and Big Butch becomes very indignant because it seems Isadore is sitting on John Ignatius Junior's doll, which says "Mamma" when you squeeze it.

It seems Big Butch figures that John Ignatius Junior may wish something to play with in case he wakes up, and it is a good thing for Little Isadore that the mamma doll is not squashed so it cannot say "Mamma" any more, or the chances are Little Isadore will get a good bust in the snoot.

We let the taxicab go a block away from the spot we are headed for in West Eighteenth Street, between Seventh and Eighth Avenues, and walk the rest of the way two by two. I walk with Big Butch, carrying my package, and Butch is lugging the baby and his satchel and the flat thing that looks like a book. It is so quiet down in West Eighteenth Street at such an hour that you can hear yourself think, and in fact I hear myself thinking very plain that I am a big sap to be on a job like this, especially with a baby, but I keep going just the same, which shows you what a very big sap I am, indeed.

There are very few people in West Eighteenth Street when we get there, and one of them is a fat guy who is leaning against a building almost in the center of the block, and who takes a walk for himself as soon as he sees us. It seems that this fat guy is the watchman at the coal company's office and is also a personal friend of Harry the Horse, which is why he takes the walk when he sees us coming.

It is agreed before we leave Big Butch's house that Harry the Horse and Spanish John are to stay outside the place as lookouts, while Big Butch is inside opening the safe, and that Little Isadore is to go with Butch. Nothing whatever is said by anybody about where I am to be at any time, and I can see that, no matter where I am, I will still be an outsider, but, as Butch gives me the package to carry, I figure he wishes me to remain with him.

It is no bother at all getting into the office of the coal company, which is on the ground floor, because it seems the watchman leaves the front door open, this watchman being a most obliging guy, indeed. In fact he is so obliging that by and by he comes back and lets Harry the Horse and Spanish John tie him up good and tight, and stick a handkerchief in his mouth and chuck him in an areaway next to the office, so nobody will think he has anything to do with opening the safe in case anybody comes around asking.

The office looks out on the street, and the safe that Harry the Horse and Little Isadore and Spanish John wish Big Butch to open is standing up against the rear wall of the office facing the street windows. There is one little electric light burning very dim over the safe so that when anybody walks past the place outside, such as a watchman, they can look in through the window and see the safe at all times, unless they are blind. It is not a tall safe, and it is not a big safe, and I can see Big Butch grin when he sees it, so I figure this safe is not much of a safe, just as Harry the Horse claims.

Well, as soon as Big Butch and the baby and Little Isadore and me get into the office, Big Butch steps over to the safe and unfolds what I think is the big flat book, and what is it but a sort of screen painted on one side to look exactly like the front of a safe. Big Butch stands this screen up on the floor in front of the real safe, leaving plenty of space in between, the idea being that the screen will keep anyone passing in the street outside from seeing Butch while he is opening the safe, because when a man is opening a safe he needs all the privacy he can get.

Big Butch lays John Ignatius Junior down on the floor on the blanket behind the phony safe front and takes his tools out of the satchel and starts to work opening the safe, while Little Isadore and me get back in a corner where it is dark, because there is not room for all of us back of the screen. However, we can see what Big Butch is doing, and I wish to say while I never before see a professional safe opener at work, and never wish to see another, this Butch handles himself like a real artist.

He starts drilling into the safe around the combination lock, working very fast and very quiet, when all of a sudden what happens but John Ignatius Junior sits up on the blanket and lets out a squall. Naturally this is most disquieting to me, and personally I am in favor of beaning John Ignatius Junior with something to make him keep still, because I am nervous enough as it is. But the squalling does not seem to bother Big Butch. He lays down his tools and picks up John Ignatius Junior and starts whispering, "There, there, there, my itty oddleums. Da-dad is here."

Well, this sounds very nonsensical to me in such a situation, and it makes no impression whatever on John Ignatius Junior. He keeps on squalling, and I judge he is squalling pretty loud because I see Harry the Horse and Spanish John both walk past the window and look in very anxious. Big Butch jiggles John Ignatius Junior up and down and keeps whispering baby talk to him, which sounds very undignified coming from a high-class safe opener, and finally Butch whispers to me to hand him the package I am carrying.

He opens the package, and what is in it but a baby's nursing bottle full of milk. Moreover, there is a little tin stew pan, and Butch hands the pan to me and whispers to me to find a water tap somewhere in the joint and fill the pan with water. So I go stumbling around in the dark in a room behind the office and bark my shins several times before I find a tap and fill the pan. I take it back to Big Butch, and he squats there with the baby on one arm, and gets a tin of what is called canned heat out of the package, and lights this canned heat with his cigar lighter, and starts heating the pan of water with the nursing bottle in it.

Big Butch keeps sticking his finger in the pan of water while it is heating, and by and by he puts the rubber nipple of the nursing bottle in his mouth and takes a pull at it to see if the milk is warm enough, just like I see dolls who have babies do. Apparently the milk is okay, as Butch hands the bottle to John Ignatius Junior, who grabs hold of it with both hands and starts sucking on the business end. Naturally he has to stop squalling, and Big Butch goes to work on the safe again, with John Ignatius Junior sitting on the blanket, pulling on the bottle and looking wiser than a treeful of owls.

It seems the safe is either a tougher job than anybody figures, or Big Butch's tools are not so good, what with being old and rusty and used for building baby cribs, because he breaks a couple of drills and works himself up into quite a sweat without getting anywhere. Butch afterwards explains to me that he is one of the first guys in this country to open safes without explosives, but he says to do this work properly you have to know the safes so as to drill to the tumblers of the lock just right, and it seems that this particular safe is a new type to him, even if it is old, and he is out of practice.

Well, in the meantime John Ignatius Junior finishes his bottle and starts mumbling again, and Big Butch gives him a tool to play with, and finally Butch needs this tool and tries to take it away from John Ignatius Junior, and the baby lets out such a squawk that Butch has to let him keep it until he can sneak it away from him, and this causes more delay.

Finally Big Butch gives up trying to drill the safe open, and he whispers to us that he will have to put a little shot in it to loosen up the lock, which is all right with us, because we are getting tired of hanging around and listening to John Ignatius Junior's glug-glugging. As far as I am personally concerned, I am wishing I am home in bed.

Well, Butch starts pawing through his satchel looking for something and it seems that what he is looking for is a little bottle of some kind of explosive with which to shake the lock on the safe up some, and at first he cannot find this bottle, but finally he discovers that John Ignatius Junior has it and is gnawing at the cork, and Butch has quite a battle making John Ignatius Junior give it up.

Anyway, he fixes the explosive in one of the holes he drills near the combination lock on the safe, and then he puts in a fuse, and just before he touches off the fuse Butch picks up John Ignatius Junior and hands him to Little Isadore, and tells us to go into the room behind the office. John Ignatius Junior does not seem to care for Little Isadore, and I do not blame him, at that, because he starts to squirm around quite some in Isadore's arms and lets out a squall, but all of a sudden he becomes very quiet indeed, and, while I am not able to prove it, something tells me that Little Isadore has his hand over John Ignatius Junior's mouth.

Well, Big Butch joins us right away in the back room, and sound comes out of John Ignatius Junior again as Butch takes him from Little Isadore, and I am thinking that it is a good thing for Isadore that the baby cannot tell Big Butch what Isadore does to him.

"I put in just a little bit of a shot," Big Butch says, "and it will not make any more noise than snapping your fingers."

But a second later there is a big whoom from the office, and the whole joint shakes, and John Ignatius Junior laughs right out loud. The chances are he thinks it is the Fourth of July.

"I guess maybe I put in too big a charge," Big Butch says, and then he rushes into the office with Little Isadore and me after him, and John Ignatius Junior still laughing very heartily for a small baby. The door of the safe is swinging loose, and the whole joint looks somewhat wrecked, but Big Butch loses no time in getting his dukes into the safe and grabbing out two big bundles of cash money, which he sticks inside his shirt.

As we go into the street Harry the Horse and Spanish

John come running up much excited, and Harry says to Big Butch like this:

"What are you trying to do," he says, "wake up the whole town?"

"Well," Butch says, "I guess maybe the charge is too strong, at that, but nobody seems to be coming, so you and Spanish John walk over to Eighth Avenue, and the rest of us will walk to Seventh, and if you go along quiet, like people minding their own business, it will be all right."

But I judge Little Isadore is tired of John Ignatius Junior's company by this time, because he says he will go with Harry the Horse and Spanish John, and this leaves Big Butch and John Ignatius Junior and me to go the other way. So we start moving, and all of a sudden two cops come tearing around the corner toward which Harry and Isadore and Spanish John are going. The chances are the cops hear the earthquake Big Butch lets off and are coming to investigate.

But the chances are, too, that if Harry the Horse and the other two keep on walking along very quietly like Butch tells them to, the coppers will pass them up entirely, because it is not likely that coppers will figure anybody to be opening safes with explosives in this neighborhood. But the minute Harry the Horse sees the coppers he loses his nut, and he outs with the old equalizer and starts blasting away, and what does Spanish John do but get his out, too, and open up.

The next thing anybody knows, the two coppers are down on the ground with slugs in them, but other coppers are coming from every which direction, blowing whistles and doing a little blasting themselves, and there is plenty

of excitement, especially when the coppers who are not
chasing Harry the Horse and Little Isadore and Spanish
John start poking around the neighborhood and find
Harry's pal, the watchman, all tied up nice and tight where
Harry leaves him, and the watchman explains that some
scoundrels blow open the safe he is watching.

All this time Big Butch and me are walking in the other
direction toward Seventh Avenue, and Big Butch has John
Ignatius in his arms, and John Ignatius is now squalling
very loud, indeed. The chances are he is still thinking of
the big whoom back there which tickles him so and is
wishing to hear some more whooms. Anyway, he is beating
his own best record for squalling, and as we go walking
along Big Butch says to me like this:

"I dast not run," he says, "because if any coppers see me
running they will start popping at me and maybe hit John
Ignatius Junior, and besides running will joggle the milk
up in him and make him sick. My old lady always warns
me never to joggle John Ignatius Junior when he is full
of milk."

"Well, Butch," I say, "there is no milk in me, and I do
not care if I am joggled up, so if you do not mind, I will
start doing a piece of running at the next corner."

But just then around the corner of Seventh Avenue toward which we are headed comes two or three coppers
with a big fat sergeant with them, and one of the coppers,
who is half out of breath as if he has been doing plenty of
sprinting, is explaining to the sergeant that somebody
blows a safe down the street and shoots a couple of coppers
in the getaway.

And there is Big Butch, with John Ignatius Junior in his arms and twenty G's in his shirt front and a tough record behind him, walking right up to them.

I am feeling very sorry, indeed, for Big Butch, and very sorry for myself, too, and I am saying to myself that if I get out of this I will never associate with anyone but ministers of the gospel as long as I live. I can remember thinking that I am getting a better break than Butch, at that, because I will not have to go to Sing Sing for the rest of my life, like him, and I also remember wondering what they will give John Ignatius Junior, who is still tearing off these squalls, with Big Butch saying, "There, there, there, Daddy's itty woogleums." Then I hear one of the coppers say to the fat sergeant:

"We better nail these guys. They may be in on this."

"Well, I can see it is good-by to Butch and John Ignatius Junior and me, as the fat sergeant steps up to Big Butch, but instead of putting the arm on Butch, the fat sergeant only points at John Ignatius Junior and asks very sympathetic:

"Teeth?"

"No," Big Butch says. "Not teeth. Colic. I just get the doctor here out of bed to do something for him, and we are going to a drug store to get some medicine."

Well, naturally I am very much surprised at this statement, because of course I am not a doctor, and if John Ignatius Junior has colic it serves him right, but I am only hoping they do not ask for my degree, when the fat sergeant says:

"Too bad. I know what it is. I got three of them at home. But," he says, "it acts more like it is teeth than colic."

Then as Big Butch and John Ignatius Junior and me go on about our business I hear the fat sergeant say to the copper, very sarcastic:

"Yea, of course a guy is out blowing safes with a baby in his arms! You will make a great detective, you will!"

I do not see Big Butch for several days after I learn that Harry the Horse and Little Isadore and Spanish John get back to Brooklyn all right, except they are a little nicked up here and there from the slugs the coppers toss at them, while the coppers they clip are not damaged so very much. Furthermore, the chances are I will not see Big Butch for several years, if it is left to me, but he comes looking for me one night, and he seems to be all pleasured up about something.

"Say," Big Butch says to me, "you know I never give a copper credit for knowing any too much about anything, but I wish to say that this fat sergeant we run into the other night is a very, very smart duck. He is right about it being teeth that is ailing John Ignatius Junior, for what happens yesterday but John cuts his first tooth."

LILLIAN

What I always say is that Wilbur Willard is nothing but a very lucky guy, because what is it but luck that has him teetering along Forty-ninth Street one cold snowy morning when Lillian is mer-owing around the sidewalk looking for her mamma?

And what is it but luck that has Wilbur Willard all

mulled up to a million, what with him having been sitting out a few seidels of Scotch with a friend by the name of Haggerty in an apartment over in Fifty-ninth Street? Because if Wilbur Willard is not mulled up he will see Lillian is nothing but a little black cat, and give her plenty of room, for everybody knows that black cats are terribly bad luck, even when they are only kittens.

But being mulled up like I tell you, things look very different to Wilbur Willard, and he does not see Lillian as a little black kitten scrabbling around in the snow. He sees a beautiful leopard, because a copper by the name of O'Hara, who is walking past about then, and who knows Wilbur Willard, hears him say:

"Oh, you beautiful leopard!"

The copper takes a quick peek himself, because he does not wish any leopards running around his beat, it being against the law, but all he sees, as he tells me afterwards, is this rumpot ham, Wilbur Willard, picking up a scrawny little black kitten and shoving it in his overcoat pocket, and he also hears Wilbur say:

"Your name is Lillian."

Then Wilbur teeters on up to his room on the top floor of an old fleabag in Eighth Avenue that is called the Hotel de Brussels, where he lives quite a while, because the management does not mind actors, the management of the Hotel de Brussels being very broadminded, indeed.

There is some complaint this same morning from one of Wilbur's neighbors, an old burlesque doll by the name of Minnie Madigan, who is not working since Abraham Lincoln is assassinated, because she hears Wilbur going on in his room about a beautiful leopard, and calls up the clerk to

say that a hotel which allows wild animals is not respectable. But the clerk looks in on Wilbur and finds him playing with nothing but a harmless-looking little black kitten,
and nothing comes of the old doll's beef, especially as nobody ever claims the Hotel de Brussels is respectable anyway, or at least not much.

Of course when Wilbur comes out from under the ether
next afternoon he can see Lillian is not a leopard, and in
fact Wilbur is quite astonished to find himself in bed with
a little black kitten, because it seems Lillian is sleeping on
Wilbur's chest to keep warm. At first Wilbur does not believe what he sees, and puts it down to Haggerty's Scotch,
but finally he is convinced, and so he puts Lillian in his
pocket, and takes her over to the Hot Box night club and
gives her some milk, of which it seems Lillian is very fond.

Now where Lillian comes from in the first place of course
nobody knows. The chances are somebody chucks her out
of a window into the snow, because people are always
chucking kittens, and one thing and another, out of windows in New York. In fact, if there is one thing this town
has plenty of, it is kittens, which finally grow up to be cats,
and go snooping around ash cans, and mer-owing on roofs,
and keeping people from sleeping good.

Personally, I have no use for cats, including kittens, because I never see one that has any too much sense, although
I know a guy by the name of Pussy McGuire who makes a
first-rate living doing nothing but stealing cats, and sometimes dogs, and selling them to old dolls who like such
things for company. But Pussy only steals Persian and Angora cats, which are very fine cats, and of course Lillian is
no such cat as this. Lillian is nothing but a black cat, and

nobody will give you a dime a dozen for black cats in this town, as they are generally regarded as very bad jinxes.

Furthermore, it comes out in a few weeks that Wilbur Willard can just as well name her Herman, or Sidney, as not, but Wilbur sticks to Lillian, because this is the name of his partner when he is in vaudeville years ago. He often tells me about Lillian Withington when he is mulled up, which is more often than somewhat, for Wilbur is a great hand for drinking Scotch, or rye, or bourbon, or gin, or whatever else there is around for drinking, except water. In fact, Wilbur Willard is a high-class drinking man, and it does no good to tell him it is against the law to drink in this country, because it only makes him mad, and he says to the dickens with the law, only Wilbur Willard uses a much rougher word than dickens.

"She is like a beautiful leopard," Wilbur says to me about Lillian Withington. "Black-haired, and black-eyed, and all ripply, like a leopard I see in an animal act on the same bill at the Palace with us once. We are headliners then," he says, "Willard and Withington, the best singing and dancing act in the country.

"I pick her up in San Antonio, which is a spot in Texas," Wilbur says. "She is not long out of a convent, and I just lose my old partner, Mary McGee, who ups and dies on me of pneumonia down there. Lillian wishes to go on the stage, and joins out with me. A natural-born actress with a great voice. But like a leopard," Wilbur says. "Like a leopard. There is cat in her, no doubt of this, and cats and women are both ungrateful. I love Lillian Withington. I wish to marry her. But she is cold to me. She says she is not going to follow the stage all her life. She says she wishes money, and luxury, and a fine home, and of course a guy like me cannot give a doll such things.

"I wait on her hand and foot," Wilbur says. "I am her slave. There is nothing I will not do for her. Then one day she walks in on me in Boston very cool and says she is quitting me. She says she is marrying a rich guy there. Well, naturally it busts up the act and I never have the heart to look for another partner, and then I get to belting that old black bottle around, and now what am I but a cabaret performer?"

Then sometimes he will bust out crying, and sometimes I will cry with him, although the way I look at it, Wilbur gets a pretty fair break, at that, in getting rid of a doll who wishes things he cannot give her. Many a guy in this town is tangled up with a doll who wishes things he cannot give her, but who keeps him tangled up just the same and busting himself trying to keep her quiet.

Wilbur makes pretty fair money as an entertainer in the Hot Box, though he spends most of it for Scotch, and he is not a bad entertainer, either. I often go to the Hot Box when I am feeling blue to hear him sing Melancholy Baby, and Moonshine Valley, and other sad songs which break my heart. Personally, I do not see why any doll cannot love Wilbur, especially if they listen to him sing such songs as Melancholy Baby when he is mulled up good, because he is a tall, nice-looking guy with long eyelashes, and sleepy brown eyes, and his voice has a low moaning sound that usually goes very big with the dolls. In fact, many a doll does do some pitching to Wilbur when he is singing in the Hot Box, but somehow Wilbur never gives them a tumble, which I suppose is because he is thinking only of Lillian Withington.

Well, after he gets Lillian, the black kitten, Wilbur seems to find a new interest in life, and Lillian turns out to be right cute, and not bad-looking after Wilbur gets her fed up good. She is blacker than a yard up a chimney, with not a white spot on her, and she grows so fast that by and by Wilbur cannot carry her in his pocket any more, so he puts a collar on her and leads her around. So Lillian becomes very well known on Broadway, what with Wilbur taking her many places, and finally she does not even have to be led around by Willard, but follows him like a pooch. And in all the Roaring Forties there is no pooch that cares to have any truck with Lillian, for she will leap aboard them quicker than you can say scat, and scratch and bite them until they are very glad indeed to get away from her.

But of course the pooches in the Forties are mainly nothing but Chows, and Pekes, and Poms, or little woolly white poodles, which are led around by blond dolls, and are not fit to take their own part against a smart cat. In fact, Wilbur Willard is finally not on speaking terms with any doll that owns a pooch between Times Square and Columbus Circle, and they are all hoping that both Wilbur and Lillian will go lay down and die somewhere. Furthermore, Wilbur has a couple of battles with guys who also belong to the dolls, but Wilbur is no sucker in a battle if he is not mulled up too much and leg-weary.

After he is through entertaining people in the Hot Box, Wilbur generally goes around to any speakeasies which may still be open, and does a little offhand drinking on top of what he already drinks down in the Hot Box, which is plenty, and although it is considered very risky in this town to mix Hot Box liquor with any other, it never seems to bother Wilbur. Along toward daylight he takes a couple of bottles of Scotch over to his room in the Hotel de Brussels and uses them for a nightcap, so by the time Wilbur Willard is ready to slide off to sleep he has plenty of liquor of one kind and another inside him, and he sleeps pretty good.

Of course nobody on Broadway blames Wilbur so very much for being such a rumpot, because they know about him loving Lillian Withington, and losing her, and it is considered a reasonable excuse in this town for a guy to do some drinking when he loses a doll, which is why there is so much drinking here, but it is a mystery to one and all how Wilbur stands off all this liquor without croaking. The cemeteries are full of guys who do a lot less drinking than Wilbur, but he never even seems to feel extra tough, or if he does he keeps it to himself and does not go around saying it is the kind of liquor you get nowadays.

He costs some of the boys around Mindy's plenty of dough one winter, because he starts in doing most of his drinking after hours in Good Time Charley's speakeasy, and the boys lay a price of four to one against him lasting until spring, never figuring a guy can drink very much of Good Time Charley's liquor and keep on living. But Wilbur Willard does it just the same, so everybody says the guy is just naturally superhuman, and lets it go at that.

Sometimes Wilbur drops into Mindy's with Lillian following him on the lookout for pooches, or riding on his shoulder if the weather is bad, and the two of them will sit with us for hours chewing the rag about one thing and another. At such times Wilbur generally has a bottle on his hip and takes a shot now and then, but of course this does not come under the head of serious drinking with him. When Lillian is with Wilbur she always lays as close to him as she can get and anybody can see that she seems to be very fond of Wilbur, and that he is very fond of her, although he sometimes forgets himself and speaks of her as a beautiful leopard. But of course this is only a slip of the tongue, and anyway if Wilbur gets any pleasure out of thinking Lillian is a leopard, it is nobody's business but his own.

"I suppose she will run away from me some day," Wilbur says, running his hand over Lillian's back until her fur crackles. "Yes, although I give her plenty of liver and catnip, and one thing and another, and all my affection, she will probably give me the shake. Cats are like women, and women are like cats. They are both very ungrateful."

"They are both generally bad luck," Big Nig, the crap shooter, says. "Especially cats, and most especially black cats."

Many other guys tell Wilbur about black cats being bad luck, and advise him to slip Lillian into the North River some night with a sinker on her, but Wilbur claims he already has all the bad luck in the world when he loses Lillian Withington, and that Lillian, the cat, cannot make it any worse, so he goes on taking extra good care of her, and Lillian goes on getting bigger and bigger until I commence thinking maybe there is some St. Bernard in her.

Finally I commence to notice something funny about Lillian. Sometimes she will be acting very loving towards

Wilbur, and then again she will be very unfriendly to him, and will spit at him, and snatch at him with her claws, very hostile. It seems to me that she is all right when Willard is mulled up, but is as sad and fretful as he is himself when he is only a little bit mulled. And when Lillian is sad and fretful she makes it very tough indeed on the pooches in the neighborhood of the Brussels.

In fact, Lillian takes to pooch-hunting, sneaking off when Wilbur is getting his rest, and running pooches bow-legged, especially when she finds one that is not on a leash. A loose pooch is just naturally cherry pie for Lillian.

Well, of course this causes great indignation among the dolls who own the pooches, particularly when Lillian comes home one day carrying a Peke as big as she is herself by the scruff of the neck, and with a very excited blond doll following her and yelling bloody murder outside Wilbur Willard's door when Lillian pops into Wilbur's room through a hole he cuts in the door for her, still lugging the Peke. But it seems that instead of being mad at Lillian and giving her a pasting for such goings on, Wilbur is somewhat pleased, because he happens to be still in a fog when Lillian arrives with the Peke, and is thinking of Lillian as a beautiful leopard.

"Why," Wilbur says, "this is devotion, indeed. My beautiful leopard goes off into the jungle and fetches me an antelope for dinner."

Now of course there is no sense whatever to this, because a Peke is certainly not anything like an antelope, but the blond doll outside Wilbur's door hears Wilbur mumble, and gets the idea that he is going to eat her Peke for dinner and the squawk she puts up is very terrible. There is plenty of trouble around the Brussels in chilling the blond doll's beef over Lillian snagging her Peke, and what is more the blond doll's ever-loving guy, who turns out to be a tough Ginney bootlegger by the name of Gregorio, shows up at the Hot Box the next night and wishes to put the slug on Wilbur Willard.

But Wilbur rounds him up with a few drinks and by singing Melancholy Baby to him, and before he leaves the Ginney gets very sentimental towards Wilbur, and Lillian, too, and wishes to give Wilbur five bucks to let Lillian grab the Peke again, if Lillian will promise not to bring it back. It seems Gregorio does not really care for the Peke, and is only acting quarrelsome to please the blond doll and make her think he loves her dearly.

But I can see Lillian is having different moods, and finally I ask Wilbur if he notices it.

"Yes," he says, very sad, "I do not seem to be holding her love. She is getting very fickle. A guy moves onto my floor at the Brussels the other day with a little boy, and Lillian becomes very fond of this kid at once. In fact, they are great friends. Ah, well," Wilbur says, "cats are like women. Their affection does not last."

I happen to go over to the Brussels a few days later to explain to a guy by the name of Crutchy, who lives on the same floor as Wilbur Willard, that some of our citizens do not like his face and that it may be a good idea for him to leave town, especially if he insists on bringing ale into their territory, and I see Lillian out in the hall with a youngster which I judge is the kid Wilbur is talking about. This kid is maybe three years old, and very cute, what with black hair, and black eyes, and he is wooling Lillian around the hall in a way that is most surprising, for Lillian is not such a cat as will stand for much wooling around, not even from Wilbur Willard.

I am wondering how anybody comes to take such a kid to a joint like the Brussels, but I figure it is some actor's kid, and that maybe there is no mamma for it. Later I am talking to Wilbur about this, and he says:

"Well, if the kid's old man is an actor, he is not working at it. He sticks close to his room all the time, and he does not allow the kid to go anywhere but in the hall, and I feel sorry for the little guy, which is why I allow Lillian to play with him."

Now it comes on a very cold spell, and a bunch of us are sitting in Mindy's along toward five o'clock in the morning when we hear fire engines going past. By and by in comes a guy by the name of Kansas, who is named Kansas because he comes from Kansas, and who is a crap shooter by trade.

"The old Brussels is on fire," this guy Kansas says.

"She is always on fire," Big Nig says, meaning there is always plenty of hot stuff going on around the Brussels.

About this time who walks in but Wilbur Willard, and anybody can see he is just naturally floating. The chances are he comes from Good Time Charley's, and he is certainly carrying plenty of pressure. I never see Wilbur Willard mulled up more. He does not have Lillian with him, but then he never takes Lillian to Good Time Charley's, because Charley hates cats.

"Hey, Wilbur," Big Nig says, "your joint, the Brussels, is on fire."

"Well," Wilbur says, "I am a little firefly, and I need a light. Let us go where there is fire."

The Brussels is only a few blocks from Mindy's, and there is nothing else to do just then, so some of us walk over to Eighth Avenue with Wilbur teetering along ahead of us. The old shack is certainly roaring good when we get in sight of it, and the firemen are tossing water into it, and the coppers have the fire lines out to keep the crowd back, although there is not much of a crowd at such an hour in the morning.

"Is it not beautiful?" Wilbur Willard says, looking up at the flames. "Is it not like a fairy palace all lighted up this way?"

You see, Wilbur does not realize the joint is on fire, although guys and dolls are running out of it every which way, most of them half dressed, or not dressed at all, and the firemen are getting out the life nets in case anybody wishes to hop out of the windows.

"It is certainly beautiful," Wilbur says. "I must get Lillian so she can see this."

And before anybody has time to think, there is Wilbur Willard walking into the front door of the Brussels as if nothing happens. The firemen and the coppers are so astonished all they can do is holler at Wilbur, but he pays no attention whatever. Well, naturally everybody figures Wilbur is a gone gosling, but in about ten minutes he comes walking out of this same door through the fire and smoke as cool as you please, and he has Lillian in his arms.

"You know," Wilbur says, coming over to where we are standing with our eyes popping out, "I have to walk all the way up to my floor because the elevators seem to be out of commission. The service is getting terrible in this hotel. I will certainly make a strong beef to the management about it as soon as I pay something on my account."

Then what happens but Lillian lets out a big mer-ow, and hops out of Wilbur's arms and skips past the coppers and the firemen with her back all humped up, and the next thing anybody knows she is tearing through the front door of the old hotel and making plenty of speed.

"Well, well," Wilbur says, looking much surprised, "there goes Lillian."

And what does this daffy Wilbur Willard do but turn and go marching back into the Brussels again, and by this time the smoke is pouring out of the front doors so thick he is out of sight in a second. Naturally he takes the coppers and firemen by surprise, because they are not used to guys walking in and out of fires on them.

This time anybody standing around will lay you plenty of odds—two and a half and maybe three to one that Wilbur never shows up again, because the old Brussels is now just popping with fire and smoke from the lower windows, although there does not seem to be quite so much fire in the upper story. Everybody seems to be out of the joint, and even the firemen are fighting the blaze from the outside because the Brussels is so old and ramshackly there is no sense in them risking the floors.

I mean everybody is out of the joint except Wilbur Willard and Lillian, and we figure they are getting a good frying somewhere inside, although Feet Samuels is around offering to take thirteen to five for a few small bets that

Lillian comes out okay, because Feet claims that a cat has nine lives and that is a fair bet at the price.

Well, up comes a swell-looking doll all heated up about something and pushing and clawing her way through the crowd up to the ropes and screaming until you can hardly hear yourself think, and about this same minute everybody hears a voice going ai-lee-hi-hee-hoo, like a Swiss yodeler, which comes from the roof of the Brussels, and looking up what do we see but Wilbur Willard standing up there on the edge of the roof, high above the fire and smoke, and yodeling very loud.

Under one arm he has a big bundle of some kind, and under the other he has the little kid I see playing in the hall with Lillian. As he stands up there going ai-lee-hi-hee-hoo, the swell-dressed doll near us begins yipping louder than Wilbur is yodeling, and the firemen rush over under him with a life net.

Wilbur lets go another ai-lee-hi-hee-hoo, and down he comes all spraddled out, with the bundle and the kid, but he hits the net sitting down and bounces up and back again for a couple of minutes before he finally settles. In fact, Wilbur is enjoying the bouncing, and the chances are he will be bouncing yet if the firemen do not drop their hold on the net and let him fall to the ground.

Then Wilbur steps out of the net, and I can see the bundle is a rolled-up blanket with Lillian's eyes peeking out of one end. He still has the kid under the other arm with his head stuck out in front, and his legs stuck out behind, and it does not seem to me that Wilbur is handling the kid as careful as he is handling Lillian. He stands there looking at the firemen with a very sneering look, and finally he says:

"Do not think you can catch me in your net unless I wish to be caught. I am a butterfly, and very hard to over-take."

Then all of a sudden the swell-dressed doll who is doing so much hollering, piles on top of Wilbur and grabs the kid from him and begins hugging and kissing it.

"Wilbur," she says, "God bless you, Wilbur, for saving my baby! Oh, thank you, Wilbur, thank you! My wretched husband kidnaps and runs away with him, and it is only a few hours ago that my detectives find out where he is."

Wilbur gives the doll a funny look for about half a minute and starts to walk away, but Lillian comes wiggling out of the blanket, looking and smelling pretty much singed up, and the kid sees Lillian and begins hollering for her, so Wilbur finally hands Lillian over to the kid. And not wishing to leave Lillian, Wilbur stands around somewhat confused, and the doll gets talking to him, and finally they go away together, and as they go Wilbur is carrying the kid, and the kid is carrying Lillian, and Lillian is not feel-ing so good from her burns.

Furthermore, Wilbur is probably more sober than he ever is before in years at this hour in the morning, but before they go I get a chance to talk some to Wilbur when he is still rambling somewhat, and I make out from what he says that the first time he goes to get Lillian he finds her in his room and does not see hide or hair of the little kid and does not even think of him, because he does not know what room the kid is in, anyway, having never noticed such a thing.

But the second time he goes up, Lillian is sniffing at the crack under the door of a room down the hall from Wilbur's and Wilbur says he seems to remember seeing a trickle of something like water coming out of the crack.

"And," Wilbur says, "as I am looking for a blanket for Lillian, and it will be a bother to go back to my room, I figure I will get one out of this room. I try the knob but the door is locked, so I kick it in, and walk in to find the room is full of smoke, and fire is shooting through the windows very lovely, and when I grab a blanket off the bed for Lillian, what is under the blanket but the kid?

"Well," Wilbur says, "the kid is squawking, and Lillian is mer-owing, and there is so much confusion generally that it makes me nervous, so I figure we better go up on the roof and let the stink blow off us, and look at the fire from there. It seems there is a guy stretched out on the floor of the room alongside an upset table between the door and the bed. He has a bottle in one hand, and he is dead. Well, naturally there is no percentage in lugging a dead guy along, so I take Lillian and the kid and go up on the roof, and we just naturally fly off like humming birds. Now I must get a drink," Wilbur says. "I wonder if anybody has anything on their hip?"

Well, the papers are certainly full of Wilbur and Lillian the next day, especially Lillian, and they are both great heroes.

But Wilbur cannot stand the publicity very long, because he never has no time to himself for his drinking, what with the scribes and the photographers hopping on him every few minutes wishing to hear his story, and to take more pictures of him and Lillian, so one night he disappears, and Lillian disappears with him.

About a year later it comes out that he marries his old doll, Lillian Withington-Harmon, and falls into a lot of dough, and what is more he cuts out the liquor and becomes quite a useful citizen one way and another. So everybody has to admit that black cats are not always bad luck, although I say Wilbur's case is a little exceptional because he does not start out knowing Lillian is a black cat, but thinking she is a leopard.

I happen to run into Wilbur one day all dressed up in good clothes and jewelry and chucking quite a swell.

"Wilbur," I say to him, "I often think how remarkable it is the way Lillian suddenly gets such an attachment for the little kid and remembers about him being in the hotel and leads you back there a second time to the right room. If I do not see this come off with my own eyes, I will never believe a cat has brains enough to do such a thing, because I consider cats extra dumb."

"Brains nothing," Wilbur says. "Lillian does not have brains enough to grease a gimlet. And what is more she has no more attachment for the kid than a jack rabbit. The time has come," Wilbur says, "to expose Lillian. She gets a lot of credit which is never coming to her. I will now tell you about Lillian, and nobody knows this but me.

"You see," Wilbur says, "when Lillian is a little kitten I always put a little Scotch in her milk, partly to help make her good and strong, and partly because I am never no hand to drink alone, unless there is nobody with me. Well, at first Lillian does not care so much for this Scotch in her milk, but finally she takes a liking to it, and I keep making her toddy stronger until in the end she will lap up a good big snort without any milk for a chaser, and yell for more. In fact, I suddenly realize that Lillian becomes a rumpot, just like I am in those days, and simply must have her grog, and it is when she is good and rummed up that Lillian goes off snatching Pekes, and acting tough generally.

"Now," Wilbur says, "the time of the fire is about the time I get home every morning and give Lillian her schnapps. But when I go into the hotel and get her the first time I forget to Scotch her up, and the reason she runs back into the hotel is because she is looking for her shot. And the reason she is sniffing at the kid's door is not because the kid is in there but because the trickle that is coming through the crack under the door is nothing but Scotch that is running out of the bottle in the dead guy's hand. I never mention this before because I figure it may be a knock to a dead guy's memory," Wilbur says. "Drinking is certainly a disgusting thing, especially secret drinking."

"But how is Lillian getting along these days?" I ask Wilbur Willard.

"I am greatly disappointed in Lillian," he says. "She refuses to reform when I do and the last I hear of her she takes up with Gregorio, the Ginney bootlegger, who keeps her well Scotched up all the time so she will lead his blond doll's Peke a dog's life."

A VERY HONORABLE GUY

OFF and on I know Feet Samuels a matter of eight or ten years, up and down Broadway, and in and out, but I never have much truck with him because he is a guy I consider no dice. In fact, he does not mean a thing.

In the first place, Feet Samuels is generally broke, and there is no percentage in hanging around brokers. The way I look at it, you are not going to get anything off a guy who has not got anything. So while I am very sorry for brokers, and I am always willing to hope that they get hold of something, I do not like to be around them. Long ago an old-timer who knows what he is talking about says to me:

"My boy," he says, "always try to rub up against money, for if you rub up against money long enough, some of it may rub off on you."

So in all the years I am around this town, I always try to keep in with the high shots and guys who carry these large coarse bank notes around with them, and I stay away from small operators and chiselers and brokers. And Feet Samuels is one of the worst brokers in this town, and has been such as long as I know him.

He is a big heavy guy with several chins and very funny feet, which is why he is called Feet. These feet are extra large feet, even for a big guy, and Dave the Dude says Feet wears violin cases for shoes. Of course this is not true, because Feet cannot get either of his feet in a violin case, unless it is a case for a very large violin, such as a cello. I see Feet one night in the Hot Box, which is a night club, dancing with a doll by the name of Hortense Hathaway, who is in Georgie White's "Scandals," and what is she doing but standing on Feet's feet as if she is on sled runners, and Feet never knows it. He only thinks the old gondolas are a little extra heavy to shove around this night, because Hortense is no invalid. In fact, she is a good rangy welterweight.

She has blond hair and plenty to say, and her square monicker is Annie O'Brien, and not Hortense Hathaway at all. Furthermore, she comes from Newark, which is in New Jersey, and her papa is a taxi jockey by the name of Skush O'Brien, and a very rough guy, at that, if anybody asks you. But of course the daughter of a taxi jockey is as good as anybody else for Georgie White's "Scandals" as long as her shape is okay, and nobody ever hears any complaint from the customers about Hortense on this proposition.

She is what is called a show girl, and all she has to do is to walk around and about Georgie White's stage with only a few light bandages on and everybody considers her very beautiful, especially from the neck down, although personally I never care much for Hortense because she is very fresh to people. I often see her around the night clubs, and when she is in these deadfalls Hortense generally is wearing quite a number of diamond bracelets and fur wraps, and one thing and another, so I judge she is not doing bad for a doll from Newark, New Jersey.

Of course Feet Samuels never knows why so many other dolls besides Hortense are wishing to dance with him, but gets to thinking maybe it is because he has the old sex appeal and he is very sore indeed when Henri, the head waiter at the Hot Box, asks him to please stay off the floor except for every tenth dance, because Feet's feet take up so much room when he is on the floor that only two other dancers can work out at the same time, it being a very small floor.

I must tell you more about Feet's feet, because they are very remarkable feet indeed. They go off at different directions under him, very sharp, so if you see Feet standing on a corner it is very difficult to tell which way he is going, because one foot will be headed one way, and the other foot the other way. In fact, guys around Mindy's restaurant often make bets on the proposition as to which way Feet is headed when he is standing still.

What Feet Samuels does for a living is the best he can, which is the same thing many other guys in this town do for a living. He hustles some around the race tracks and crap games and prize fights, picking up a few bobs here and there as a runner for the bookmakers, or scalping bets, or steering suckers, but he is never really in the money in his whole life. He is always owing and always paying off, and I never see him but what he is troubled with the shorts as regards to dough.

The only good thing you can say about Feet Samuels is he is very honorable about his debts, and what he owes he pays when he can. Anybody will tell you this about Feet Samuels, although of course it is only what any hustler such as Feet must do if he wishes to protect his credit and keep in action. Still, you will be surprised how many guys forget to pay.

It is because Feet's word is considered good at all times that he is nearly always able to raise a little dough, even off The Brain, and The Brain is not an easy guy for anybody to raise dough off of. In fact, The Brain is very tough about letting people raise dough off of him.

If anybody gets any dough off of The Brain he wishes to know right away what time they are going to pay it back, with certain interest, and if they say at five-thirty Tuesday morning, they better not make it five-thirty-one Tuesday morning, or The Brain will consider them very unreliable and never let them have any money again. And when a guy loses his credit with The Brain he is in a very tough spot indeed in this town, for The Brain is the only man who always has dough.

Furthermore, some very unusual things often happen to guys who get money off of The Brain and fail to kick it back just when they promise, such as broken noses and sprained ankles and other injuries, for The Brain has people around him who seem to resent guys getting dough off of him and not kicking it back. Still, I know of The Brain letting some very surprising guys have dough, because he has a bug that he is a wonderful judge of guys' characters, and that he is never wrong on them, although I must say that no guy who gets dough off of The Brain is more surprising than Feet Samuels.

The Brain's right name is Armand Rosenthal, and he is called The Brain because he is so smart. He is well known to one and all in this town as a very large operator in gambling, and one thing and another, and nobody knows how much dough The Brain has, except that he must have plenty, because no matter how much dough is around,

The Brain sooner or later gets hold of all of it. Some day I will tell you more about The Brain, but right now I wish to tell you about Feet Samuels.

It comes on a tough winter in New York, what with nearly all hands who have the price going to Miami and Havana and New Orleans, leaving the brokers behind. There is very little action of any kind in town with the high shots gone, and one night I run into Feet Samuels in Mindy's, and he is very sad indeed. He asks me if I happen to have a finnif on me, but of course I am not giving finnifs to guys like Feet Samuels, and finally he offers to compromise with me for a deuce, so I can see things must be very bad with Feet for him to come down from five dollars to two.

"My rent is away overdue for the shovel and broom," Feet says, "and I have a hard-hearted landlady who will not listen to reason. She says she will give me the wind if I do not lay something on the line at once. Things are never so bad with me," Feet says, "and I am thinking of doing something very desperate."

I cannot think of anything very desperate for Feet Samuels to do, except maybe go to work, and I know he is not going to do such a thing no matter what happens. In fact, in all the years I am around Broadway I never know any broker to get desperate enough to go to work.

I once hear Dave the Dude offer Feet Samuels a job riding rum between here and Philly at good wages, but Feet turns it down because he claims he cannot stand the open air, and anyway Feet says he hears riding rum is illegal and may land a guy in the pokey. So I know whatever Feet is going to do will be nothing difficult.

"The Brain is still in town," I say to Feet. "Why do you not put the lug on him? You stand okay with him."

"There is the big trouble," Feet says. "I owe The Brain a C note already, and I am supposed to pay him back by four o'clock Monday morning, and where I am going to get a hundred dollars I do not know, to say nothing of the other ten I must give him for interest."

"What are you figuring on doing?" I ask, for it is now a Thursday, and I can see Feet has very little time to get together such a sum.

"I am figuring on scragging myself," Feet says, very sad. "What good am I to anybody? I have no family and no friends, and the world is packing enough weight without me. Yes, I think I will scrag myself."

"It is against the law to commit suicide in this man's town," I say, "although what the law can do to a guy who commits suicide I am never able to figure out."

"I do not care," Feet says. "I am sick and tired of it all. I am especially sick and tired of being broke. I never have more than a few quarters to rub together in my pants pocket. Everything I try turns out wrong. The only thing that keeps me from scragging myself at once is the C note I owe The Brain, because I do not wish to have him going around after I am dead and gone saying I am no good. And the toughest thing of all," Feet says, "is I am in love. I am in love with Hortense."

"Hortense?" I say, very much astonished indeed. "Why, Hortense is nothing but a big——"

"Stop!" Feet says. "Stop right here! I will not have her called a big boloney or whatever else big you are going to call her, because I love her. I cannot live without her. In fact," Feet says, "I do not wish to live without her."

"Well," I say, "what does Hortense think about you loving her."

"She does not know it," Feet says. "I am ashamed to tell her, because naturally if I tell her I love her, Hortense will expect me to buy her some diamond bracelets, and naturally I cannot do this. But I think she likes me more than somewhat, because she looks at me in a certain way. But," Feet says, "there is some other guy who likes her also, and who is buying her diamond bracelets and what goes with them, which makes it very tough on me. I do not know who the guy is, and I do not think Hortense cares for him so much, but naturally any doll must give serious consideration to a guy who can buy her diamond bracelets. So I guess there is nothing for me to do but scrag myself."

Naturally I do not take Feet Samuels serious, and I forget about his troubles at once, because I figure he will wiggle out some way, but the next night he comes into Mindy's all pleasured up, and I figure he must make a scratch somewhere, for he is walking like a man with about sixty-five dollars on him.

But it seems Feet only has an idea, and very few ideas are worth sixty-five dollars.

"I am laying in bed thinking this afternoon," Feet says, "and I get to thinking how I can raise enough dough to pay off The Brain, and maybe a few other guys, and my landlady, and leave a few bobs over to help bury me. I am going to sell my body."

Well, naturally I am somewhat bewildered by this statement, so I ask Feet to explain, and here is his idea: He is going to find some doctor who wishes a dead body and sell his body to this doctor for as much as he can get, the body to be delivered after Feet scrags himself, which is to be within a certain time.

"I understand," Feet says, "that these croakers are always looking for bodies to practice on, and that good bodies are not easy to get nowadays."

"How much do you figure your body is worth?" I ask.

"Well," Feet says, "a body as big as mine ought to be worth at least a *G*."

"Feet," I say, "this all sounds most gruesome to me. Personally I do not know much about such a proposition, but I do not believe if doctors buy bodies at all that they buy them by the pound. And I do not believe you can get a thousand dollars for your body, especially while you are still alive, because how does a doctor know if you will deliver your body to him?"

"Why," Feet says, very indignant, "everybody knows I pay what I owe. I can give The Brain for reference, and he will okay me with anybody for keeping my word."

Well, it seems to me that there is very little sense to what Feet Samuels is talking about, and anyway I figure that maybe he blows his topper, which is what often happens to brokers, so I pay no more attention to him. But on Monday morning, just before four o'clock, I am in Mindy's, and what happens but in walks Feet with a handful of money, looking much pleased.

The Brain is also there at the table where he always sits facing the door so nobody can pop in on him without him seeing them first, because there are many people in this town that The Brain likes to see first if they are coming in where he is. Feet steps up to the table and lays a C note in front of The Brain and also a sawbuck, and The Brain looks up at the clock and smiles and says:

"Okay, Feet, you are on time."

It is very unusual for The Brain to smile about anything, but afterwards I hear he wins two C's off of Manny Mandelbaum, who bets him Feet will not pay off on time, so The Brain has a smile coming.

"By the way, Feet," The Brain says, "some doctor calls me up today and asks me if your word is good and you may be glad to know I tell him you are one hundred percent. I put the okay on you because I know you never fail to deliver on a promise. Are you sick, or something?"

"No," Feet says, "I am not sick. I just have a little business deal on with the guy. Thanks for the okay."

Then he comes over to the table where I am sitting, and I can see he still has money left in his duke. Naturally I am anxious to know where he makes the scratch, and by and by he tells me.

"I put over the proposition I am telling you about," Feet says. "I sell my body to a doctor over on Park Avenue by the name of Bodeeker, but I do not get a G for it as I expect. It seems bodies are not worth much right now because there are so many on the market, but Doc Bodeeker gives me four C's on thirty days' delivery.

"I never know it is so much trouble selling a body before," Feet says. "Three doctors call the cops on me when I proposition them, thinking I am daffy, but Doc Bodeeker is a nice old guy and is glad to do business with me, especially when I give The Brain as reference. Doc Bodeeker says he is looking for a head shaped just like mine for years, because it seems he is a shark on heads. But," Feet says, "I got to figure out some way of scragging myself besides jumping out a window, like I plan, because Doc Bodeeker does not wish my head mussed up."

"Well," I say, "this is certainly most ghastly to me and does not sound legitimate. Does The Brain know you sell your body?"

"No," Feet says, "Doc Bodeeker only asks him over the phone if my word is good and does not tell him why he wishes to know, but he is satisfied with The Brain's okay. Now I am going to pay my landlady, and take up a few other markers here and there, and feed myself up good until it is time to leave this bad old world behind."

But it seems Feet Samuels does not go to pay his land-lady right away. Where he goes is to Johnny Crackow's crap game downtown, which is a crap game with a $500 limit where the high shots seldom go, but where there is always some action for a small operator. And as Feet walks into the joint it seems that Big Nig is trying to make four with the dice, and everybody knows that four is a hard point for Big Nig, or anybody else, to make.

So Feet Samuels looks on awhile watching Big Nig try-ing to make four, and a guy by the name of Whitey offers to take two to one for a C note that Big Nig makes his four, which is certainly more confidence that I will ever have in Big Nig. Naturally Feet hauls out a couple of his C notes at once, as anybody must do who has a couple of C notes, and bets Whitey two hundred to a hundred that Big Nig does not make the four. And right away Big Nig outs with a seven, so Feet wins the bet.

Well, to make a long story short, Feet stands there for some time betting guys that other guys will not make four, or whatever it is they are trying to make with the dice, and the first thing anybody knows Feet Samuels is six *G's* winner, and has the crap game all cripped up. I see him the next night up in the Hot Box, and this big first base-man, Hortense, is with him, sliding around on Feet's feet, and a blind man can see that she has on at least three more diamond bracelets than ever before.

A night or two later I hear of Feet beating Long George McCormack, a high shot from Los Angeles, out of eighteen *G's* playing a card game that is called low ball, and Feet Samuels has no more license to beat a guy like Long George playing low ball than I have to lick Jack Dempsey. But when a guy finally gets his rushes in gambling nothing can stop him for awhile, and this is the way it is with Feet. Every night you hear of him winning plenty of dough at this or that.

He comes into Mindy's one morning, and naturally I move over to his table at once, because Feet is now in the money and is a guy anybody can associate with freely. I am just about to ask him how things are going with him, although I know they are going pretty good, when in pops a fierce-looking old guy with his face all covered with gray whiskers that stick out every which way, and whose eyes peek out of these whiskers very wild indeed. Feet turns pale as he sees the guy, but nods at him, and the guy nods back and goes out.

"Who is the Whiskers?" I ask Feet. "He is in here the other morning looking around, and he makes people very nervous because nobody can figure who he is or what his dodge may be."

"It is old Doc Bodeeker," Feet says. "He is around checking up on me to make sure I am still in town. Say, I am in a very hot spot one way and another."

"What are you worrying about?" I ask. "You got plenty of dough and about two weeks left to enjoy yourself before this Doc Bodeeker forecloses on you."

"I know," Feet says, very sad. "But now I get this dough things do not look as tough to me as formerly, and I am very sorry I make the deal with the doctor. Especially," Feet says, "on account of Hortense."

"What about Hortense?" I ask.

"I think she is commencing to love me since I am able to buy her more diamond bracelets than the other guy," Feet says. "If it is not for this thing hanging over me, I will ask her to marry me, and maybe she will do it, at that."

"Well, then," I say, "why do you not go to old Whiskers and pay him his dough back, and tell him you change your mind about selling your body, although of course if it is not for Whiskers' buying your body you will not have all this dough."

"I do go to him," Feet says, and I can see there are big tears in his eyes. "But he says he will not cancel the deal. He says he will not take the money back; what he wants is my body, because I have such a funny-shaped head. I offer him four times what he pays me, but he will not take it. He says my body must be delivered to him promptly on March first."

"Does Hortense know about this deal?" I ask.

"Oh, no, no!" Feet says. "And I will never tell her, because she will think I am crazy, and Hortense does not care for crazy guys. In fact, she is always complaining about the other guy who buys her the diamond bracelets, claiming he is a little crazy, and if she thinks I am the same way the chances are she will give me the breeze."

Now this is a situation, indeed, but what to do about it I do not know. I put the proposition up to a lawyer friend of mine the next day, and he says he does not believe the deal will hold good in court, but of course I know Feet Samuels does not wish to go to court, because the last time Feet goes to court he is held as a material witness and is in the Tombs ten days.

The lawyer says Feet can run away, but personally I consider this a very dishonorable idea after The Brain putting the okay on Feet with old Doc Bodeeker, and anyway I can see Feet is not going to do such a thing as long as Hortense is around. I can see that one hair of her head is stronger than the Atlantic cable with Feet Samuels.

A week slides by, and I do not see so much of Feet, but I hear of him murdering crap games and short card players, and winning plenty, and also going around the night clubs with Hortense who finally has so many bracelets there is no more room on her arms, and she puts a few of them on her ankles, which are not bad ankles to look at, at that, with or without bracelets.

Then goes another week, and it just happens I am standing in front of Mindy's about four-thirty one morning and thinking that Feet's time must be up and wondering how he makes out with old Doc Bodeeker, when all of a sudden I hear a ploppity-plop coming up Broadway, and what do I see but Feet Samuels running so fast he is passing taxis that are going thirty-five miles an hour like they are standing still. He is certainly stepping along.

There are no traffic lights and not much traffic at such an hour in the morning, and Feet passes me in a terrible hurry. And about twenty yards behind him comes an old guy with gray whiskers, and I can see it is nobody but Doc Bodeeker. What is more, he has a big long knife in one hand, and he seems to be reaching for Feet at every jump with the knife.

Well, this seems to me a most surprising spectacle, and I follow them to see what comes of it, because I can see at once that Doc Bodeeker is trying to collect Feet's body himself. But I am not much of a runner, and they are out of my sight in no time, and only that I am able to follow them by ear through Feet's feet going ploppity-plop I will never trail them.

They turn east into Fifty-fourth Street off Broadway, and when I finally reach the corner I see a crowd halfway down the block in front of the Hot Box, and I know this crowd has something to do with Feet and Doc Bodeeker even before I get to the door to find that Feet goes on in while Doc Bodeeker is arguing with Soldier Sweeney, the door man, because as Feet passes the Soldier he tells the Soldier not to let the guy who is chasing him in. And the Soldier, being a good friend of Feet's, is standing the doc off.

Well, it seems that Hortense is in the Hot Box waiting for Feet, and naturally she is much surprised to see him come in all out of breath, and so is everybody else in the joint, including Henri, the head waiter, who afterwards tells me what comes off there, because you see I am out in front.

"A crazy man is chasing me with a butcher knife," Feet says to Hortense. "If he gets inside I am a goner. He is down at the door trying to get in."

Now I will say one thing for Hortense, and this is she has plenty of nerve, but of course you will expect a daughter of Skush O'Brien to have plenty of nerve. Nobody ever has more moxie than Skush. Henri, the head waiter, tells me that Hortense does not get excited, but says she will just have a little peek at the guy who is chasing Feet.

The Hot Box is over a garage, and the kitchen windows look down into Fifty-fourth Street, and while Doc Bodeeker is arguing with Soldier Sweeney, I hear a window lift, and who looks out but Hortense. She takes one squint and yanks her head in quick, and Henri tells me afterwards she shrieks:

"My Lord, Feet! This is the same daffy old guy who sends me all the bracelets, and who wishes to marry me!"

"And he is the guy I sell my body to," Feet says, and then he tells Hortense the story of his deal with Doc Bodeeker.

"It is all for you, Horty," Feet says, although of course this is nothing but a big lie, because it is all for The Brain in the beginning. "I love you, and I only wish to get a little dough to show you a good time before I die. If it is not for this deal I will ask you to be my ever-loving wife."

Well, what happens but Hortense plunges right into Feet's arms, and gives him a big kiss on his ugly smush, and says to him like this:

"I love you too, Feet, because nobody ever makes such a sacrifice as to hock their body for me. Never mind the deal. I will marry you at once, only we must first get rid of this daffy old guy downstairs."

Then Hortense peeks out of the window again and hollers down at old Doc Bodeeker. "Go away," she says. "Go away, or I will chuck a moth in your whiskers, you old fool."

But the sight of her only seems to make old Doc Bodeeker a little wilder than somewhat, and he starts struggling with Soldier Sweeney very ferocious, so the Soldier takes the knife away from the doc and throws it away before somebody gets hurt with it.

Now it seems Hortense looks around the kitchen for something to chuck out the window at old Doc Bodeeker, and all she sees is a nice new ham which the chef just lays out on the table to slice up for ham sandwiches. This ham is a very large ham, such as will last the Hot Box a month, for they slice the ham in their ham sandwiches very, very thin up at the Hot Box. Anyway, Hortense grabs up the ham and runs to the window with it and gives it a heave without even stopping to take aim.

Well, this ham hits poor old Doc Bodeeker kerbowie smack dab on the noggin. The doc does not fall down, but he commences staggering around with his legs bending under him like he is drunk.

I wish to help him because I feel sorry for a guy in such a spot as this, and what is more I consider it a dirty trick for a doll such as Hortense to slug anybody with a ham.

Well, I take charge of the old doc and lead him back down Broadway and into Mindy's, where I set him down

and get him a cup of coffee and a Bismarck herring to
revive him, while quite a number of citizens gather about
him very sympathetic.

"My friends," the old doc says finally, looking around,
"you see in me a broken-hearted man. I am not a crack-
pot, although of course my relatives may give you an argument on this proposition. I am in love with Hortense. I
am in love with her from the night I first see her playing
the part of a sunflower in 'Scandals.' I wish to marry her,
as I am a widower of long standing, but somehow the
idea of me marrying anybody never appeals to my sons
and daughters.

"In fact," the doc says, dropping his voice to a whisper,
"sometimes they even talk of locking me up when I wish
to marry somebody. So naturally I never tell them about
Hortense, because I fear they may try to discourage me.
But I am deeply in love with her and send her many
beautiful presents, although I am not able to see her often
on account of my relatives. Then I find out Hortense is
carrying on with this Feet Samuels.

"I am desperately jealous," the doc says, "but I do not
know what to do. Finally Fate sends this Feet to me offering to sell his body. Of course I am not practicing for
years, but I keep an office on Park Avenue just for old
times' sake, and it is to this office he comes. At first I think
he is crazy, but he refers me to Mr. Armand Rosenthal,
the big sporting man, who assures me that Feet Samuels
is all right.

"The idea strikes me that if I make a deal with Feet
Samuels for his body as he proposes, he will wait until
the time comes to pay his obligation and run away, and,"

the doc says, "I will never be troubled by his rivalry for the affection of Hortense again. But he does not depart. I do not reckon on the holding power of love.

"Finally in a jealous frenzy I take after him with a knife, figuring to scare him out of town. But it is too late. I can see now Hortense loves him in return, or she will not drop a scuttle of coal on me in his defense as she does.

"Yes, gentlemen," the old doc says, "I am broken-hearted. I also seem to have a large lump on my head. Besides, Hortense has all my presents, and Feet Samuels has my money, so I get the worst of it all around. I only hope and trust that my daughter Eloise, who is Mrs. Sidney Simmons Bragdon, does not hear of this or she may be as mad as she is the time I wish to marry the beautiful cigaret girl in Jimmy Kelley's."

Here Doc Bodeeker seems all busted up by his feelings and starts to shed tears, and everybody is feeling very sorry for him indeed, when up steps The Brain who is taking everything in.

"Do not worry about your presents and your dough," The Brain says. "I will make everything good, because I am the guy who okays Feet Samuels with you. I am wrong on a guy for the first time in my life, and I must pay, but Feet Samuels will be very, very sorry when I find him. Of course I do not figure on a doll in the case, and this always makes quite a difference, so I am really not a hundred percent wrong on the guy, at that.

"But," The Brain says, in a very loud voice so everybody can hear, "Feet Samuels is nothing but a dirty welsher for not turning in his body to you as per agreement, and as long as he lives he will never get another dollar or another okay off of me, or anybody I know. His credit is ruined forever on Broadway."

But I judge that Feet and Hortense do not care. The last time I hear of them they are away over in New Jersey where not even The Brain's guys dast to bother them on account of Skush O'Brien, and I understand they are raising chickens and children right and left, and that all of Hortense's bracelets are now in Newark municipal bonds, which I am told are not bad bonds, at that.

MADAME LA GIMP

ONE night I am passing the corner of Fiftieth Street and Broadway, and what do I see but Dave the Dude standing in a doorway talking to a busted-down old Spanish doll by the name of Madame La Gimp. Or rather Madame La Gimp is talking to Dave the Dude, and what is more he is listening to her, because I can hear him say yes, yes, as he always does when he is really listening to anybody, which is very seldom.

Now this is a most surprising sight to me, because Madame La Gimp is not such an old doll as anybody will wish to listen to, especially Dave the Dude. In fact, she is nothing but an old haybag, and generally somewhat ginned up. For fifteen years, or maybe sixteen, I see Madame La Gimp up and down Broadway, or sliding along through the Forties, sometimes selling newspapers, and sometimes selling flowers, and in all these years I seldom see her but what she seems to have about half a heat on from drinking gin.

Of course nobody ever takes the newspapers she sells, even after they buy them off of her, because they are generally yesterday's papers, and sometimes last week's, and nobody ever wants her flowers, even after they pay her for them, because they are flowers such as she gets off an undertaker over on Tenth Avenue, and they are very tired flowers, indeed.

Personally, I consider Madame La Gimp nothing but an old pest, but kind-hearted guys like Dave the Dude always stake her to a few pieces of silver when she comes shuffling along putting on the moan about her tough luck. She walks with a gimp in one leg, which is why she is called Madame La Gimp, and years ago I hear somebody say Madame La Gimp is once a Spanish dancer, and a big shot on Broadway, but that she meets up with an accident which puts her out of the dancing dodge, and that a busted romance makes her become a ginhead.

I remember somebody telling me once that Madame La Gimp is quite a beauty in her day, and has her own servants, and all this and that, but I always hear the same thing about every bum on Broadway, male and female, including some I know are bums, in spades, right from taw, so I do not pay any attention to these stories.

Still, I am willing to allow that maybe Madame La Gimp is once a fair looker, at that, and the chances are has a fair shape, because once or twice I see her when she is not ginned up, and has her hair combed, and she is not so bad-looking, although even then if you put her in a claiming race I do not think there is any danger of anybody claiming her out of it.

Mostly she is wearing raggedy clothes, and busted shoes, and her gray hair is generally hanging down her face, and when I say she is maybe fifty years old I am giving her plenty the best of it. Although she is Spanish, Madame La Gimp talks good English, and in fact she can cuss in English as good as anybody I ever hear, barring Dave the Dude.

Well, anyway, when Dave the Dude sees me as he is listening to Madame La Gimp, he motions me to wait, so I wait until she finally gets through gabbing to him and goes gimping away. Then Dave the Dude comes over to me looking much worried.

"This is quite a situation," Dave says. "The old doll is in a tough spot. It seems that she once has a baby which she calls by the name of Eulalie, being it is a girl baby, and she ships this baby off to her sister in a little town in Spain to raise up, because Madame La Gimp figures a baby is not apt to get much raising-up off of her as long as she is on Broadway. Well, this baby is on her way here. In fact," Dave says, "she will land next Saturday and here it is Wednesday already."

"Where is the baby's papa?" I ask Dave the Dude.

"Well," Dave says, "I do not ask Madame La Gimp this, because I do not consider it a fair question. A guy who goes around this town asking where babies' papas are, or even who they are, is apt to get the name of being nosey. Anyway, this has nothing whatever to do with the proposition, which is that Madame La Gimp's baby, Eulalie, is arriving here.

"Now," Dave says, "it seems that Madame La Gimp's baby, being now eighteen years old, is engaged to marry the son of a very proud old Spanish nobleman who lives in this little town in Spain, and it also seems that the very proud old Spanish nobleman, and his ever-loving wife, and the son, and Madame La Gimp's sister, are all with the baby. They are making a tour of the whole world, and will stop over here a couple of days just to see Madame La Gimp."

"It is commencing to sound to me like a movie such as a guy is apt to see at a midnight show," I say.

"Wait a minute," Dave says, getting impatient. "You are too gabby to suit me. Now it seems that the proud old Spanish nobleman does not wish his son to marry any lob, and one reason he is coming here is to look over Madame La Gimp, and see that she is okay. He thinks that Madame La Gimp's baby's own papa is dead, and that Madame La Gimp is now married to one of the richest and most aristocratic guys in America."

"How does the proud old Spanish nobleman get such an idea as this?" I ask. "It is a sure thing he never sees Madame La Gimp, or even a photograph of her as she is at present."

"I will tell you how," Dave the Dude says. "It seems Madame La Gimp gives her baby the idea that such is the case in her letters to her. It seems Madame La Gimp does a little scrubbing business around a swell apartment hotel in Park Avenue that is called the Marberry, and she cops stationery there and writes her baby in Spain on this stationery saying this is where she lives, and how rich and aristocratic her husband is. And what is more, Madame La Gimp has letters from her baby sent to her in care of the hotel and gets them out of the employees' mail."

"Why," I say, "Madame La Gimp is nothing but an old fraud to deceive people in this manner, especially a proud old Spanish nobleman. And," I say, "this proud old Spanish nobleman must be something of a chump to believe a mother will keep away from her baby all these years, especially if the mother has plenty of dough, although of course I do not know just how smart a proud old Spanish nobleman can be."

"Well," Dave says, "Madame La Gimp tells me the thing that makes the biggest hit of all with the proud old Spanish nobleman is that she keeps her baby in Spain all these years because she wishes her raised up a true Spanish baby in every respect until she is old enough to know what time it is. But I judge the proud old Spanish nobleman is none too bright, at that," Dave says, "because Madame La Gimp tells me he always lives in this little town which does not even have running water in the bathrooms.

"But what I am getting at is this," Dave says. "We must have Madame La Gimp in a swell apartment in the Marberry with a rich and aristocratic guy for a husband by the time her baby gets here, because if the proud old Spanish nobleman finds out Madame La Gimp is nothing but a bum, it is a hundred to one he will cancel his son's engagement to Madame La Gimp's baby and break a lot of people's hearts, including his son's.

"Madame La Gimp tells me her baby is daffy about the young guy, and he is daffy about her, and there are enough broken hearts in this town as it is. I know how I will get the apartment, so you go and bring me Judge Henry G. Blake for a rich and aristocratic husband, or anyway for a husband."

Well, I know Dave the Dude to do many a daffy thing but never a thing as daffy as this. But I know there is no use arguing with him when he gets an idea, because if you argue with Dave the Dude too much he is apt to reach over and lay his Sunday punch on your snoot, and no argument is worth a punch on the snoot, especially from Dave the Dude.

So I go out looking for Judge Henry G. Blake to be Madame La Gimp's husband, although I am not so sure Judge Henry G. Blake will care to be anybody's husband, and especially Madame La Gimp's after he gets a load of her, for Judge Henry G. Blake is kind of a classy old guy.

To look at Judge Henry G. Blake, with his gray hair, and his nose glasses, and his stomach, you will think he is very important people, indeed. Of course Judge Henry G. Blake is not a judge, and never is a judge, but they call him Judge because he looks like a judge, and talks slow, and puts in many long words, which very few people understand.

They tell me Judge Blake once has plenty of dough, and is quite a guy in Wall Street, and a high shot along Broadway, but he misses a few guesses at the market, and winds up without much dough, as guys generally do who miss guesses at the market. What Judge Henry G. Blake does for a living at this time nobody knows, because he does nothing much whatever, and yet he seems to be a producer in a small way at all times.

Now and then he makes a trip across the ocean with

such as Little Manuel, and other guys who ride the tubs,
and sits in with them on games of bridge, and one thing
and another, when they need him. Very often when he
is riding the tubs, Little Manuel runs into some guy he
cannot cheat, so he has to call in Judge Henry G. Blake to
outplay the guy on the level, although of course Little
Manuel will much rather get a guy's dough by cheating
him than by outplaying him on the level. Why this is, I
do not know, but this is the way Little Manuel is.

Anyway, you cannot say Judge Henry G. Blake is a
bum, especially as he wears good clothes, with a wing collar, and a derby hat, and most people consider him a very
nice old man. Personally I never catch the judge out of
line on any proposition whatever, and he always says hello
to me, very pleasant.

It takes me several hours to find Judge Henry G. Blake,
but finally I locate him in Derle's billiard room playing a
game of pool with a guy from Providence, Rhode Island.
It seems the judge is playing the guy from Providence for
five cents a ball, and the judge is about thirteen balls behind when I step into the joint, because naturally at
five cents a ball the judge wishes the guy from Providence to win, so as to encourage him to play for maybe
twenty-five cents a ball, the judge being very cute this
way.

Well, when I step in I see the judge miss a shot anybody can make blindfolded, but as soon as I give him the
office I wish to speak to him, the judge hauls off and belts
in every ball on the table, bingity-bing, the last shot being
a bank that will make Al de Oro stop and think, because

when it comes to pool, the old judge is just naturally a
curly wolf.

Afterwards he tells me he is very sorry I make him hurry
up this way, because of course after the last shot he is
never going to get the guy from Providence to play him
pool even for fun, and the judge tells me the guy sizes up
as a right good thing, at that.

Now Judge Henry G. Blake is not so excited when I
tell him what Dave the Dude wishes to see him about, but
naturally he is willing to do anything for Dave, because
he knows that guys who are not willing to do things for
Dave the Dude often have bad luck. The judge tells me
that he is afraid he will not make much of a husband because he tries it before several times on his own hook and
is always a bust, but as long as this time it is not to be
anything serious, he will tackle it. Anyway, Judge Henry
G. Blake says, being aristocratic will come natural to him.

Well, when Dave the Dude starts out on any proposition,
he is a wonder for fast working. The first thing he does is
to turn Madame La Gimp over to Miss Billy Perry, who
is now Dave's ever-loving wife which he takes out of tap-
dancing in Miss Missouri Martin's Sixteen Hundred Club,
and Miss Billy Perry calls in Miss Missouri Martin to help.

This is water on Miss Missouri Martin's wheel, because
if there is anything she loves it is to stick her nose in other
people's business, no matter what it is, but she is quite a
help at that, although at first they have a tough time keeping her from telling Waldo Winchester, the scribe, about
the whole cat-hop, so he will put a story in the *Morning
Item* about it, with Miss Missouri Martin's name in it.

Miss Missouri Martin does not believe in ever overlooking any publicity bets on the layout.

Anyway, it seems that between them Miss Billy Perry and Miss Missouri Martin get Madame La Gimp dolled up in a lot of new clothes, and run her through one of these beauty joints until she comes out very much changed, indeed. Afterwards I hear Miss Billy Perry and Miss Missouri Martin have quite a few words, because Miss Missouri Martin wishes to paint Madame La Gimp's hair the same color as her own, which is a high yellow, and buy her the same kind of dresses which Miss Missouri Martin wears herself, and Miss Missouri Martin gets much insulted when Miss Billy Perry says no, they are trying to dress Madame La Gimp to look like a lady.

They tell me Miss Missouri Martin thinks some of putting the slug on Miss Billy Perry for this crack, but happens to remember just in time that Miss Billy Perry is now Dave the Dude's ever-loving wife, and that nobody in this town can put the slug on Dave's ever-loving wife, except maybe Dave himself.

Now the next thing anybody knows, Madame La Gimp is in a swell eight- or nine-room apartment in the Marberry, and the way this comes about is as follows: It seems that one of Dave the Dude's most important champagne customers is a guy by the name of Rodney B. Emerson, who owns the apartment, but who is at his summer home in Newport, with his family, or anyway with his ever-loving wife.

This Rodney B. Emerson is quite a guy along Broadway, and a great hand for spending dough and looking for laughs, and he is very popular with the mob. Furthermore, he is obligated to Dave the Dude, because Dave sells him good champagne when most guys are trying to hand him the old phonus bolonus, and naturally Rodney B. Emerson appreciates this kind of treatment.

He is a short, fat guy, with a round, red face, and a big laugh, and the kind of a guy Dave the Dude can call up at his home in Newport and explain the situation and ask for the loan of the apartment, which Dave does.

Well, it seems Rodney B. Emerson gets a big bang out of the idea, and he says to Dave the Dude like this:

"You not only can have the apartment, Dave, but I will come over and help you out. It will save a lot of explaining around the Marberry if I am there."

So he hops right over from Newport, and joins in with Dave the Dude, and I wish to say Rodney B. Emerson will always be kindly remembered by one and all for his co-operation, and nobody will every again try to hand him the phonus bolonus when he is buying champagne, even if he is not buying it off of Dave the Dude.

Well, it is coming on Saturday and the boat from Spain is due, so Dave the Dude hires a big town car, and puts his own driver, Wop Sam, on it, as he does not wish any strange driver tipping off anybody that it is a hired car. Miss Missouri Martin is anxious to go to the boat with Madame La Gimp, and take her jazz band, the Hi Hi Boys, from her Sixteen Hundred Club with her to make it a real welcome, but nobody thinks much of this idea. Only Madame La Gimp and her husband, Judge Henry G. Blake, and Miss Billy Perry go, though the judge holds out for some time for Little Manuel, because Judge Blake says he wishes somebody around to tip him off in case there are any bad cracks made about him as a husband in Spanish, and Little Manuel is very Spanish.

The morning they go to meet the boat is the first time Judge Henry G. Blake gets a load of his ever-loving wife, Madame La Gimp, and by this time Miss Billy Perry and Miss Missouri Martin give Madame La Gimp such a going-over that she is by no means the worst looker in the world. In fact, she looks first-rate, especially as she is off gin and says she is off it for good.

Judge Henry G. Blake is really quite surprised by her looks as he figures all along she will turn out to be a crow. In fact, Judge Blake hurls a couple of shots into himself to nerve himself for the ordeal, as he explains it, before he appears to go to the boat. Between these shots, and the nice clothes, and the good cleaning-up Miss Billy Perry and Miss Missouri Martin give Madame La Gimp, she is really a pleasant sight to the judge.

They tell me the meeting at the dock between Madame La Gimp and her baby is very affecting indeed, and when the proud old Spanish nobleman and his wife, and their son, and Madame La Gimp's sister, all go into action, too, there are enough tears around there to float all the battle-ships we once sink for Spain. Even Miss Billy Perry and Judge Henry G. Blake do some first-class crying, although the chances are the judge is worked up to the crying more by the shots he takes for his courage than by the meeting.

Still, I hear the old judge does himself proud, what with kissing Madame La Gimp's baby plenty, and duking the proud old Spanish nobleman, and his wife, and son, and giving Madame La Gimp's sister a good strong hug that squeezes her tongue out.

It turns out that the proud old Spanish nobleman has white sideburns, and is entitled Conde de Something, so his ever-loving wife is the Condesa, and the son is a very nice-looking quiet young guy any way you take him, who blushes every time anybody looks at him. As for Madame La Gimp's baby, she is as pretty as they come, and many guys are sorry they do not get Judge Henry G. Blake's job as stepfather, because he is able to take a kiss at Madame La Gimp's baby on what seems to be very small excuse. I never see a nicer-looking young couple, and anybody can see they are very fond of each other, indeed.

Madame La Gimp's sister is not such a doll as I will wish to have sawed off on me, and is up in the paints as regards to age, but she is also very quiet. None of the bunch talk any English, so Miss Billy Perry and Judge Henry G. Blake are pretty much outsiders on the way uptown. Anyway, the judge takes the wind as soon as they reach the Marberry, because the judge is now getting a little tired of being a husband. He says he has to take a trip out to Pittsburgh to buy four or five coal mines, but will be back the next day.

Well, it seems to me that everything is going perfect so far, and that it is good judgment to let it lay as it is, but nothing will do Dave the Dude but to have a reception the following night. I advise Dave the Dude against this idea, because I am afraid something will happen to spoil the whole cat-hop, but he will not listen to me, especially as Rodney B. Emerson is now in town and is a strong booster for the party, as he wishes to drink some of the good champagne he has planted in his apartment.

Furthermore, Miss Billy Perry and Miss Missouri Martin are very indignant at me when they hear about my advice, as it seems they both buy new dresses out of Dave the Dude's bank roll when they are dressing up Madame La Gimp, and they wish to spring these dresses somewhere where they can be seen. So the party is on.

I get to the Marberry around nine o'clock and who opens the door of Madame La Gimp's apartment for me but Moosh, the door man from Miss Missouri Martin's Sixteen Hundred Club. Furthermore, he is in his Sixteen Hundred Club uniform, except he has a clean shave. I wish Moosh a hello, and he never raps to me but only bows, and takes my hat.

The next guy I see is Rodney B. Emerson in evening clothes, and the minute he sees me he yells out, "Mister O. O. McIntyre." Well, of course I am not Mister O. O. McIntyre, and never put myself away as Mister O. O. McIntyre, and furthermore there is no resemblance whatever between Mister O. O. McIntyre and me, because I am a fairly good-looking guy, and I start to give Rodney B. Emerson an argument, when he whispers to me like this:

"Listen," he whispers, "we must have big names at this affair, so as to impress these people. The chances are they read the newspapers back there in Spain, and we must let them meet the folks they read about, so they will see Madame La Gimp is a real big shot to get such names to a party."

Then he takes me by the arm and leads me to a group of people in a corner of the room, which is about the size of the Grand Central waiting room.

"Mister O. O. McIntyre, the big writer!" Rodney B. Emerson says, and the next thing I know I am shaking hands with Mr. and Mrs. Conde, and their son, and with

Madame La Gimp and her baby, and Madame La Gimp's sister, and finally with Judge Henry G. Blake, who has on a swallowtail coat, and does not give me much of a tumble. I figure the chances are Judge Henry G. Blake is getting a swelled head already, not to tumble up a guy who helps him get his job, but even at that I wish to say the old judge looks immense in his swallowtail coat, bowing and giving one and all the old castor oil smile.

Madame La Gimp is in a low-neck black dress and is wearing a lot of Miss Missouri Martin's diamonds, such as rings and bracelets, which Miss Missouri Martin insists on hanging on her, although I hear afterwards that Miss Missouri Martin has Johnny Brannigan, the plain clothes copper, watching these diamonds. I wonder at the time why Johnny is there but figure it is because he is a friend of Dave the Dude's. Miss Missouri Martin is no sucker, even if she is kind-hearted.

Anybody looking at Madame La Gimp will bet you all the coffee in Java that she never lives in a cellar over in Tenth Avenue, and drinks plenty of gin in her day. She has her gray hair piled up high on her head, with a big Spanish comb in it, and she reminds me of a picture I see somewhere, but I do not remember just where. And her baby, Eulalie, in a white dress is about as pretty a little doll as you will wish to see, and nobody can blame Judge Henry G. Blake for copping a kiss off of her now and then.

Well, pretty soon I hear Rodney B. Emerson bawling, "Mister Willie K. Vanderbilt," and in comes nobody but Big Nig, and Rodney B. Emerson leads him over to the group and introduces him.

Little Manuel is standing alongside Judge Henry G.

Blake, and he explains in Spanish to Mr. and Mrs. Conde and the others that "Willie K. Vanderbilt" is a very large millionaire, and Mr. and Mrs. Conde seem much interested, anyway, though naturally Madame La Gimp and Judge Henry G. Blake are jerry to Big Nig, while Madame La Gimp's baby and the young guy are interested in nobody but each other.

Then I hear, "Mister Al Jolson," and in comes nobody but Tony Bertazzola, from the Chicken Club, who looks about as much like Al as I do like O. O. McIntyre, which is not at all. Next comes "the Very Reverend John Roach Straton," who seems to be Skeets Bolivar to me, then "the Honorable Mayor James J. Walker," and who is it but Good-Time Charley Bernstein.

"Mister Otto H. Kahn" turns out to be Rochester Red, and "Mister Heywood Broun" is Nick the Greek, who asks me privately who Heywood Broun is, and gets very sore at Rodney B. Emerson when I describe Heywood Broun to him.

Finally there is quite a commotion at the door and Rodney B. Emerson announces, "Mister Herbert Bayard Swope" in an extra loud voice which makes everybody look around, but it is nobody but the Pale Face Kid. He gets me to one side, too, and wishes to know who Herbert Bayard Swope is, and when I explain to him, the Pale Face Kid gets so swelled up he will not speak to Death House Donegan, who is only "Mister William Muldoon."

Well, it seems to me they are getting too strong when they announce, "Vice-President of the United States, the Honorable Charles Curtis," and in pops Guinea Mike, and I say as much to Dave the Dude, who is running around every which way looking after things, but he only says, "Well, if you do not know it is Guinea Mike, will you know it is not Vice-President Curtis?"

But it seems to me all this is most disrespectful to our leading citizens, especially when Rodney B. Emerson calls, "The Honorable Police Commissioner, Mister Grover A. Whalen," and in pops Wild William Wilkins, who is a very hot man at this time, being wanted in several spots for different raps. Dave the Dude takes personal charge of Wild William and removes a rod from his pants pocket, because none of the guests are supposed to come rodded up, this being strictly a social matter.

I watch Mr. and Mrs. Conde, and I do not see that these names are making any impression on them, and I afterwards find out that they never get any newspapers in their town in Spain except a little local bladder which only prints the home news. In fact, Mr. and Mrs. Conde seem somewhat bored, although Mr. Conde cheers up no little and looks interested when a lot of dolls drift in. They are mainly dolls from Miss Missouri Martin's Sixteen Hundred Club, and the Hot Box, but Rodney B. Emerson introduces them as "Sophie Tucker," and "Theda Bara," and "Jeanne Eagles," and "Helen Morgan" and "Aunt Jemima," and one thing and another.

Well, pretty soon in comes Miss Missouri Martin's jazz band, the Hi Hi Boys, and the party commences getting up steam, especially when Dave the Dude gets Rodney B. Emerson to breaking out the old grape. By and by there is dancing going on, and a good time is being had by one and all, including Mr. and Mrs. Conde. In fact, after Mr. Conde gets a couple of jolts of the old grape, he turns out to be a pretty nice old skate, even if nobody can understand what he is talking about.

As for Judge Henry G. Blake, he is full of speed, indeed. By this time anybody can see that the judge is commencing to believe that all this is on the level and that he is really entertaining celebrities in his own home. You put a quart of good grape inside the old judge and he will believe anything. He soon dances himself plumb out of wind, and then I notice he is hanging around Madame La Gimp a lot.

Along about midnight, Dave the Dude has to go out into the kitchen and settle a battle there over a crap game, but otherwise everything is very peaceful. It seems that "Herbert Bayard Swope," "Vice-President Curtis" and "Grover Whalen" get a little game going, when "the Reverend John Roach Straton" steps up and cleans them in four passes, but it seems that they soon discover that "the Reverend John Roach Straton" is using tops on them, which are very dishonest dice, and so they put the slug on "the Reverend John Roach Straton" and Dave the Dude has to split them out.

By and by I figure on taking the wind, and I look for Mr. and Mrs. Conde to tell them good night, but Mr. Conde and Miss Missouri Martin are still dancing, and Miss Missouri Martin is pouring conversation into Mr. Conde's ear by the bucketful, and while Mr. Conde does not savvy a word she says, this makes no difference to Miss Missouri Martin. Let Miss Missouri Martin do all the talking, and she does not care a whoop if anybody understands her.

Mrs. Conde is over in a corner with "Herbert Bayard Swope," or the Pale Face Kid, who is trying to find out from her by using hog Latin and signs on her if there is any chance for a good twenty-one dealer in Spain, and of course Mrs. Conde is not able to make heads or tails of what he means, so I hunt up Madame La Gimp.

She is sitting in a darkish corner off by herself and I really do not see Judge Henry G. Blake leaning over her until I am almost on top of them, so I cannot help hearing what the judge is saying.

"I am wondering for two days," he says, "if by any chance you remember me. Do you know who I am?"

"I remember you," Madame La Gimp says. "I remember you—oh, so very well, Henry. How can I forget you? But I have no idea you recognize me after all these years."

"Twenty of them now," Judge Henry G. Blake says. "You are beautiful then. You are still beautiful."

Well, I can see the old grape is working first-class on Judge Henry G. Blake to make such remarks as this, although at that, in the half light, with the smile on her face, Madame La Gimp is not so bad. Still, give me them carrying a little less weight for age.

"Well, it is all your fault," Judge Henry G. Blake says. "You go and marry that chile con carne guy, and look what happens!"

I can see there is no sense in me horning in on Madame La Gimp and Judge Henry G. Blake while they are cutting up old touches in this manner, so I think I will just say good-by to the young people and let it go at that, but while I am looking for Madame La Gimp's baby, and her guy, I run into Dave the Dude.

"You will not find them here," Dave says. "By this time they are being married over at Saint Malachy's with my ever-loving wife and Big Nig standing up with them. We get the license for them yesterday afternoon. Can you imagine a couple of young saps wishing to wait until they go plumb around the world before getting married?"

Well, of course this elopement creates much excitement for a few minutes, but by Monday Mr. and Mrs. Conde and the young folks and Madame La Gimp's sister take a train for California to keep on going around the world, leaving us nothing to talk about but about old Judge Henry G. Blake and Madame La Gimp getting themselves married too, and going to Detroit where Judge Henry G. Blake claims he has a brother in the plumbing business who will give him a job, although personally I think Judge Henry G. Blake figures to do a little booting on his own hook in and out of Canada. It is not like Judge Henry G. Blake to tie himself up to the plumbing business.

So there is nothing more to the story, except that Dave the Dude is around a few days later with a big sheet of paper in his duke and very, very indignant.

"If every single article listed here is not kicked back to the owners of the different joints in the Marberry that they are taken from by next Tuesday night, I will bust a lot of noses around this town," Dave says. "I am greatly mortified by such happenings at my social affairs, and everything must be returned at once. Especially," Dave says, "the baby grand piano that is removed from Apartment 9-D."

THE HOTTEST GUY IN THE WORLD

I WISH to say I am very nervous indeed when Big Jule pops into my hotel room one afternoon, because anybody will tell you that Big Jule is the hottest guy in the whole world at the time I am speaking about.

In fact, it is really surprising how hot he is. They wish to see him in Pittsburgh, Pa., about a matter of a mail truck being robbed, and there is gossip about him in Minneapolis, Minn., where somebody takes a fifty *G* pay roll off a messenger in cash money, and slugs the messenger around somewhat for not holding still.

Furthermore, the Bankers' Association is willing to pay good dough to talk to Big Jule out in Kansas City, Mo., where a jug is knocked off by a stranger, and in the confusion the paying teller, and the cashier, and the second vice president are clouted about, and the day watchman is hurt, and two coppers are badly bruised, and over fifteen *G's* is removed from the counters, and never returned.

Then there is something about a department store in Canton, O., and a flour mill safe in Toledo, and a grocery in Spokane, Wash., and a branch postoffice in San Francisco, and also something about a shooting match in Chicago, but of course this does not count so much, as only one party is fatally injured. However, you can see that Big Jule is really very hot, what with the coppers all over the country looking for him high and low. In fact, he is practically on fire.

Of course I do not believe Big Jule does all the things the coppers say, because coppers always blame everything no matter where it happens on the most prominent guy they can think of, and Big Jule is quite prominent all over the U. S. A. The chances are he does not do more than half these things, and he probably has a good alibi for the half he does do, at that, but he is certainly hot, and I do not care to have hot guys around me, or even guys who are only just a little bit warm.

But naturally I am not going to say this to Big Jule when he pops in on me, because he may think I am inhospitable, and I do not care to have such a rap going around and about on me, and furthermore Jule may become indignant if he thinks I am inhospitable, and knock me on my potato, because Big Jule is quick to take offense.

So I say hello to Big Jule, very pleasant, and ask him to have a chair by the window where he can see the citizens walking to and fro down in Eighth Avenue and watch the circus wagons moving into Madison Square Garden by way of the Forty-ninth Street side, for the circus always shows in the Garden in the spring before going out on the road. It is a little warm, and Big Jule takes off his coat, and I can see he has one automatic slung under his arm, and another sticking down in the waistband of his pants, and I hope and trust that no copper steps into the room while Big Jule is there because it is very much against the law for guys to go around rodded up this way in New York City.

"Well, Jule," I say, "this is indeed a very large surprise to me, and I am glad to see you, but I am thinking maybe it is very foolish for you to be popping into New York just now, what with all the heat around here, and the coppers looking to arrest people for very little."

"I know," Jule says. "I know. But they do not have so very much on me around here, no matter what people say, and a guy gets homesick for his old home town, especially a guy who is stuck away where I am for the past few months. I get homesick for the lights and the crowds on Broadway, and for the old neighborhood. Furthermore, I wish to see my Maw. I hear she is sick and may not live, and I wish to see her before she goes."

Well, naturally anybody will wish to see their Maw under such circumstances, but Big Jule's Maw lives over in West Forty-ninth Street near Eleventh Avenue, and who is living in the very same block but Johnny Brannigan, the strong arm copper, and it is a hundred to one if Big Jule goes nosing around his old neighborhood, Johnny Brannigan will hear of it, and if there is one guy Johnny Brannigan does not care for, it is Big Jule, although they are kids together.

But it seems that even when they are kids they have very little use for each other, and after they grow up and Johnny gets on the strong arm squad, he never misses a chance to push Big Jule around, and sometimes trying to boff Big Jule with his blackjack, and it is well known to one and all that before Big Jule leaves town the last time, he takes a punch at Johnny Brannigan, and Johnny swears he will never rest until he puts Big Jule where he belongs, although where Big Jule belongs, Johnny does not say.

So I speak of Johnny living in the same block with Big Jule's Maw to Big Jule, but it only makes him mad.

"I am not afraid of Johnny Brannigan," he says. "In

fact," he says, "I am thinking for some time lately that maybe I will clip Johnny Brannigan good while I am here. I owe Johnny Brannigan a clipping. But I wish to see my Maw first, and then I will go around and see Miss Kitty Clancy. I guess maybe she will be much surprised to see me, and no doubt very glad."

Well, I figure it is a sure thing Miss Kitty Clancy will be surprised to see Big Jule, but I am not so sure about her being glad, because very often when a guy is away from a doll for a year or more, no matter how ever-loving she may be, she may get to thinking of someone else, for this is the way dolls are, whether they live on Eleventh Avenue or over on Park. Still, I remember hearing that this Miss Kitty Clancy once thinks very well of Big Jule, although her old man, Jack Clancy, who runs a speakeasy, always claims it is a big knock to the Clancy family to have such a character as Big Jule hanging around.

"I often think of Miss Kitty Clancy the past year or so," Big Jule says, as he sits there by the window, watching the circus wagons, and the crowds. "I especially think of her the past few months. In fact," he says, "thinking of Miss Kitty Clancy is about all I have to do where I am at, which is in an old warehouse on the Bay of Fundy outside of a town that is called St. Johns, or some such, up in Canada, and thinking of Miss Kitty Clancy all this time, I find out I love her very much indeed.

"I go to this warehouse," Big Jule says, "after somebody takes a jewelry store in the town, and the coppers start in blaming me. This warehouse is not such a place as I will choose myself if I am doing the choosing, because it is an old fur warehouse, and full of strange smells, but in the

excitement around the jewelry store, somebody puts a slug
in my hip, and Leon Pierre carries me to the old warehouse,
and there I am until I get well.

"It is very lonesome," Big Jule says. "In fact, you will
be surprised how lonesome it is, and it is very, very cold,
and all I have for company is a lot of rats. Personally, I
never care for rats under any circumstances because they
carry disease germs, and are apt to bite a guy when he is
asleep, if they are hungry, which is what these rats try to
do to me.

"The warehouse is away off by itself," Jule says, "and
nobody ever comes around there except Leon Pierre to
bring me grub and dress my hip, and at night it is very
still, and all you can hear is the wind howling around outside, and the rats running here and there. Some of them
are very, very large rats. In fact, some of them seem about
the size of rabbits, and they are pretty fresh, at that. At
first I am willing to make friends with these rats, but they
seem very hostile, and after they take a few nips at me I
can see there is no use trying to be nice to them, so I have
Leon Pierre bring me a lot of ammunition for my rods
every day and I practice shooting at the rats.

"The warehouse is so far off there is no danger of anybody hearing the shooting," Big Jule says, "and it helps
me pass the time away. I get so I can hit a rat sitting, or
running, or even flying through the air, because these warehouse rats often leap from place to place like mountain
sheep, their idea being generally to take a good nab at me
as they fly past.

"Well, sir," Jule says, "I keep score on myself one day,
and I hit fifty rats hand running without a miss, which I

claim makes me the champion rat shooter of the world
with a 45 automatic, although of course," he says, "if anybody wishes to challenge me to a rat shooting match I am
willing to take them on for a side bet. I get so I can call
my shots on the rats, and in fact several times I say to
myself, I will hit this one in the right eye, and this one in
the left eye, and it always turns out just as I say, although
sometimes when you hit a rat with a 45 up close it is not
always possible to tell afterwards just where you hit him,
because you seem to hit him all over.

"By and by," Jule says, "I seem to discourage the rats
somewhat, and they get so they play the chill for me, and
do not try to nab me even when I am asleep. They find
out that no rat dast poke his whiskers out at me or he will
get a very close shave. So I have to look around for other
amusement, but there is not much doing in such a place,
although I finally find a bunch of doctors' books which
turn out to be very interesting reading. It seems these books
are left there by some croaker who retires there to think
things over after experimenting on his ever-loving wife
with a knife. In fact, it seems he cuts his ever-loving wife's
head off, and she does not continue living, so he takes his
books and goes to the warehouse and remains there until
the law finds him, and hangs him up very high, indeed.

"Well, the books are a great comfort to me, and I learn
many astonishing things about surgery, but after I read
all the books there is nothing for me to do but think, and
what I think about is Miss Kitty Clancy, and how much
pleasure we have together walking around and about and
seeing movie shows, and all this and that, until her old man
gets so tough with me. Yes, I will be very glad to see Miss

Kitty Clancy, and the old neighborhood, and my Maw again."

Well, finally nothing will do Big Jule but he must take a stroll over into his old neighborhood, and see if he cannot see Miss Kitty Clancy, and also drop in on his Maw, and he asks me to go along with him. I can think of a million things I will rather do than take a stroll with Big Jule, but I do not wish him to think I am snobbish, because as I say, Big Jule is quick to take offense. Furthermore, I figure that at such an hour of the day he is less likely to run into Johnny Brannigan or any other coppers who know him than at any other time, so I say I will go with him, but as we start out, Big Jule puts on his rods.

"Jule," I say, "do not take any rods with you on a stroll, because somebody may happen to see them, such as a copper, and you know they will pick you up for carrying a rod in this town quicker than you can say Jack Robinson, whether they know who you are or not. You know the Sullivan law is very strong against guys carrying rods in this town."

But Big Jule says he is afraid he will catch cold if he goes out without his rods, so we go down into Forty-ninth Street and start west toward Madison Square Garden, and just as we reach Eighth Avenue and are standing there waiting for the traffic to stop, so we can cross the street, I see there is quite some excitement around the Garden on the Forty-ninth Street side, with people running every which way, and yelling no little, and looking up in the air.

So I look up myself, and what do I see sitting up there on the edge of the Garden roof but a big ugly faced monkey. At first I do not recognize it as a monkey, be-

cause it is so big I figure maybe it is just one of the prize
fight managers who stand around on this side of the Garden all afternoon waiting to get a match for their fighters,
and while I am somewhat astonished to see a prize fight
manager in such a position, I figure maybe he is doing it
on a bet. But when I take a second look I see that it is
indeed a big monk, and an exceptionally homely monk at
that, although personally I never see any monks I consider
so very handsome, anyway.

Well, this big monk is holding something in its arms,
and what it is I am not able to make out at first, but then
Big Jule and I cross the street to the side opposite the
Garden, and now I can see that the monk has a baby in
its arms. Naturally I figure it is some kind of advertising
dodge put on by the Garden to ballyhoo the circus, or
maybe the fight between Sharkey and Risko which is coming off after the circus, but guys are still yelling and
running up and down, and dolls are screaming until
finally I realize that a most surprising situation prevails.

It seems that the big monk up on the roof is nobody but
Bongo, who is a gorilla belonging to the circus, and one
of the very few gorillas of any account in this country, or
anywhere else, as far as this goes, because good gorillas are
very scarce, indeed. Well, it seems that while they are
shoving Bongo's cage into the Garden, the door becomes
unfastened, and the first thing anybody knows, out pops
Bongo, and goes bouncing along the street where a lot of
the neighbors' children are playing games on the sidewalk,
and a lot of Mammas are sitting out in the sun alongside
baby buggies containing their young. This is a very common sight in side streets such as West Forty-ninth on nice

days, and by no means unpleasant, if you like Mammas
and their young.

Now what does this Bongo do but reach into a baby
buggy which a Mamma is pushing past on the sidewalk on
the Garden side of the street, and snatch out a baby, though
what Bongo wants with this baby nobody knows to this
day. It is a very young baby, and not such a baby as is
fit to give a gorilla the size of Bongo any kind of struggle,
so Bongo has no trouble whatever in handling it. Anyway,
I always hear a gorilla will make a sucker out of a grown
man in a battle, though I wish to say I never see a battle
between a gorilla and a grown man. It ought to be a first
class drawing card, at that.

Well, naturally the baby's Mamma puts up quite a
squawk about Bongo grabbing her baby, because no
Mamma wishes her baby to keep company with a gorilla,
and this Mamma starts in screaming very loud, and trying
to take the baby away from Bongo, so what does Bongo
do but run right up on the roof of the Garden by way of
a big electric sign which hangs down on the Forty-ninth
Street side. And there old Bongo sits on the edge of the
roof with the baby in his arms, and the baby is squalling
quite some, and Bongo is making funny noises, and showing his teeth as the folks commence gathering in the street
below.

There is a big guy in his shirt sleeves running through
the crowd waving his hands, and trying to shush everybody, and saying "quiet, please" over and over, but nobody
pays any attention to him. I figure this guy has something
to do with the circus, and maybe with Bongo, too. A
traffic copper takes a peek at the situation, and calls for

the reserves from the Forty-seventh Street station, and somebody else sends for the fire truck down the street, and pretty soon cops are running from every direction, and the fire engines are coming, and the big guy in his shirt sleeves is more excited than ever.

"Quiet, please," he says. "Everybody keep quiet, because if Bongo becomes disturbed by the noise he will throw the baby down in the street. He throws everything he gets his hands on," the guy says. "He acquires this habit from throwing coconuts back in his old home country. Let us get a life net, and if you all keep quiet we may be able to save the baby before Bongo starts heaving it like a coconut."

Well, Bongo is sitting up there on the edge of the roof about seven stories above the ground peeking down with the baby in his arms, and he is holding this baby just like a Mamma would, but anybody can see that Bongo does not care for the row below, and once he lifts the baby high above his head as if to bean somebody with it. I see Big Nig, the crap shooter, in the mob, and afterwards I hear he is around offering to lay 7 to 5 against the baby, but everybody is too excited to bet on such a proposition, although it is not a bad price, at that.

I see one doll in the crowd on the sidewalk on the side of the street opposite the Garden who is standing perfectly still staring up at the monk and the baby with a very strange expression on her face, and the way she is looking makes me take a second gander at her, and who is it but Miss Kitty Clancy. Her lips are moving as she stands there staring up, and something tells me Miss Kitty Clancy is saying prayers to herself, because she is such a doll as will know how to say prayers on an occasion like this.

Big Jule sees her about the same time I do, and Big Jule steps up beside Miss Kitty Clancy, and says hello to her, and though it is over a year since Miss Kitty Clancy sees Big Jule she turns to him and speaks to him as if she is talking to him just a minute before. It is very strange indeed the way Miss Kitty Clancy speaks to Big Jule as if he has never been away at all.

"Do something, Julie," she says. "You are always the one to do something. Oh, please do something, Julie."

Well Big Jule never answers a word, but steps back in the clear of the crowd and reaches for the waistband of his pants, when I grab him by the arm and say to him like this:

"My goodness, Jule," I say, "what are you going to do?"

"Why," Jule says, "I am going to shoot this thieving monk before he takes a notion to heave the baby on somebody down here. For all I know," Jule says, "he may hit me with it, and I do not care to be hit with anybody's baby."

"Jule," I say, very earnestly, "do not pull a rod in front of all these coppers, because if you do they will nail you sure, if only for having the rod, and if you are nailed you are in a very tough spot, indeed, what with being wanted here and there. Jule," I say, "you are hotter than a forty-five all over this country, and I do not wish to see you nailed. Anyway," I say, "you may shoot the baby instead of the monk, because anybody can see it will be very difficult to hit the monk up there without hitting the baby.

Furthermore, even if you do hit the monk it will fall into
the street, and bring the baby with it."

"You speak great foolishness," Jule says. "I never miss
what I shoot at. I will shoot the monk right between the
eyes, and this will make him fall backwards, not forwards,
and the baby will not be hurt because anybody can see it
is no fall at all from the ledge to the roof behind. I make
a study of such propositions," Jule says, "and I know if a
guy is in such a position as this monk sitting on a ledge
looking down from a high spot his defensive reflexes tend
backwards, so this is the way he is bound to fall if anything
unexpected comes up on him such as a bullet between the
eyes. I read all about it in the doctor's books," Jule says.

Then all of a sudden up comes his hand, and in his
hand is one of his rods, and I hear a sound like ker-bap.
When I come to think about it afterwards, I do not remember Big Jule even taking aim like a guy will generally
do if he is shooting at something sitting, but old Bongo
seems to lift up a little bit off the ledge at the crack of the
gun and then he keels over backwards, the baby still in his
arms, and squalling more than somewhat, and Big Jule
says to me like this:

"Right between the eyes, and I will bet on it," he says,
"although it is not much of a target, at that."

Well, nobody can figure what happens for a minute,
and there is much silence except from the guy in his shirt
sleeves who is expressing much indignation with Big Jule
and saying the circus people will sue him for damages
sure if he has hurt Bongo because the monk is worth
$100,000, or some such. I see Miss Kitty Clancy kneeling on
the sidewalk with her hands clasped, and looking upward,

and Big Jule is sticking his rod back in his waistband again.

By this time some guys are out on the roof getting through from the inside of the building with the idea of heading Bongo off from that direction, and they let out a yell, and pretty soon I see one of them holding the baby up so everyone in the street can see it. A couple of other guys get down near the edge of the roof and pick up Bongo and show him to the crowd, as dead as a mackerel, and one of the guys puts a finger between Bongo's eyes to show where the bulleet hits the monk, and Miss Kitty Clancy walks over to Big Jule and tries to say something to him, but only busts out crying very loud.

Well, I figure this is a good time for Big Jule and me to take a walk, because everybody is interested in what is going on up on the roof, and I do not wish the circus people to get a chance to serve a summons in a damage suit on Big Jule for shooting the valuable monk. Furthermore, a couple of coppers in harness are looking Big Jule over very critically, and I figure they are apt to put the old sleeve on Jule any second.

All of a sudden a slim young guy steps up to Big Jule and says to him like this:

"Jule," he says, "I want to see you," and who is it but Johnny Brannigan. Naturally Big Jule starts reaching for a rod, but Johnny starts him walking down the street so fast Big Jule does not have time to get in action just then.

"No use getting it out, Jule," Johnny Brannigan says. "No use, and no need. Come with me, and hurry."

Well, Big Jule is somewhat puzzled, because Johnny Brannigan is not acting like a copper making a collar, so he goes along with Johnny, and I follow after them, and half way down the block Johnny stops a Yellow short, and hustles us into it and tells the driver to keep shoving down Eighth Avenue.

"I am trailing you ever since you get in town, Jule," Johnny Brannigan says. "You never have a chance around here. I was going over to your Maw's house to put the arm on you figuring you are sure to go there, when the thing over by the Garden comes off. Now I am getting out of this cab at the next corner, and you go on and see your Maw, and then screw out of town as quick as you can, because you are red hot around here, Jule.

"By the way," Johnny Brannigan says, "do you know it is my kid you save, Jule? Mine and Kitty Clancy's? We are married a year ago today."

Well, Big Jule looks very much surprised for a moment, and then he laughs, and says like this: "Well, I never know it is Kitty Clancy's but I figure it for yours the minute I see it because it looks like you."

"Yes," Johnny Brannigan says, very proud. "Everybody says he does."

"I can see the resemblance even from a distance," Big Jule says. "In fact," he says, "it is remarkable how much you look alike. But," he says, "for a minute, Johnny, I am afraid I will not be able to pick out the right face between the two on the roof because it is very hard to tell the monk and your baby apart."

BRED FOR BATTLE

ONE night a guy by the name of Bill Corum, who is one of these sport scribes, gives me a Chinee for a fight at Madison Square Garden, a Chinee being a ducket with holes punched in it like old-fashioned Chink money, to show that it is a free ducket, and the reason I am explaining to you how I get this ducket is because I do not wish anybody to think I am ever simple enough to pay out my own potatoes for a ducket to a fight, even if I have any potatoes.

Personally, I will not give you a bad two-bit piece to see a fight anywhere, because the way I look at it, half the time the guys who are supposed to do the fighting go in there and put on the old do-se-do, and I consider this a great fraud upon the public, and I do not believe in encouraging dishonesty.

But of course I never refuse a Chinee to such events, because the way I figure it, what can I lose except my time, and my time is not worth more than a bob a week the way things are. So on the night in question I am standing in the lobby of the Garden with many other citizens, and I am trying to find out if there is any skullduggery doing in connection with the fight, because any time there is any skullduggery doing I love to know it, as it is something worth knowing in case a guy wishes to get a small wager down.

Well, while I am standing there, somebody comes up

behind me and hits me an awful belt on the back, knocking my wind plumb out of me, and making me very indignant indeed. As soon as I get a little of my wind back
again, I turn around figuring to put a large blast on the
guy who slaps me, but who is it but a guy by the name of
Spider McCoy, who is known far and wide as a manager
of fighters.

Well, of course I do not put the blast on Spider McCoy,
because he is an old friend of mine, and furthermore,
Spider McCoy is such a guy as is apt to let a left hook go
at anybody who puts the blast on him, and I do not believe in getting in trouble, especially with good left-hookers.

So I say hello to Spider, and am willing to let it go at
that, but Spider seems glad to see me, and says to me like
this:

"Well, well, well, well, well!" Spider says.

"Well," I say to Spider McCoy, "how many wells does
it take to make a river?"

"One, if it is big enough," Spider says, so I can see he
knows the answer all right. "Listen," he says, "I just think
up the greatest proposition I ever think of in my whole
life, and who knows but what I can interest you in same."

"Well, Spider," I say, "I do not care to hear any propositions at this time, because it may be a long story, and I
wish to step inside and see the impending battle. Anyway,"
I say, "if it is a proposition involving financial support, I
wish to state that I do not have any resources whatever
at this time."

"Never mind the battle inside," Spider says. "It is nothing but a tank job, anyway. And as for financial support,"
Spider says, "this does not require more than a

pound note, tops, and I know you have a pound note because I know you put the bite on Overcoat Obie for this
amount not an hour ago. Listen," Spider McCoy says, "I
know where I can place my hands on the greatest heavyweight prospect in the world to-day, and all I need is the
price of car-fare to where he is."

Well, off and on, I know Spider McCoy twenty years,
and in all this time I never know him when he is not looking for the greatest heavyweight prospect in the world.
And as long as Spider knows I have the pound note, I
know there is no use trying to play the duck for him, so I
stand there wondering who the stool pigeon can be who
informs him of my financial status.

"Listen," Spider says, "I just discover that I am all out
of line in the way I am looking for heavyweight prospects
in the past. I am always looking for nothing but plenty of
size," he says. "Where I make my mistake is not looking
for blood lines. Professor D just smartens me up," Spider
says.

Well, when he mentions the name of Professor D, I
commence taking a little interest, because it is well known
to one and all that Professor D is one of the smartest old
guys in the world. He is once a professor in a college out
in Ohio, but quits this dodge to handicap the horses, and
he is a first-rate handicapper, at that. But besides knowing
how to handicap the horses, Professor D knows many other
things, and is highly respected in all walks of life, especially on Broadway.

"Now then," Spider says, "Professor D calls my attention
this afternoon to the fact that when a guy is looking for
a race horse, he does not take just any horse that comes

along, but he finds out if the horse's papa is able to run
in his day, and if the horse's mamma can get out of her
own way when she is young. Professor D shows me how
a guy looks for speed in a horse's breeding away back to
its great-great-great-great-grandpa and grandmamma,"
Spider McCoy says.

"Well," I say, "anybody knows this without asking Professor D. In fact," I say, "you can look up a horse's parents
to see if they can mud before betting on a plug to win in
heavy going."

"All right," Spider says, "I know all this myself, but I
never think much about it before Professor D mentions
it. Professor D says if a guy is looking for a hunting dog
he does not pick a Pekingese pooch, but he gets a dog that
is bred to hunt from away back yonder, and if he is after
a game chicken he does not take a Plymouth Rock out of
the back yard.

"So then," Spider says, "Professor D wishes to know
why, when I am looking for a fighter, I do not look for
one who comes of fighting stock. Professor D wishes to
know," Spider says, "why I do not look for some guy who
is bred to fight, and when I think this over, I can see the
professor is right.

"And then all of a sudden," Spider says, "I get the largest
idea I ever have in all my life. Do you remember a guy
I have about twenty years back by the name of Shamus
Mulrooney, the Fighting Harp?" Spider says. "A big,
rough, tough heavyweight out of Newark?"

"Yes," I say, "I remember Shamus very well indeed. The
last time I see him is the night Pounder Pat O'Shea almost
murders him in the old Garden," I say. "I never see a

guy with more ticker than Shamus, unless maybe it is Pat."

"Yes," Spider says, "Shamus has plenty of ticker. He is about through the night of the fight you speak of, otherwise Pat will never lay a glove on him. It is not long after this fight that Shamus packs in and goes back to bricklaying in Newark, and it is also about this same time," Spider says, "that he marries Pat O'Shea's sister, Bridget.

"Well, now," Spider says, "I remember they have a boy who must be around nineteen years old now, and if ever a guy is bred to fight it is a boy by Shamus Mulrooney out of Bridget O'Shea, because," Spider says, "Bridget herself can lick half the heavyweights I see around nowadays if she is half as good as she is the last time I see her. So now you have my wonderful idea. We will go to Newark and get this boy and make him heavyweight champion of the world."

"What you state is very interesting indeed, Spider," I say. "But," I say, "how do you know this boy is a heavyweight?"

"Why," Spider says, "how can he be anything else but a heavyweight, what with his papa as big as a house, and his mamma weighing maybe a hundred and seventy pounds in her step-ins? Although of course," Spider says, "I never see Bridget weigh in in such manner.

"But," Spider says, "even if she does carry more weight than I will personally care to spot a doll, Bridget is by no means a pelican when she marries Shamus. In fact," he says, "she is pretty good-looking. I remember their wedding well, because it comes out that Bridget is in love with some other guy at the time, and this guy comes to see the

nuptials, and Shamus runs him all the way from Newark
to Elizabeth, figuring to break a couple of legs for the guy
if he catches him. But," Spider says, "the guy is too speedy
for Shamus, who never has much foot anyway."

Well, all that Spider says appeals to me as a very sound
business proposition, so the upshot of it is, I give him my
pound note to finance his trip to Newark.

Then I do not see Spider McCoy again for a week, but
one day he calls me up and tells me to hurry over to the
Pioneer gymnasium to see the next heavyweight champion
of the world, Thunderbolt Mulrooney.

I am personally somewhat disappointed when I see
Thunderbolt Mulrooney, and especially when I find out
his first name is Raymond and not Thunderbolt at all, because I am expecting to see a big, fierce guy with red hair
and a chest like a barrel, such as Shamus Mulrooney has
when he is in his prime. But who do I see but a tall, pale
looking young guy with blond hair and thin legs.

Furthermore, he has pale blue eyes, and a far-away look
in them, and he speaks in a low voice, which is nothing
like the voice of Shamus Mulrooney. But Spider seems
satisfied with Thunderbolt, and when I tell him Thunderbolt does not look to me like the next heavyweight champion of the world, Spider says like this:

"Why," he says, "the guy is nothing but a baby, and
you must give him time to fill out. He may grow to be
bigger than his papa. But you know," Spider says, getting
indignant as he thinks about it, "Bridget Mulrooney does
not wish to let this guy be the next heavyweight champion
of the world. In fact," Spider says, "she kicks up an awful

row when I go to get him, and Shamus finally has to speak to her severely. Shamus says he does not know if I can ever make a fighter of this guy because Bridget coddles him until he is nothing but a mush-head, and Shamus says he is sick and tired of seeing the guy sitting around the house doing nothing but reading and playing the zither."

"Does he play the zither yet?" I ask Spider McCoy.

"No," Spider says, "I do not allow my fighters to play zithers. I figure it softens them up. This guy does not play anything at present. He seems to be in a daze most of the time, but of course everything is new to him. He is bound to come out okay, because," Spider says, "he is certainly bred right. I find out from Shamus that all the Mulrooneys are great fighters back in the old country," Spider says, "and furthermore he tells me Bridget's mother once licks four Newark cops who try to stop her from pasting her old man, so," Spider says, "this lad is just naturally steaming with fighting blood."

Well, I drop around to the Pioneer once or twice a week after this, and Spider McCoy is certainly working hard with Thunderbolt Mulrooney. Furthermore, the guy seems to be improving right along, and gets so he can box fairly well and punch the bag, and all this and that, but he always has that far-away look in his eyes, and personally I do not care for fighters with far-away looks.

Finally one day Spider calls me up and tells me he has Thunderbolt Mulrooney matched in a four-round preliminary bout at the St. Nick with a guy by the name of Bubbles Browning, who is fighting almost as far back as the first battle of Bull Run, so I can see Spider is being very careful in matching Thunderbolt. In fact, I congratulate Spider on his carefulness.

"Well," Spider says, "I am taking this match just to give Thunderbolt the feel of the ring. I am taking Bubbles because he is an old friend of mine, and very deserving, and furthermore," Spider says, "he gives me his word he will not hit Thunderbolt very hard and will become unconscious the instant Thunderbolt hits him. You know," Spider says, "you must encourage a young heavyweight, and there is nothing that encourages one so much as knocking somebody unconscious."

Now of course it is nothing for Bubbles to promise not to hit anybody very hard because even when he is a young guy, Bubbles cannot punch his way out of a paper bag, but I am glad to learn that he also promises to become unconscious very soon, as naturally I am greatly interested in Thunderbolt's career, what with owning a piece of him, and having an investment of one pound in him already.

So the night of the fight, I am at the St. Nick very early, and many other citizens are there ahead of me, because by this time Spider McCoy gets plenty of publicity for Thunderbolt by telling the boxing scribes about his wonderful fighting blood lines, and everybody wishes to see a guy who is bred for battle, like Thunderbolt.

I take a guest with me to the fight by the name of Harry the Horse, who comes from Brooklyn, and as I am anxious to help Spider McCoy all I can, as well as to protect my investment in Thunderbolt, I request Harry to call on Bubbles Browning in his dressing room and remind him of his promise about hitting Thunderbolt.

Harry the Horse does this for me, and furthermore he shows Bubbles a large revolver and tells Bubbles that he will be compelled to shoot his ears off if Bubbles forgets his promise, but Bubbles says all this is most unnecessary, as his eyesight is so bad he cannot see to hit anybody, anyway.

Well, I know a party who is a friend of the guy who is going to referee the preliminary bouts, and I am looking for this party to get him to tell the referee to disqualify Bubbles in case it looks as if he is forgetting his promise and is liable to hit Thunderbolt, but before I can locate the party, they are announcing the opening bout, and there is Thunderbolt in the ring looking very far away indeed, with Spider McCoy behind him.

It seems to me I never see a guy who is so pale all over as Thunderbolt Mulrooney, but Spider looks down at me and tips me a large wink, so I can see that everything is as right as rain, especially when Harry the Horse makes motions at Bubbles Browning like a guy firing a large revolver at somebody, and Bubbles smiles, and also winks.

Well, when the bell rings, Spider gives Thunderbolt a shove toward the center, and Thunderbolt comes out with his hands up, but looking more far away than somewhat, and something tells me that Thunderbolt by no means feels the killer instinct such as I love to see in fighters. In fact, something tells me that Thunderbolt is not feeling enthusiastic about this proposition in any way, shape, manner, or form.

Old Bubbles almost falls over his own feet coming out of his corner, and he starts bouncing around making passes at Thunderbolt, and waiting for Thunderbolt to hit him so he can become unconscious. Naturally, Bubbles does not wish to become unconscious without getting hit, as this may look suspicious to the public. .

Well, instead of hitting Bubbles, what does Thunderbolt Mulrooney do but turn around and walk over to a neutral corner, and lean over the ropes with his face in his gloves, and bust out crying. Naturally, this is a most surprising incident to one and all, and especially to Bubbles Browning.

The referee walks over to Thunderbolt Mulrooney and tries to turn him around, but Thunderbolt keeps his face in his gloves and sobs so loud that the referee is deeply touched and starts sobbing with him. Between sobs he asks Thunderbolt if he wishes to continue the fight, and Thunderbolt shakes his head, although as a matter of fact no fight whatever starts so far, so the referee declares Bubbles Browning the winner, which is a terrible surprise to Bubbles.

Then the referee puts his arm around Thunderbolt and leads him over to Spider McCoy, who is standing in his corner with a very strange expression on his face. Personally, I consider the entire spectacle so revolting that I go out into the air, and stand around awhile expecting to hear any minute that Spider McCoy is in the hands of the gendarmes on a charge of mayhem. .

But it seems that nothing happens, and when Spider finally comes out of the St. Nick, he is only looking sorrowful because he just hears that the promoter declines to pay him the fifty bobs he is supposed to receive for Thunderbolt's services, the promoter claiming that Thunderbolt renders no service.

"Well," Spider says, "I fear this is not the next heavy-weight champion of the world after all. There is nothing in Professor D's idea about blood lines as far as fighters are concerned, although," he says, "it may work out all right with horses and dogs, and one thing and another. I am greatly disappointed," Spider says, "but then I am always being disappointed in heavyweights. There is noth-ing we can do but take this guy back home, because," Spider says, "the last thing I promised Bridget Mulrooney is that I will personally return him to her in case I am not able to make him heavyweight champion, as she is afraid he will get lost if he tries to find his way home alone."

So the next day, Spider McCoy and I take Thunderbolt Mulrooney over to Newark and to his home, which turns out to be a nice little house in a side street with a yard all around and about, and Spider and I are just as well pleased that old Shamus Mulrooney is absent when we arrive, because Spider says that Shamus is just such a guy as will be asking a lot of questions about the fifty bobbos that Thunderbolt does not get.

Well, when we reach the front door of the house, out comes a big, fine-looking doll with red cheeks, all excited, and she takes Thunderbolt in her arms and kisses him, so I know this is Bridget Mulrooney, and I can see she knows what happens, and in fact I afterwards learn that Thunder-bolt telephones her the night before.

After a while she pushes Thunderbolt into the house and stands at the door as if she is guarding it against us entering to get him again, which of course is very un-necessary. And all this time Thunderbolt is sobbing no little, although by and by the sobs die away, and from somewhere in the house comes the sound of music I seem to recognize as the music of a zither.

Well, Bridget Mulrooney never says a word to us as she stands in the door, and Spider McCoy keeps staring at her in a way that I consider very rude indeed. I am wondering if he is waiting for a receipt for Thunderbolt, but finally he speaks as follows:

"Bridget," Spider says, "I hope and trust that you will not consider me too fresh, but I wish to learn the name of the guy you are going around with just before you marry Shamus. I remember him well," Spider says, "but I cannot think of his name, and it bothers me not being able to think of names. He is a tall, skinny, stoop-shouldered guy," Spider says, "with a hollow chest and a soft voice, and he loves music."

Well, Bridget Mulrooney stands there in the doorway, staring back at Spider, and it seems to me that the red suddenly fades out of her cheeks, and just then we hear a lot of yelling, and around the corner of the house comes a bunch of five or six kids, who seem to be running from another kid.

This kid is not very big, and is maybe fifteen or sixteen years old, and he has red hair and many freckles, and he seems very mad at the other kids. In fact, when he catches up with them, he starts belting away at them with his fists, and before anybody can as much as say boo, he has three of them on the ground as flat as pancakes, while the others are yelling bloody murder.

Personally, I never see such wonderful punching by a kid, especially with his left hand, and Spider McCoy is also much impressed, and is watching the kid with great interest. Then Bridget Mulrooney runs out and grabs the frecklefaced kid with one hand and smacks him with the other hand and hauls him, squirming and kicking, over to Spider McCoy and says to Spider like this:

"Mr. McCoy," Bridget says, "this is my youngest son, Terence, and though he is not a heavyweight, and will never be a heavyweight, perhaps he will answer your purpose. Suppose you see his father about him sometime," she says, "and hoping you will learn to mind your own business, I wish you a very good day."

Then she takes the kid into the house under her arm and slams the door in our kissers, and there is nothing for us to do but walk away. And as we are walking away, all of a sudden Spider McCoy snaps his fingers as guys will do when they get an unexpected thought, and says like this:

"I remember the guy's name," he says. "It is Cedric Tilbury, and he is a floorwalker in Hamburgher's department store, and," Spider says, "how he can play the zither!"

I see in the papers the other day where Jimmy Johnston, the match maker at the Garden, matches Tearing Terry Mulrooney, the new sensation in the lightweight division, to fight for the championship, but it seems from what Spider McCoy tells me that my investment with him does not cover any fighters in his stable except maybe heavyweights.

And it also seems that Spider McCoy is not monkeying with heavyweights since he gets Tearing Terry.

A STORY GOES WITH IT

ONE night I am in a gambling joint in Miami watching the crap game and thinking what a nice thing it is, indeed, to be able to shoot craps without having to worry about losing your potatoes.

Many of the high shots from New York and Detroit and St. Louis and other cities are around the table, and there is quite some action in spite of the hard times. In fact, there is so much action that a guy with only a few bobs on him, such as me, will be considered very impolite to be pushing into this game, because they are packed in very tight around the table.

I am maybe three guys back from the table, and I am watching the game by standing on tiptoe peeking over their shoulders, and all I can hear is Goldie, the stick man, hollering money-money-money every time some guy makes a number, so I can see the dice are very warm indeed, and that the right betters are doing first-rate.

By and by a guy by the name of Guinea Joe, out of Trenton, picks up the dice and starts making numbers right and left, and I know enough about this Guinea Joe to know that when he starts making numbers anybody will be very foolish indeed not to follow his hand, although personally I am generally a wrong better against the dice, if I bet at all.

Now all I have in my pocket is a sawbuck, and the hotel stakes are coming up on me the next day, and I need this

saw, but with Guinea Joe hotter than a forty-five it will
be overlooking a big opportunity not to go along with
him, so when he comes out on an eight, which is a very
easy number for Joe to make when he is hot, I dig up my
sawbuck, and slide it past the three guys in front of me
to the table, and I say to Lefty Park, who is laying against
the dice, as follows:

"I will take the odds, Lefty."

Well, Lefty looks at my sawbuck and nods his head, for
Lefty is not such a guy as will refuse any bet, even though
it is as modest as mine, and right away Goldie yells money-
money-money, so there I am with twenty-two dollars.

Next Guinea Joe comes out on a nine, and naturally I
take thirty to twenty for my sugar, because nine is nothing
for Joe to make when he is hot. He makes the nine just as
I figure, and I take two to one for my half a yard when he
starts looking for a ten, and when he makes the ten I am
right up against the table, because I am now a guy with
means.

Well, the upshot of the whole business is that I finally
find myself with three hundred bucks, and when it looks
as if the dice are cooling off, I take out and back off from
the table, and while I am backing off I am trying to look
like a guy who loses all his potatoes, because there are
always many wolves waiting around crap games and one
thing and another in Miami this season, and what they are
waiting for is to put the bite on anybody who happens to
make a little scratch.

In fact, nobody can remember when the bite is as painful
as it is in Miami this season, what with the unemployment
situation among many citizens who come to Miami ex-

pecting to find work in the gambling joints, or around the
race track. But almost as soon as these citizens arrive, the
gambling joints are all turned off, except in spots, and the
bookmakers are chased off the track and the mutuels put
in, and the consequences are the suffering is most intense.
It is not only intense among the visiting citizens, but it is
quite intense among the Miami landlords, because naturally
if a citizen is not working, nobody can expect him to pay
any room rent, but the Miami landlords do not seem to
understand this situation, and are very unreasonable about
their room rent.

Anyway, I back through quite a crowd without anybody
biting me, and I am commencing to figure I may escape altogether and get to my hotel and hide my dough before the
news gets around that I win about five *G's,* which is what
my winning is sure to amount to by the time the rumor
reaches all quarters of the city.

Then, just as I am thinking I am safe, I find I am looking a guy by the name of Hot Horse Herbie in the face,
and I can tell from Hot Horse Herbie's expression that
he is standing there watching me for some time, so there
is no use in telling him I am washed out in the game. In
fact, I cannot think of much of anything to tell Hot Horse
Herbie that may keep him from putting the bite on me for
at least a few bobs, and I am greatly astonished when he
does not offer to bite me at all, but says to me like this:

"Well," he says, "I am certainly glad to see you make
such a nice score. I will be looking for you tomorrow at
the track, and will have some big news for you."

Then he walks away from me and I stand there with
my mouth open looking at him, as it is certainly a most

unusual way for Herbie to act. It is the first time I ever
knew Herbie to walk away from a chance to bite somebody, and I can scarcely understand such actions, for
Herbie is such a guy as will not miss a bite, even if he
does not need it.

He is a tall, thin guy, with a sad face and a long chin,
and he is called Hot Horse Herbie because he nearly
always has a very hot horse to tell you about. He nearly always has a horse that is so hot it is fairly smoking, a hot
horse being a horse that cannot possibly lose a race unless it
falls down dead, and while Herbie's hot horses often lose
without falling down dead, this does not keep Herbie from
coming up with others just as hot.

In fact, Hot Horse Herbie is what is called a hustler
around the race tracks, and his business is to learn about
these hot horses, or even just suspect about them, and then
get somebody to bet on them, which is a very legitimate
business indeed, as Herbie only collects a commission if
the hot horses win, and if they do not win Herbie just
keeps out of sight awhile from whoever he gets to bet on
the hot horses. There are very few guys in this world who
can keep out of sight better than Hot Horse Herbie, and
especially from old Cap Duhaine, of the Pinkertons, who
is always around pouring cold water on hot horses.

In fact, Cap Duhaine, of the Pinkertons, claims that
guys such as Hot Horse Herbie are nothing but touts, and
sometimes he heaves them off the race track altogether,
but of course Cap Duhaine is a very unsentimental old guy
and cannot see how such characters as Hot Horse Herbie
add to the romance of the turf.

Anyway, I escape from the gambling joint with all my

scratch on me, and hurry to my room and lock myself in
for the night, and I do not show up in public until along
about noon the next day, when it is time to go over to the
coffee shop for my java. And of course by this time the
news of my score is all over town, and many guys are
taking dead aim at me.

But naturally I am now able to explain to them that I
have to wire most of the three yards I win to Nebraska
to save my father's farm from being seized by the sheriff,
and while everybody knows I do not have a father, and
that if I do have a father I will not be sending him money
for such a thing as saving his farm, with times what they
are in Miami, nobody is impolite enough to doubt my
word except a guy by the name of Pottsville Legs, who
wishes to see my receipts from the telegraph office when I
explain to him why I cannot stake him to a double
sawbuck.

I do not see Hot Horse Herbie until I get to the track,
and he is waiting for me right inside the grand-stand gate,
and as soon as I show up he motions me off to one side
and says to me like this:

"Now," Herbie says, "I am very smart indeed about a
certain race to-day. In fact," he says, "if any guy knowing
what I know does not bet all he can rake and scrape together on a certain horse, such a guy ought to cut his own
throat and get himself out of the way forever. What I
know," Herbie says, "is enough to shake the foundations
of this country if it gets out. Do not ask any questions," he
says, "but get ready to bet all the sugar you win last night
on this horse I am going to mention to you, and all I ask
you in return is to bet fifty on me. And," Herbie says,

"kindly do not tell me you leave your money in your other pants, because I know you do not have any other pants."

"Now, Herbie," I say, "I do not doubt your information, because I know you will not give out information unless it is well founded. But," I say, "I seldom stand for a tip, and as for betting fifty for you, you know I will not bet fifty even for myself if somebody guarantees me a winner. So I thank you, Herbie, just the same," I say, "but I must do without your tip," and with this I start walking away.

"Now," Herbie says, "wait a minute. A story goes with it," he says.

Well, of course this is a different matter entirely. I am such a guy as will always listen to a tip on a horse if a story goes with the tip. In fact, I will not give you a nickel for a tip without a story, but it must be a first-class story, and most horse players are the same way. In fact, there are very few horse players who will not listen to a tip if a story goes with it, for this is the way human nature is. So I turn and walk back to Hot Horse Herbie, and say to him like this:

"Well," I say, "let me hear the story, Herbie."

"Now," Herbie says, dropping his voice away down low, in case old Cap Duhaine may be around somewhere listening, "it is the third race, and the horse is a horse by the name of Never Despair. It is a boat race," Herbie says. "They are going to shoo in Never Despair. Everything else in the race is a cooler," he says.

"Well," I say, "this is just an idea, Herbie, and not a story."

"Wait a minute," Herbie says. "The story that goes with it is a very strange story indeed. In fact," he says, "it is such a story as I can scarcely believe myself, and I will generally believe almost any story, including," he says, "the ones I make up out of my own head. Anyway, the story is as follows:

"Never Despair is owned by an old guy by the name of Seed Mercer," Herbie says. "Maybe you remember seeing him around. He always wears a black slouch hat and gray whiskers," Herbie says, "and he is maybe a hundred years old, and his horses are very terrible horses indeed. In fact," Herbie says, "I do not remember seeing any more terrible horses in all the years I am around the track, and," Herbie says, "I wish to say I see some very terrible horses indeed.

"Now," Herbie says, "old Mercer has a granddaughter who is maybe sixteen years old, come next grass, by the name of Lame Louise, and she is called Lame Louise because she is all crippled up from childhood by infantile what-is-this, and can scarcely navigate, and," Herbie says, "her being crippled up in such a way makes old Mercer feel very sad, for she is all he has in the world, except these terrible horses."

"It is a very long story, Herbie," I say, "and I wish to see Moe Shapoff about a very good thing in the first race."

"Never mind Moe Shapoff," Herbie says. "He will only tell you about a bum by the name of Zachary in the first race, and Zachary has no chance whatever. I make Your John a stand-out in the first," he says.

"Well," I say, "let us forget the first and go on with your story, although it is commencing to sound all mixed up to me."

"Now," Herbie says, "it not only makes old man Mercer very sad because Lame Louise is all crippled up, but," he says, "it makes many of the jockeys and other guys around the race track very sad, because," he says, "they know Lame Louise since she is so high and she always has a smile for them, and especially for Jockey Scroon. In fact," Herbie says, "Jockey Scroon is even more sad about Lame Louise than old man Mercer, because Jockey Scroon loves Lame Louise."

"Why," I say, very indignant, "Jockey Scroon is nothing but a little burglar. Why," I say, "I see Jockey Scroon do things to horses I bet on that he will have to answer for on the Judgment Day, if there is any justice at such a time. Why," I say, "Jockey Scroon is nothing but a Gerald Chapman in his heart, and so are all other jockeys."

"Yes," Hot Horse Herbie says, "what you say is very, very true, and I am personally in favor of the electric chair for all jockeys, but," he says, "Jockey Scroon loves Lame Louise just the same, and is figuring on making her his ever-loving wife when he gets a few bobs together, which," Herbie says, "makes Louise eight to five in my line to be an old maid. Jockey Scroon rooms with me downtown," Herbie says, "and he speaks freely to me about his love for Louise. Furthermore," Herbie says, "Jockey Scroon is personally not a bad little guy, at that, although of course being a jockey he is sometimes greatly misunderstood by the public.

"Anyway," Hot Horse Herbie says, "I happen to go home early last night before I see you at the gambling joint, and I hear voices coming out of my room, and naturally I pause outside the door to listen, because for all I know it may be the landlord speaking about the room rent, although," Herbie says, "I do not figure my landlord to be much worried at this time because I see him sneak into my room a few days before and take a lift at my trunk to make sure I have belongings in the same, and it happens I nail the trunk to the floor beforehand, so not being able to lift it, the landlord is bound to figure me a guy with property.

"These voices," Herbie says, "are mainly soprano voices, and at first I think Jockey Scroon is in there with some dolls, which is by no means permissible in my hotel, but, after listening awhile, I discover they are the voices of young boys, and I make out that these boys are nothing but jockeys, and they are the six jockeys who are riding in the third race, and they are fixing up this race to be a boat race, and to shoo in Never Despair, which Jockey Schroon is riding.

"And," Hot Horse Herbie says, "the reason they are fixing up this boat race is the strangest part of the story. It seems," he says, "that Jockey Schroon hears old man Mercer talking about a great surgeon from Europe who is a shark on patching up cripples such as Lame Louise, and who just arrives at Palm Beach to spend the winter, and old man Mercer is saying how he wishes he has dough enough to take Lame Louise to this guy so he can operate on her, and maybe make her walk good again.

"But of course," Herbie says, "it is well known to one and all that old man Mercer does not have a quarter, and that he has no way of getting a quarter unless one of his terrible horses accidentally wins a purse. So," Herbie says, "it seems these jockeys get to talking it over among themselves, and they figure it will be a nice thing to let old man Mercer win a purse such as the thousand bucks that goes with the third race to-day, so he can take Lame Louise to Palm Beach, and now you have a rough idea of what is coming off.

"Furthermore," Herbie says, "these jockeys wind up their meeting by taking a big oath among themselves that they will not tell a living soul what is doing so nobody will bet on Never Despair, because," he says, "these little guys are smart enough to see if there is any betting on such a horse there may be a very large squawk afterwards. And," he says, "I judge they keep their oath because Never Despair is twenty to one in the morning line, and I do not hear a whisper about him, and you have the tip all to yourself."

"Well," I say, "so what?" For this story is now commencing to make me a little tired, especially as I hear the bell for the first race, and I must see Moe Shapoff.

"Why," Hot Horse Herbie says, "so you bet every nickel you can rake and scrape together on Never Despair, including the twenty you are to bet for me for giving you this tip and the story that goes with it."

"Herbie," I say, "it is a very interesting story indeed, and also very sad, but," I say, "I am sorry it is about a horse Jockey Scroon is to ride, because I do not think I will ever bet on anything Jockey Scroon rides if they pay off in advance. And," I say, "I am certainly not going to bet twenty for you or anybody else."

"Well," Hot Horse Herbie says, "I will compromise with you for a pound note, because I must have something going for me on this boat race."

So I give Herbie a fiver, and the chances are this is about as strong as he figures from the start, and I forget all about

his tip and the story that goes with it, because while I
enjoy a story with a tip, I feel that Herbie overdoes this
one.

Anyway, no handicapper alive can make Never Despair
win the third race off the form, because this race is at six
furlongs, and there is a barrel of speed in it, and anybody
can see that old man Mercer's horse is away over his head.
In fact, The Dancer tells me that any one of the other
five horses in this race can beat Never Despair doing anything from playing hockey to putting the shot, and everybody else must think the same thing because Never Despair
goes to forty to one.

Personally, I like a horse by the name of Loose Living,
which is a horse owned by a guy by the name of Bill
Howard, and I hear Bill Howard is betting plenty away
on his horse, and any time Bill Howard is betting away on
his horse a guy will be out of his mind not to bet on this
horse, too, as Bill Howard is very smart indeed. Loose
Living is two to one in the first line, but by and by I
judge the money Bill Howard bets away commences to
come back to the track, and Loose Living winds up seven
to ten, and while I am generally not a seven-to-ten guy, I
can see that here is a proposition I cannot overlook.

So, naturally, I step up to the mutuel window and invest in Loose Living. In fact, I invest everything I have on
me in the way of scratch, amounting to a hundred and
ten bucks, which is all I have left after taking myself out
of the hotel stakes and giving Hot Horse Herbie the finnif,
and listening to what Moe Shapoff has to say about the first
race, and also getting beat a snoot in the second.

When I first step up to the window, I have no idea of

betting all my scratch on Loose Living, but while waiting
in line there I get to thinking what a cinch Loose Living
is, and how seldom such an opportunity comes into a guy's
life, so I just naturally set it all in.

Well, this is a race which will be remembered by one and
all to their dying day, as Loose Living beats the barrier
a step, and is two lengths in front before you can say Jack
Robinson, with a thing by the name of Callipers second by
maybe half a length, and with the others bunched except
Never Despair, and where is Never Despair but last, where
he figures.

Now any time Loose Living busts on top there is no
need worrying any more about him, and I am thinking I
better get in line at the pay-off window right away, so I will
not have to wait long to collect my sugar. But I figure I
may as well stay and watch the race, although personally I
am never much interested in watching races. I am interested only in how a race comes out.

As the horses hit the turn into the stretch, Loose Living
is just breezing, and anybody can see that he is going to
laugh his way home from there. Callipers is still second,
and a thing called Goose Pimples is third, and I am surprised to see that Never Despair now struggles up to fourth
with Jockey Scroon belting away at him with his bat quite
earnestly. Furthermore, Never Despair seems to be running
very fast, though afterwards I figure this may be because
the others are commencing to run very slow.

Anyway, a very strange spectacle now takes place in the
stretch, as all of a sudden Loose Living seems to be stopping, as if he is waiting for a street car, and what is all
the more remarkable Callipers and Goose Pimples also

seem to be hanging back, and the next thing anybody knows, here comes Jockey Scroon on Never Despair sneaking through on the rail, and personally it looks to me as if the jock on Callipers moves over to give Jockey Scroon plenty of elbow room, but of course the jock on Callipers may figure Jockey Scroon has diphtheria, and does not wish to catch it.

Loose Living is out in the middle of the track, anyway, so he does not have to move over. All Loose Living has to do is to keep on running backwards as he seems to be doing from the top of the stretch, to let Jockey Scroon go past on Never Despair to win the heat by a length.

Well, the race is practically supernatural in many respects, and the judges are all upset over it, and they haul all the jocks up in the stand and ask them many questions, and not being altogether satisfied with the answers, they ask these questions over several times. But all the jocks will say is that Never Despair sneaks past them very unexpectedly indeed, while Jockey Scroon, who is a pretty fresh duck at that, wishes to know if he is supposed to blow a horn when he is slipping through a lot of guys sound asleep.

But the judges are still not satisfied, so they go prowling around investigating the betting, because naturally when a boat race comes up there is apt to be some reason for it, such as the betting, but it seems that all the judges find is that one five-dollar win ticket is sold on Never Despair in the mutuels, and they cannot learn of a dime being bet away on the horse. So there is nothing much the judges can do about the proposition, except give the jocks many hard looks, and the jocks are accustomed to hard looks from the judges, anyway.

Personally, I am greatly upset by this business, especially when I see that Never Despair pays $86.34, and for two cents I will go right up in the stand and start hollering copper on these little Jesse Jameses for putting on such a boat race and taking all my hard-earned potatoes away from me, but before I have time to do this, I run into The Dancer, and he tells me that Dedicate in the next race is the surest thing that ever goes to the post, and at five to one, at that. So I have to forget everything while I bustle about to dig up a few bobs to bet on Dedicate, and when Dedicate is beat a whisker, I have to do some more bustling to dig up a few bobs to bet on Vesta in the fifth, and by this time the third race is such ancient history that nobody cares what happens in it.

It is nearly a week before I see Hot Horse Herbie again, and I figure he is hiding out on everybody because he has this dough he wins off the fiver I give him, and personally I consider him a guy with no manners not to be kicking back the fin, at least. But before I can mention the fin, Herbie gives me a big hello, and says to me like this:

"Well," he says, "I just see Jockey Scroon, and Jockey Scroon just comes back from Palm Beach, and the operation is a big success, and Lame Louise will walk as good as anybody again, and old Mercer is tickled silly. But," Herbie says, "do not say anything out loud, because the judges may still be trying to find out what comes off in the race."

"Herbie," I say, very serious, "do you mean to say the story you tell me about Lame Louise, and all this and that, the other day is on the level?"

"Why," Herbie says, "certainly it is on the level, and I

am sorry to hear you do not take advantage of my information. But," he says, "I do not blame you for not believing my story, because it is a very long story for anybody to believe. It is not such a story," Herbie says, "as I will tell to any one if I expect them to believe it. In fact," he says, "it is so long a story that I do not have the heart to tell it to anybody else but you, or maybe I will have something running for me on the race.

"But," Herbie says, "never mind all this. I will be plenty smart about a race to-morrow. Yes," Herbie says, "I will be wiser than a treeful of owls, so be sure and see me if you happen to have any coconuts."

"There is no danger of me seeing you," I say, very sad, because I am all sorrowed up to think that the story he tells me is really true. "Things are very terrible with me at this time," I say, "and I am thinking maybe you can hand me back my finnif, because you must do all right for yourself with the fiver you have on Never Despair at such a price."

Now a very strange look comes over Hot Horse Herbie's face, and he raises his right hand, and says to me like this:

"I hope and trust I drop down dead right here in front of you," Herbie says, "if I bet a quarter on the horse. It is true," he says, "I am up at the window to buy a ticket on Never Despair, but the guy who is selling the tickets is a friend of mine by the name of Heeby Rosenbloom, and Heeby whispers to me that Big Joe Gompers, the guy who owns Callipers, just bets half a hundred on his horse, and," Herbie says, "I know Joe Gompers is such a guy as will not bet half a hundred on anything he does not get a Federal Reserve guarantee with it.

"Anyway," Herbie says, "I get to thinking about what a bad jockey this Jockey Scroon is, which is very bad indeed, and," he says, "I figure that even if it is a boat race it is no even-money race they can shoo him in, so I buy a ticket on Callipers."

"Well," I say, "somebody buys one five-dollar ticket on Never Despair, and I figure it can be nobody but you."

"Why," Hot Horse Herbie says, "do you not hear about this? Why," he says, "Cap Duhaine, of the Pinkertons, traces this ticket and finds it is bought by a guy by the name of Steve Harter, and the way this guy Harter comes to buy it is very astonishing. It seems," Herbie says, "that this Harter is a tourist out of Indiana who comes to Miami for the sunshine, and who loses all his dough but six bucks against the faro bank at Hollywood.

"At the same time," Herbie says, "the poor guy gets a telegram from his ever-loving doll back in Indiana saying she no longer wishes any part of him.

"Well," Herbie says, "between losing his dough and his doll, the poor guy is practically out of his mind, and he figures there is nothing left for him to do but knock himself off.

"So," Herbie says, "this Harter spends one of his six bucks to get to the track, figuring to throw himself under the feet of the horses in the first race and let them kick him to a jelly. But he does not get there until just as the third race is coming up and," Herbie says, "he sees this name 'Never Despair,' and he figures it may be a hunch, so he buys himself a ticket with his last fiver. Well, naturally," Herbie says, "when Never Despair pops down, the guy forgets about letting the horses kick him to a jelly, and he keeps sending his dough along until he runs nothing but a nubbin into six *G's* on the day.

"Then," Herbie says, "Cap Duhaine finds out that the guy, still thinking of Never Despair, calls his ever-loving doll on the phone, and finds she is very sorry she sends him the wire and that she really loves him more than somewhat, especially," Herbie says, "when she finds out about the six *G's*. And the last anybody hears of the matter, this Harter is on his way home to get married, so Never Despair does quite some good in this wicked old world, after all.

"But," Herbie says, "let us forget all this, because to-morrow is another day. To-morrow," he says, "I will tell you about a thing that goes in the fourth which is just the same as wheat in the bin. In fact," Hot Horse Herbie says, "if it does not win, you can never speak to me again."

"Well," I say, as I start to walk away, "I am not interested in any tip at this time."

"Now," Herbie says, "wait a minute. A story goes with it."

"Well," I say, coming back to him, "let me hear the story."

SENSE OF HUMOR

ONE night I am standing in front of Mindy's restaurant on Broadway, thinking of practically nothing whatever, when all of a sudden I feel a very terrible pain in my left foot.

In fact, this pain is so very terrible that it causes me to leap up and down like a bullfrog, and to let out loud cries of agony, and to speak some very profane language, which is by no means my custom, although of course I recognize the pain as coming from a hot foot, because I often experience this pain before.

Furthermore, I know Joe the Joker must be in the neighborhood, as Joe the Joker has the most wonderful sense of humor of anybody in this town, and is always around giving people the hot foot, and gives it to me more times than I can remember. In fact, I hear Joe the Joker invents the hot foot, and it finally becomes a very popular idea all over the country.

The way you give a hot foot is to sneak up behind some guy who is standing around thinking of not much, and stick a paper match in his shoe between the sole and the upper along about where his little toe ought to be, and then light the match. By and by the guy will feel a terrible pain in his foot, and will start stamping around, and hollering, and carrying on generally, and it is always a most comical sight and a wonderful laugh to one and all to see him suffer.

No one in the world can give a hot foot as good as Joe the Joker, because it takes a guy who can sneak up very quiet on the guy who is to get the hot foot, and Joe can sneak up so quiet many guys on Broadway are willing to lay you odds that he can give a mouse a hot foot if you can find a mouse that wears shoes. Furthermore, Joe the Joker can take plenty of care of himself in case the guy who gets the hot foot feels like taking the matter up, which sometimes happens, especially with guys who get their shoes made to order at forty bobs per copy and do not care to have holes burned in these shoes.

But Joe does not care what kind of shoes the guys are wearing when he feels like giving out hot foots, and furthermore, he does not care who the guys are, although many citizens think he makes a mistake the time he gives a hot foot to Frankie Ferocious. In fact, many citizens are greatly horrified by this action, and go around saying no good will come of it.

This Frankie Ferocious comes from over in Brooklyn, where he is considered a rising citizen in many respects, and by no means a guy to give hot foots to, especially as Frankie Ferocious has no sense of humor whatever. In fact, he is always very solemn, and nobody ever sees him laugh, and he certainly does not laugh when Joe the Joker gives him a hot foot one day on Broadway when Frankie Ferocious is standing talking over a business matter with some guys from the Bronx.

He only scowls at Joe, and says something in Italian, and while I do not understand Italian, it sounds so unpleasant that I guarantee I will leave town inside of the next two hours if he says it to me.

Of course Frankie Ferocious' name is not really Ferocious, but something in Italian like Feroccio, and I hear he originally comes from Sicily, although he lives in Brooklyn for quite some years, and from a modest beginning he builds himself up until he is a very large operator in merchandise of one kind and another, especially alcohol. He is a big guy of maybe thirty-odd, and he has hair blacker than a yard up a chimney, and black eyes, and black eyebrows, and a slow way of looking at people.

Nobody knows a whole lot about Frankie Ferocious, because he never has much to say, and he takes his time saying it, but everybody gives him plenty of room when he comes around, as there are rumors that Frankie never likes to be crowded. As far as I am concerned, I do not care for any part of Frankie Ferocious, because his slow way of looking at people always makes me nervous, and I am always sorry Joe the Joker gives him a hot foot, because I figure Frankie Ferocious is bound to consider it a most disrespectful action, and hold it against everybody that lives on the Island of Manhattan.

But Joe the Joker only laughs when anybody tells him he is out of line in giving Frankie the hot foot, and says it is not his fault if Frankie has no sense of humor. Further-more, Joe says he will not only give Frankie another hot foot if he gets a chance, but that he will give hot foots to the Prince of Wales or Mussolini, if he catches them in the right spot, although Regret, the horse player, states that Joe can have twenty to one any time that he will not give Mussolini any hot foots and get away with it.

Anyway, just as I suspect, there is Joe the Joker watching me when I feel the hot foot, and he is laughing very heartily, and furthermore, a large number of other citizens are also laughing heartily, because Joe the Joker never sees any fun in giving people the hot foot unless others are present to enjoy the joke.

Well, naturally when I see who it is gives me the hot foot I join in the laughter, and go over and shake hands with Joe, and when I shake hands with him there is more laughter, because it seems Joe has a hunk of Limburger cheese in his duke, and what I shake hands with is this

Limburger. Furthermore, it is some of Mindy's Limburger
cheese, and everybody knows Mindy's Limburger is very
squashy, and also very loud.

Of course I laugh at this, too, although to tell the truth
I will laugh much more heartily if Joe the Joker drops dead
in front of me, because I do not like to be made the subject
of laughter on Broadway. But my laugh is really quite
hearty when Joe takes the rest of the cheese that is not on
my fingers and smears it on the steering wheels of some
automobiles parked in front of Mindy's, because I get to
thinking of what the drivers will say when they start steering their cars.

Then I get to talking to Joe the Joker, and I ask him
how things are up in Harlem, where Joe and his younger
brother, Freddy, and several other guys have a small or-
ganization operating in beer, and Joe says things are as
good as can be expected considering business conditions.
Then I ask him how Rosa is getting along, this Rosa being
Joe the Joker's ever-loving wife, and a personal friend of
mine, as I know her when she is Rosa Midnight and is singing in the old Hot Box before Joe hauls off and marries her.

Well, at this question Joe the Joker starts laughing, and
I can see that something appeals to his sense of humor,
and finally he speaks as follows:

"Why," he says, "do you not hear the news about Rosa?
She takes the wind on me a couple of months ago for my
friend Frankie Ferocious, and is living in an apartment
over in Brooklyn, right near his house, although," Joe says,
"of course you understand I am telling you this only to answer your question, and not to holler copper on Rosa."

Then he lets out another large ha-ha, and in fact Joe the

Joker keeps laughing until I am afraid he will injure himself internally. Personally, I do not see anything comical in a guy's ever-loving wife taking the wind on him for a guy like Frankie Ferocious, so when Joe the Joker quiets down a bit I ask him what is funny about the proposition.

"Why," Joe says, "I have to laugh every time I think of how the big greaseball is going to feel when he finds out how expensive Rosa is. I do not know how many things Frankie Ferocious has running for him in Brooklyn," Joe says, "but he better try to move himself in on the mint if he wishes to keep Rosa going."

Then he laughs again, and I consider it wonderful the way Joe is able to keep his sense of humor even in such a situation as this, although up to this time I always think Joe is very daffy indeed about Rosa, who is a little doll, weighing maybe ninety pounds with her hat on and quite cute.

Now I judge from what Joe the Joker tells me that Frankie Ferocious knows Rosa before Joe marries her and is always pitching to her when she is singing in the Hot Box, and even after she is Joe's ever-loving wife, Frankie occasionally calls her up, especially when he commences to be a rising citizen of Brooklyn, although of course Joe does not learn about these calls until later. And about the time. Frankie Ferocious commences to be a rising citizen of Brooklyn, things begin breaking a little tough for Joe the Joker, what with the depression and all, and he has to economize on Rosa in spots, and if there is one thing Rosa cannot stand it is being economized on.

Along about now, Joe the Joker gives Frankie Ferocious the hot foot, and just as many citizens state at the time, it is a mistake, for Frankie starts calling Rosa up more than somewhat, and speaking of what a nice place Brooklyn is to live in—which it is, at that—and between these boosts for Brooklyn and Joe the Joker's economy, Rosa hauls off and takes the subway to Borough Hall, leaving Joe a note telling him that if he does not like it he knows what he can do.

"Well, Joe," I say, after listening to his story, "I always hate to hear of these little domestic difficulties among my friends, but maybe this is all for the best. Still, I feel sorry for you, if it will do you any good," I say.

"Do not feel sorry for me," Joe says. "If you wish to feel sorry for anybody, feel sorry for Frankie Ferocious, and," he says, "if you can spare a little more sorrow, give it to Rosa."

And Joe the Joker laughs very heartily again and starts telling me about a little scatter that he has up in Harlem where he keeps a chair fixed up with electric wires so he can give anybody that sits down in it a nice jolt, which sounds very humorous to me, at that, especially when Joe tells me how they turn on too much juice one night and almost kill Commodore Jake.

Finally Joe says he has to get back to Harlem, but first he goes to the telephone in the corner cigar store and calls up Mindy's and imitates a doll's voice, and tells Mindy he is Peggy Joyce, or somebody, and orders fifty dozen sandwiches sent up at once to an apartment in West Seventy-second Street for a birthday party, although of course there is no such number as he gives, and nobody there will wish fifty dozen sandwiches if there is such a number.

Then Joe gets in his car and starts off, and while he is waiting for the traffic lights at Fiftieth Street, I see citizens on the sidewalks making sudden leaps, and looking around very fierce, and I know Joe the Joker is plugging them with pellets made out of tin foil, which he fires from a rubber band hooked between his thumb and forefinger.

Joe the Joker is very expert with this proposition, and it is very funny to see the citizens jump, although once or twice in his life Joe makes a miscue and knocks out somebody's eye. But it is all in fun, and shows you what a wonderful sense of humor Joe has.

Well, a few days later I see by the papers where a couple of Harlem guys Joe the Joker is mobbed up with are found done up in sacks over in Brooklyn, very dead indeed, and the coppers say it is because they are trying to move in on certain business enterprises that belong to nobody but Frankie Ferocious. But of course the coppers do not say Frankie Ferocious puts these guys in the sacks, because in the first place Frankie will report them to Headquarters if the coppers say such a thing about him, and in the second place putting guys in sacks is strictly a St. Louis idea and to have a guy put in a sack properly you have to send to St. Louis for experts in this matter.

Now, putting a guy in a sack is not as easy as it sounds, and in fact it takes quite a lot of practice and experience. To put a guy in a sack properly, you first have to put him to sleep, because naturally no guy is going to walk into a sack wide awake unless he is a plumb sucker. Some people claim the best way to put a guy to sleep is to give him a sleeping powder of some kind in a drink, but the real experts just tap the guy on the noggin with a blackjack, which saves the expense of buying the drink.

Anyway, after the guy is asleep, you double him up like a pocketknife, and tie a cord or a wire around his neck and under his knees. Then you put him in a gunny sack, and leave him some place, and by and by when the guy wakes up and finds himself in the sack, naturally he wants to get out and the first thing he does is to try to straighten out his knees. This pulls the cord around his neck up so tight that after a while the guy is all out of breath.

So then when somebody comes along and opens the sack they find the guy dead, and nobody is responsible for this unfortunate situation, because after all the guy really commits suicide, because if he does not try to straighten out his knees he may live to a ripe old age, if he recovers from the tap on the noggin.

Well, a couple of days later I see by the papers where three Brooklyn citizens are scragged as they are walking peaceably along Clinton Street, the scragging being done by some parties in an automobile who seem to have a machine gun, and the papers state that the citizens are friends of Frankie Ferocious, and that it is rumored the parties with the machine gun are from Harlem.

I judge by this that there is some trouble in Brooklyn, especially as about a week after the citizens are scragged in Clinton Street, another Harlem guy is found done up in a sack like a Virginia ham near Prospect Park, and now who is it but Joe the Joker's brother, Freddy, and I know Joe is going to be greatly displeased by this.

By and by it gets so nobody in Brooklyn will open as much as a sack of potatoes without first calling in the gendarmes, for fear a pair of No. 8 shoes will jump out at them.

Now one night I see Joe the Joker, and this time he is all alone, and I wish to say I am willing to leave him all alone, because something tells me he is hotter than a stove. But he grabs me as I am going past, so naturally I stop to talk to him, and the first thing I say is how sorry I am about his brother.

"Well," Joe the Joker says, "Freddy is always a kind of a sap. Rosa calls him up and asks him to come over to Brooklyn to see her. She wishes to talk to Freddy about getting me to give her a divorce," Joe says, "so she can marry Frankie Ferocious, I suppose. Anyway," he says, "Freddy tells Commodore Jake why he is going to see her. Freddy always likes Rosa, and thinks maybe he can patch it up between us. So," Joe says, "he winds up in a sack. They get him after he leaves her apartment. I do not claim Rosa will ask him to come over if she has any idea he will be sacked," Joe says, "but," he says, "she is responsible. She is a bad-luck doll."

Then he starts to laugh, and at first I am greatly horrified, thinking it is because something about Freddy being sacked strikes his sense of humor, when he says to me like this:

"Say," he says, "I am going to play a wonderful joke on Frankie Ferocious."

"Well, Joe," I say, "you are not asking me for advice, but I am going to give you some free gratis, and for nothing. Do not play any jokes on Frankie Ferocious, as I hear he has no more sense of humor than a nanny goat. I hear Frankie Ferocious will not laugh if you have Al Jolson,

Eddie Cantor, Ed Wynn and Joe Cook telling him jokes all at once. In fact," I say, "I hear he is a tough audience."

"Oh," Joe the Joker says, "he must have some sense of humor somewhere to stand for Rosa. I hear he is daffy about her. In fact, I understand she is the only person in the world he really likes, and trusts. But I must play a joke on him. I am going to have myself delivered to Frankie Ferocious in a sack."

Well, of course I have to laugh at this myself, and Joe the Joker laughs with me. Personally, I am laughing just at the idea of anybody having themselves delivered to Frankie Ferocious in a sack, and especially Joe the Joker, but of course I have no idea Joe really means what he says.

"Listen," Joe says, finally. "A guy from St. Louis who is a friend of mine is doing most of the sacking for Frankie Ferocious. His name is Ropes McGonnigle. In fact," Joe says, "he is a very dear old pal of mine, and he has a wonderful sense of humor like me. Ropes McGonnigle has nothing whatever to do with sacking Freddy," Joe says, "and he is very indignant about it since he finds out Freddy is my brother, so he is anxious to help me play a joke on Frankie.

"Only last night," Joe says, "Frankie Ferocious sends for Ropes and tells him he will appreciate it as a special favor if Ropes will bring me to him in a sack. I suppose," Joe says, "that Frankie Ferocious hears from Rosa what Freddy is bound to tell her about my ideas on divorce. I have very strict ideas on divorce," Joe says, "especially where Rosa is concerned. I will see her in what's-this before I ever do her and Frankie Ferocious such a favor as giving her a divorce.

"Anyway," Joe the Joker says, "Ropes tells me about Frankie Ferocious propositioning him, so I send Ropes back to Frankie Ferocious to tell him he knows I am to be in Brooklyn to-morrow night, and furthermore, Ropes tells Frankie that he will have me in a sack in no time. And so he will," Joe says.

"Well," I say, "personally, I see no percentage in being delivered to Frankie Ferocious in a sack, because as near as I can make out from what I read in the papers, there is no future for a guy in a sack that goes to Frankie Ferocious. What I cannot figure out," I say, "is where the joke on Frankie comes in."

"Why," Joe the Joker says, "the joke is, I will not be asleep in the sack, and my hands will not be tied, and in each of my hands I will have a John Roscoe, so when the sack is delivered to Frankie Ferocious and I pop out blasting away, can you not imagine his astonishment?"

Well, I can imagine this, all right. In fact, when I get to thinking of the look of surprise that is bound to come to Frankie Ferocious' face when Joe the Joker comes out of the sack I have to laugh, and Joe the Joker laughs right along with me.

"Of course," Joe says, "Ropes McGonnigle will be there to start blasting with me, in case Frankie Ferocious happens to have any company."

Then Joe the Joker goes on up the street, leaving me still laughing from thinking of how amazed Frankie Ferocious will be when Joe bounces out of the sack and starts throwing slugs around and about. I do not hear of Joe from that time to this, but I hear the rest of the story from very reliable parties.

It seems that Ropes McGonnigle does not deliver the sack himself, after all, but sends it by an expressman to Frankie Ferocious' home. Frankie Ferocious receives many sacks such as this in his time, because it seems that it is a sort of passion with him to personally view the contents of the sacks and check up on them before they are distributed about the city, and of course Ropes McGonnigle knows about this passion from doing so much sacking for Frankie.

When the expressman takes the sack into Frankie's house, Frankie personally lugs it down into his basement, and there he outs with a big John Roscoe and fires six shots into the sack, because it seems Ropes McGonnigle tips him off to Joe the Joker's plan to pop out of the sack and start blasting.

I hear Frankie Ferocious has a very strange expression on his pan and is laughing the only laugh anybody ever hears from him when the gendarmes break in and put the arm on him for murder, because it seems that when Ropes McGonnigle tells Frankie of Joe the Joker's plan, Frankie tells Ropes what he is going to do with his own hands before opening the sack. Naturally, Ropes speaks to Joe the Joker of Frankie's idea about filling the sack full of slugs, and Joe's sense of humor comes right out again.

So, bound and gagged, but otherwise as right as rain in the sack that is delivered to Frankie Ferocious, is by no means Joe the Joker, but Rosa.

UNDERTAKER SONG

Now this story I am going to tell you is about the game of football, a very healthy pastime for the young, and a great character builder from all I hear, but to get around to this game of football I am compelled to bring in some most obnoxious characters, beginning with a guy by the name of Joey Perhaps, and all I can conscientiously say about Joey is you can have him.

It is a matter of maybe four years since I see this Joey Perhaps until I notice him on a train going to Boston, Mass., one Friday afternoon. He is sitting across from me in the dining-car, where I am enjoying a small portion of baked beans and brown bread, and he looks over to me once, but he does not rap to me.

There is no doubt but what Joey Perhaps is bad company, because the last I hear of him he is hollering copper on a guy by the name of Jack Ortega, and as a result of Joey Perhaps hollering copper, this Jack Ortega is taken to the city of Ossining, N. Y., and placed in an electric chair, and given a very, very, very severe shock in the seat of his pants.

It is something about plugging a most legitimate business guy in the city of Rochester, N. Y., when Joey Perhaps and Jack Ortega are engaged together in a little enterprise to shake the guy down, but the details of this transaction are dull, sordid, and quite uninteresting, except that Joey Perhaps turns state's evidence and announces that Jack Ortega fires the shot which cools the legitimate guy off, for which service he is rewarded with only a small stretch.

I must say for Joey Perhaps that he looks good, and he is very well dressed, but then Joey is always particular about clothes, and he is quite a handy guy with the dolls in his day and, to tell the truth, many citizens along Broadway are by no means displeased when Joey is placed in the state institution, because they are generally pretty uneasy about their dolls when he is around.

Naturally, I am wondering why Joey Perhaps is on this train going to Boston, Mass., but for all I know maybe he is wondering the same thing about me, although personally I am making no secret about it. The idea is I am en route to Boston, Mass., to see a contest of skill and science that is to take place there this very Friday night between a party by the name of Lefty Ledoux and another party by the name of Mickey McCoy, who are very prominent middleweights.

Now ordinarily I will not go around the corner to see a contest of skill and science between Lefty Ledoux and Mickey McCoy, or anybody else, as far as that is concerned, unless they are using blackjacks and promise to hurt each other, but I am the guest on this trip of a party by the name of Meyer Marmalade, and I will go anywhere to see anything if I am a guest.

This Meyer Marmalade is really a most superior character, who is called Meyer Marmalade because nobody can ever think of his last name, which is something like Marmalodowski, and he is known far and wide for the way he likes to make bets on any sporting proposition, such as baseball, or horse races, or ice hockey, or contests of skill and science, and especially contests of skill and science.

So he wishes to be present at this contest in Boston, Mass., between Lefty Ledoux and Mickey McCoy to have a nice wager on McCoy, as he has reliable information that McCoy's manager, a party by the name of Koons, has both judges and the referee in the satchel.

If there is one thing Meyer Marmalade dearly loves, it is to have a bet on a contest of skill and science of this nature, and so he is going to Boston, Mass. But Meyer Marmalade is such a guy as loathes and despises traveling all alone, so when he offers to pay my expenses if I will go along to keep him company, naturally I am pleased to accept, as I have nothing on of importance at the moment and, in fact, I do not have anything on of importance for the past ten years.

I warn Meyer Marmalade in advance that if he is looking to take anything off of anybody in Boston, Mass., he may as well remain at home, because everybody knows that statistics show that the percentage of anything being taken off of the citizens of Boston, Mass., is less per capita than anywhere else in the United States, especially when it comes to contests of skill and science, but Meyer Marmalade says this is the first time they ever had two judges and a referee running against the statistics, and he is very confident.

Well, by and by I go from the dining-car back to my seat in another car, where Meyer Marmalade is sitting reading a detective magazine, and I speak of seeing Joey Perhaps to him. But Meyer Marmalade does not seem greatly interested, although he says to me like this:

"Joey Perhaps, eh?" he says. "A wrong gee. A dead wrong gee. He must just get out. I run into the late Jack Ortega's brother, young Ollie, in Mindy's restaurant last week," Meyer Marmalade says, "and when we happen to get to talking of wrong gees, naturally Joey Perhaps' name comes up, and Ollie remarks he understands Joey Perhaps is about due out, and that he will be pleased to see him some day. Personally," Meyer Marmalade says, "I do not care for any part of Joey Perhaps at any price."

Now our car is loaded with guys and dolls who are going to Boston, Mass., to witness a large football game between the Harvards and the Yales at Cambridge, Mass., the next day, and the reason I know this is because they are talking of nothing else.

So this is where the football starts getting into this story.

One old guy that I figure must be a Harvard from the way he talks seems to have a party all his own, and he is getting so much attention from one and all in the party that I figure he must be a guy of some importance, because they laugh heartily at his remarks, and although I listen very carefully to everything he says he does not sound so very humorous to me.

He is a heavy-set guy with a bald head and a deep voice, and anybody can see that he is such a guy as is accustomed to plenty of authority. I am wondering out loud to Meyer Marmalade who the guy can be, and Meyer Marmalade states as follows:

"Why," he says, "he is nobody but Mr. Phillips Randolph, who makes the automobiles. He is the sixth richest guy in this country," Meyer says, "or maybe it is the seventh. Anyway, he is pretty well up with the front runners. I spot his monicker on his suitcase, and then I ask the porter, to make sure. It is a great honor for us to be traveling with Mr. Phillips Randolph," Meyer says, "because of him being such a public benefactor and having so much dough, especially having so much dough."

Well, naturally everybody knows who Mr. Phillips Randolph is, and I am surprised that I do not recognize his face myself from seeing it so often in the newspapers alongside the latest model automobile his factory turns out, and I am as much pleasured up as Meyer Marmalade over being in the same car with Mr. Phillips Randolph.

He seems to be a good-natured old guy, at that, and he is having a grand time, what with talking, and laughing, and taking a dram now and then out of a bottle, and when old Crip McGonnigle comes gimping through the car selling his football souvenirs, such as red and blue feathers, and little badges and pennants, and one thing and another, as Crip is doing around the large football games since Hickory Slim is a two-year-old, Mr. Phillips Randolph stops him and buys all of Crip's red feathers, which have a little white H on them to show they are for the Harvards.

Then Mr. Phillips Randolph distributes the feathers around among his party, and the guys and dolls stick them in their hats, or pin them on their coats, but he has quite a number of feathers left over, and about this time who comes through the car but Joey Perhaps, and Mr. Phillips Randolph steps out in the aisle and stops Joey and politely offers him a red feather, and speaks as follows:

"Will you honor us by wearing our colors?"

Well, of course Mr. Phillips Randolph is only full of good spirits, and means no harm whatever, and the guys and dolls in his party laugh heartily as if they consider his action very funny, but maybe because they laugh, and maybe because he is just naturally a hostile guy, Joey Perhaps knocks Mr. Phillips Randolph's hand down, and says like this:

"Get out of my way," Joey says. "Are you trying to make a sucker out of somebody?"

Personally, I always claim that Joey Perhaps has a right to reject the red feather, because for all I know he may prefer a blue feather, which means the Yales, but what I say is he does not need to be so impolite to an old guy such as Mr. Phillips Randolph, although of course Joey has no way of knowing at this time about Mr. Phillips Randolph having so much dough.

Anyway, Mr. Phillips Randolph stands staring at Joey as if he is greatly startled, and the chances are he is, at that, for the chances are nobody ever speaks to him in such a manner in all his life, and Joey Perhaps also stands there a minute staring back at Mr. Phillips Randolph, and finally Joey speaks as follows:

"Take a good peek," Joey Perhaps says. "Maybe you will remember me if you ever see me again."

"Yes," Mr. Phillips Randolph says, very quiet. "Maybe I will. They say I have a good memory for faces. I beg your pardon for stopping you, sir. It is all in fun, but I am sorry," he says.

Then Joey Perhaps goes on, and he does not seem to notice Meyer Marmalade and me sitting there in the car, and Mr. Phillips Randolph sits down, and his face is redder than somewhat, and all the joy is gone out of him, and out of his party, too. Personally, I am very sorry Joey Perhaps comes along, because I figure Mr. Phillips Randolph will give me one of his spare feathers, and I will consider it a wonderful keepsake.

But now there is not much more talking, and no laughing whatever in Mr. Phillips Randolph's party, and he just sits there as if he is thinking, and for all I know he may be thinking that there ought to be a law against a guy speaking so disrespectfully to a guy with all his dough as Joey Perhaps speaks to him.

Well, the contest of skill and science between Lefty Ledoux and Mickey McCoy turns out to be something of a disappointment, and, in fact, it is a stinkeroo, because there is little skill and no science whatever in it, and by the fourth round the customers are scuffling their feet, and saying throw these bums out, and making other derogatory remarks, and furthermore it seems that this Koons does not have either one of the judges, or even as much as the referee, in the satchel, and Ledoux gets the duke by unanimous vote of the officials.

So Meyer Marmalade is out a couple of C's, which is all he can wager at the ringside, because it seems that nobody in Boston, Mass., cares a cuss about who wins the contest, and Meyer is much disgusted with life, and so am I, and we go back to the Copley Plaza Hotel, where we are stopping, and sit down in the lobby to meditate on the injustice of everything.

Well, the lobby is a scene of gayety, as it seems there are a number of football dinners and dances going on in the hotel, and guys and dolls in evening clothes are all around and about, and the dolls are so young and beautiful that I get to thinking that this is not such a bad old world, after all, and even Meyer Marmalade begins taking notice.

All of a sudden, a very, very beautiful young doll who is about 40 per cent in and 60 per cent out of an evening gown walks right up to us sitting there, and holds out her hand to me, and speaks as follows:

"Do you remember me?"

Naturally, I do not remember her, but naturally I am not going to admit it, because it is never my policy to discourage any doll who wishes to strike up an acquaintance with me, which is what I figure this doll is trying to do; then I see that she is nobody but Doria Logan, one of the prettiest dolls that ever hits Broadway, and about the same time Meyer Marmalade also recognizes her.

Doria changes no little since last I see her, which is quite some time back, but there is no doubt the change is for the better, because she is once a very rattle-headed young doll, and now she seems older, and quieter, and even prettier than ever. Naturally, Meyer Marmalade and I are glad to see her looking so well, and we ask her how are tricks, and what is the good word, and all this and that, and finally Doria Logan states to us as follows:

"I am in great trouble," Doria says. "I am in terrible trouble, and you are the first ones I see that I can talk to about it."

Well, at this, Meyer Marmalade begins to tuck in somewhat, because he figures it is the old lug coming up, and Meyer Marmalade is not such a guy as will go for the lug from a doll unless he gets something more than a story. But I can see Doria Logan is in great earnest.

"Do you remember Joey Perhaps?" she says.

"A wrong gee," Meyer Marmalade says. "A dead wrong gee."

"I not only remember Joey Perhaps," I say, "but I see him on the train today."

"Yes," Doria says, "he is here in town. He hunts me up only a few hours ago. He is here to do me great harm. He is here to finish ruining my life."

"A wrong gee," Meyer Marmalade puts in again. "Always a 100 per cent wrong gee."

Then Doria Logan gets us to go with her to a quiet corner of the lobby, and she tells us a strange story, as follows, and also to wit:

It seems that she is once tangled up with Joey Perhaps, which is something I never know before, and neither does Meyer Marmalade, and, in fact, the news shocks us quite some. It is back in the days when she is just about sixteen and is in the chorus of Earl Carroll's Vanities, and I remember well what a standout she is for looks, to be sure.

Naturally, at sixteen, Doria is quite a chump doll, and does not know which way is south, or what time it is, which is the way all dolls at sixteen are bound to be, and she has no idea what a wrong gee Joey Perhaps is, as he is good-looking and young, and seems very romantic, and is always speaking of love and one thing and another.

Well, the upshot of it all is the upshot of thousands of other cases since chump dolls commence coming to Broadway, and the first thing she knows, Doria Logan finds herself mixed up with a very bad character, and does not know what to do about it.

By and by, Joey Perhaps commences mistreating her no

little, and finally he tries to use her in some nefarious schemes of his, and of course everybody along Broadway knows that most of Joey's schemes are especially nefarious, because Joey is on the shake almost since infancy.

Well, one day Doria says to herself that if this is love, she has all she can stand, and she hauls off and runs away from Joey Perhaps. She goes back to her people, who live in the city of Cambridge, Mass., which is the same place where the Harvards have their college, and she goes there because she does not know of any other place to go.

It seems that Doria's people are poor, and Doria goes to a business school and learns to be a stenographer, and she is working for a guy in the real estate dodge by the name of Poopnoodle, and doing all right for herself, and in the meantime she hears that Joey Perhaps gets sent away, so she figures her troubles are all over as far as he is concerned.

Now Doria Logan goes along quietly through life, working for Mr. Poopnoodle, and never thinking of love, or anything of a similar nature, when she meets up with a young guy who is one of the Harvards, and who is maybe twenty-one years old, and is quite a football player, and where Doria meets up with this guy is in a drug store over a banana split.

Well, the young Harvard takes quite a fancy to Doria and, in fact, he is practically on fire about her, but by this time Doria is going on twenty, and is no longer a chump doll, and she has no wish to get tangled up in love again.

In fact, whenever she thinks of Joey Perhaps, Doria takes to hating guys in general, but somehow she cannot seem to get up a real good hate on the young Harvard,

because, to hear her tell it, he is handsome, and noble, and
has wonderful ideals.

Now as time goes on, Doria finds she is growing pale,
and is losing her appetite, and cannot sleep, and this wor-
ries her no little, as she is always a first-class feeder, and
finally she comes to the conclusion that what ails her is that
she is in love with the young Harvard, and can scarcely
live without him, so she admits as much to him one night
when the moon is shining on the Charles River, and everything is a dead cold setup for love.

Well, naturally, after a little offhand guzzling, which is
quite permissible under the circumstances, the young guy
wishes her to name the happy day, and Doria has half a
notion to make it the following Monday, this being a Sunday night, but then she gets to thinking about her past with
Joey Perhaps, and all, and she figures it will be bilking the
young Harvard to marry him unless she has a small talk
with him first about Joey, because she is well aware that
many young guys may have some objection to wedding a
doll with a skeleton in her closet, and especially a skeleton
such as Joey Perhaps.

But she is so happy she does not wish to run the chance
of spoiling everything by these narrations right away, so
she keeps her trap closed about Joey, although she promises to marry the young Harvard when he gets out of college, which will be the following year, if he still insists,
because Doria figures that by then she will be able to break
the news to him about Joey very gradually, and gently, and
especially gently.

Anyway, Doria says she is bound and determined to tell
him before the wedding, even if he takes the wind on her

as a consequence, and personally I claim this is very considerate of Doria, because many dolls never tell before the wedding, or even after. So Doria and the young Harvard are engaged, and great happiness prevails, when, all of a sudden, in pops Joey Perhaps.

It seems that Joey learns of Doria's engagement as soon as he gets out of the state institution, and he hastens to Boston, Mass., with an inside coat pocket packed with letters that Doria writes him long ago, and also a lot of pictures they have taken together, as young guys and dolls are bound to do, and while there is nothing much out of line about these letters and pictures, put them all together they spell a terrible pain in the neck to Doria at this particular time.

"A wrong gee," Meyer Marmalade says. "But," he says, "he is only going back to his old shakedown dodge, so all you have to do is to buy him off."

Well, at this, Doria Logan laughs one of these little short dry laughs that go "hah," and says like this:

"Of course he is looking to get bought off, but," she says, "where will I get any money to buy him off? I do not have a dime of my own, and Joey is talking large figures, because he knows my fiancé's papa has plenty. He wishes me to go to my fiancé and make him get the money off his papa, or he threatens to personally deliver the letters and pictures to my fiancé's papa.

"You can see the predicament I am in," Doria says, "and you can see what my fiancé's papa will think of me if he learns I am once mixed up with a blackmailer such as Joey Perhaps.

"Besides," Doria says, "it is something besides money with

Joey Perhaps, and I am not so sure he will not doublecross me even if I can pay him his price. Joey Perhaps is very angry at me. I think," she says, "if he can spoil my happiness, it will mean more to him than money."

Well, Doria states that all she can think of when she is talking to Joey Perhaps is to stall for time, and she tells Joey that, no matter what, she cannot see her fiancé until after the large football game between the Harvards and the Yales as he has to do a little football playing for the Harvards, and Joey asks her if she is going to see the game, and naturally she is.

And then Joey says he thinks he will look up a ticket speculator, and buy a ticket and attend the game himself, as he is very fond of football, and where will she be sitting, as he hopes and trusts he will be able to see something of her during the game, and this statement alarms Doria Logan no little, for who is she going with but her fiancé's papa, and a party of his friends, and she feels that there is no telling what Joey Perhaps may be up to.

She explains to Joey that she does not know exactly where she will be sitting, except that it will be on the Harvards' side of the field, but Joey is anxious for more details than this.

"In fact," Doria says, "he is most insistent, and he stands at my elbow while I call up Mr. Randolph at this very hotel, and he tells me the exact location of our seats. Then Joey says he will endeavor to get a seat as close to me as possible, and he goes away."

"What Mr. Randolph?" Meyer says. "Which Mr. Randolph?" he says. "You do not mean Mr. Phillips Randolph, by any chance, do you?"

"Why, to be sure," Doria says. "Do you know him?"

Naturally, from now on Meyer Marmalade gazes at Doria Logan with deep respect, and so do I, although by now she is crying a little, and I am by no means in favor of crying dolls. But while she is crying, Meyer Marmalade seems to be doing some more thinking, and finally he speaks as follows:

"Kindly see if you can recall these locations you speak of."

So here is where the football game comes in once more.

Only I regret to state that personally I do not witness this game, and the reason I do not witness it is because nobody wakes me up the next day in time for me to witness it, and the way I look at it, this is all for the best, as I am scarcely a football enthusiast.

So from now on the story belongs to Meyer Marmalade, and I will tell it to you as Meyer tells it to me.

It is a most exciting game (Meyer says). The place is full of people, and there are bands playing, and much cheering, and more lovely dolls than you can shake a stick at, although I do not believe there are any lovelier present than Doria Logan.

It is a good thing she remembers the seat locations, otherwise I will never find her, but there she is surrounded by some very nice-looking people, including Mr. Phillips Randolph, and there I am two rows back of Mr. Phillips Randolph, and the ticket spec I get my seat off of says he cannot understand why everybody wishes to sit near Mr. Phillips Randolph to-day when there are other seats just as good, and maybe better, on the Harvards' side.

So I judge he has other calls similar to mine for this location, and a sweet price he gets for it, too, and I judge that maybe at least one call is from Joey Perhaps, as I see Joey a couple of rows on back up of where I am sitting, but off to my left on an aisle, while I am almost in a direct line with Mr. Phillips Randolph.

To show you that Joey is such a guy as attracts attention, Mr. Phillips Randolph stands up a few minutes before the game starts, peering around and about to see who is present that he knows, and all of a sudden his eyes fall on Joey Perhaps, and then Mr. Phillips Randolph proves he has a good memory for faces, to be sure, for he states as follows:

"Why," he says, "there is the chap who rebuffs me so churlishly on the train when I offer him our colors. Yes," he says, "I am sure it is the same chap."

Well, what happens in the football game is much pulling and hauling this way and that, and to and fro, between the Harvards and the Yales without a tally right down to the last five minutes of play, and then all of a sudden the Yales shove the football down to within about three-eighths of an inch of the Harvards' goal line.

At this moment quite some excitement prevails. Then the next thing anybody knows, the Yales outshove the Harvards, and now the game is over, and Mr. Phillips Randolph gets up out of his seat, and I hear Mr. Phillips Randolph say like this:

"Well," he says, "the score is not so bad as it might be, and it is a wonderful game, and," he says, "we seem to make one convert to our cause, anyway, for see who is wearing our colors."

And with this he points to Joey Perhaps, who is still sitting down, with people stepping around him and over him, and he is still smiling a little smile, and Mr. Phillips Randolph seems greatly pleased to see that Joey Perhaps has a big, broad crimson ribbon where he once wears his white silk muffler.

But the chances are Mr. Phillips Randolph will be greatly surprised if he knows that the crimson ribbon across Joey's bosom comes of Ollie Ortega planting a short knife in Joey's throat, or do I forget to mention before that Ollie Ortega is among those present?

I send for Ollie after I leave you last night, figuring he may love to see a nice football game. He arrives by plane this morning, and I am not wrong in my figuring. Ollie thinks the game is swell.

Well, personally, I will never forget this game, it is so exciting. Just after the tally comes off, all of a sudden, from the Yales in the stand across the field from the Harvards, comes a long-drawn-out wail that sounds so mournful it makes me feel very sad, to be sure. It starts off something like Oh-oh-oh-oh-oh, with all the Yales Oh-oh-oh-oh-oh-ing at once, and I ask a guy next to me what it is all about.

"Why," the guy says, "it is the Yales' 'Undertaker Song.' They always sing it when they have the other guy licked. I am an old Yale myself, and I will now personally sing this song for you."

And with this the guy throws back his head, and opens his mouth wide and lets out a yowl like a wolf calling to its mate.

Well, I stop the guy, and tell him it is a very lovely song, to be sure, and quite appropriate all the way around, and then I hasten away from the football game without getting a chance to say good-by to Doria, although afterwards I mail her the package of letters and pictures that Ollie gets out of Joey Perhaps' inside coat pocket during the confusion that prevails when the Yales make their tally, and I hope and trust that she will think the crimson streaks across the package are just a little touch of color in honor of the Harvards.

But the greatest thing about the football game (Meyer Marmalade says) is I win two C's off of one of the Harvards sitting near me, so I am now practically even on my trip.

THAT EVER-LOVING WIFE OF HYMIE'S

IF anybody ever tells me I will wake up some morning to find myself sleeping with a horse, I will consider them very daffy indeed, especially if they tell me it will be with such a horse as old Mahogany, for Mahogany is really not much horse. In fact, Mahogany is nothing but an old bum, and you can say it again, and many horse players wish he is dead ten thousand times over.

But I will think anybody is daffier still if they tell me I will wake up some morning to find myself sleeping with Hymie Banjo Eyes, because as between Mahogany and Hymie Banjo Eyes to sleep with, I will take Mahogany every time, even though Mahogany snores more than somewhat when he is sleeping. But Mahogany is by no means as offensive to sleep with as Hymie Banjo Eyes, as Hymie not only snores when he is sleeping, but he hollers and kicks around and takes on generally.

He is a short, pudgy little guy who is called Hymie Banjo Eyes because his eyes bulge out as big and round as banjos, although his right name is Weinstein, or some such, and he is somewhat untidy-looking in spots, for Hymie Banjo Eyes is a guy who does not care if his breakfast gets on his vest, or what. Furthermore, he gabs a lot and thinks he is very smart, and many citizens consider him a pest, in spades. But personally I figure Hymie Banjo Eyes as very harmless, although he is not such a guy as I will ordinarily care to have much truck with.

But there I am one morning waking up to find myself sleeping with both Mahogany and Hymie, and what are we sleeping in but a horse car bound for Miami, and we are passing through North Carolina in a small-time blizzard when I wake up, and Mahogany is snoring and shivering, because it seems Hymie cops the poor horse's blanket to wrap around himself, and I am half frozen and wishing I am back in Mindy's restaurant on Broadway, where all is bright and warm, and that I never see either Mahogany or Hymie in my life.

Of course it is not Mahogany's fault that I am sleeping with him and Hymie, and in fact, for all I know, Mahogany may not consider me any bargain whatever to sleep with. It is Hymie's fault for digging me up in Mindy's one night and explaining to me how wonderful the weather is in Miami in the winter-time, and how we can go there for the races with his stable and make plenty of potatoes for ourselves, although of course I know when Hymie is speaking of his stable he means Mahogany, for Hymie never has more than one horse at any one time in his stable.

Generally it is some broken-down lizard that he buys for

about the price of an old wool hat and patches up the best
he can, as Hymie Banjo Eyes is a horse trainer by trade,
and considering the kind of horses he trains he is not a bad
trainer, at that. He is very good indeed at patching up
cripples and sometimes winning races with them until
somebody claims them on him or they fall down dead, and
then he goes and gets himself another cripple and starts all
over again.

I hear he buys Mahogany off a guy by the name of O'Shea
for a hundred bucks, although the chances are if Hymie
waits awhile the guy will pay him at least two hundred to
take Mahogany away and hide him, for Mahogany has bad
legs and bum feet, and is maybe nine years old, and does
not win a race since the summer of 1924, and then it is an
accident. But anyway, Mahogany is the stable Hymie Banjo
Eyes is speaking of taking to Miami when he digs me up in
Mindy's.

"And just think," Hymie says, "all we need to get there
is the price of a drawing-room on the Florida Special."

Well, I am much surprised by this statement, because it
is the first time I ever hear of a horse needing a drawing-
room, especially such a horse as Mahogany, but it seems the
drawing-room is not to be for Mahogany, or even for
Hymie or me. It seems it is to be for Hymie's ever-loving
wife, a blond doll by the name of 'Lasses, which he marries
out of some night club where she is what is called an
adagio dancer.

It seems that when 'Lasses is very young somebody once
says she is just as sweet as Molasses, and this is how she
comes to get the name of 'Lasses, although her right name
is Maggie Something, and I figure she must change quite a

lot since they begin calling her 'Lasses because at the time I meet her she is sweet just the same as green grapefruit.

She has a partner in the adagio business by the name of Donaldo, who picks her up and heaves her around the night club as if she is nothing but a baseball, and it is very thrilling indeed to see Donaldo giving 'Lasses a sling as if he is going to throw her plum away, which many citizens say may not be a bad idea, at that, and then catching her by the foot in mid-air and hauling her back to him.

But one night it seems that Donaldo takes a few slugs of gin before going into this adagio business, and he muffs 'Lasses' foot, although nobody can see how this is possible, because 'Lasses' foot is no more invisible than a box car, and 'Lasses keeps on sailing through the air. She finally sails into Hymie Banjo Eyes' stomach as he is sitting at a table pretty well back, and this is the way Hymie and 'Lasses meet, and a romance starts, although it is nearly a week before Hymie recovers enough from the body beating he takes off 'Lasses to go around and see her.

The upshot of the romance is 'Lasses and Hymie get married, although up to the time Donaldo slings her into Hymie's stomach, 'Lasses is going around with Brick McCloskey, the bookmaker, and is very loving with him indeed, but they have a row about something and are carrying the old torch for each other when Hymie happens along.

Some citizens say the reason 'Lasses marries Hymie is because she is all sored up on Brick and that she acts without thinking, as dolls often do, especially blond dolls, although personally I figure Hymie takes all the worst of the situation, as 'Lasses is not such a doll as any guy shall marry without talking it over with his lawyer. 'Lasses is one of these little blonds who is full of short answers, and personally I will just as soon marry a porcupine. But Hymie loves her more than somewhat, and there is no doubt Brick McCloskey is all busted up because 'Lasses takes this run-out powder on him, so maybe after all 'Lasses has some kind of appeal which I cannot notice offhand.

"But," Hymie explains to me when he is speaking to me about this trip to Miami, " 'Lasses is not well, what with nerves and one thing and another, and she will have to travel to Miami along with her Pekingese dog, Sooey-pow, because," Hymie says, "it will make her more nervous than somewhat if she has to travel with anybody else. And of course," Hymie says, "no one can expect 'Lasses to travel in anything but a drawing-room on account of her health."

Well, the last time I see 'Lasses she is making a sucker of a big sirloin in Bobby's restaurant, and she strikes me as a pretty healthy doll, but of course I never examine her close, and anyway, her health is none of my business.

"Now," Hymie says, "I get washed out at Empire, and I am pretty much in hock here and there and have no dough to ship my stable to Miami, but," he says, "a friend of mine is shipping several horses there and he has a whole car, and he will kindly let me have room in one end of the car for my stable, and you and I can ride in there, too.

"That is," Hymie says, "we can ride in there if you will dig up the price of a drawing-room and the two tickets that go with it so 'Lasses' nerves will not be disturbed. You see," Hymie says, "I happen to know you have two hundred and fifty bucks in the jug over here on the corner, because one of the tellers in the jug is a friend of mine, and he tips me off you have this sugar, even though," Hymie says, "you have it in there under another name."

Well, a guy goes up against many daffy propositions as he goes along through life, and the first thing I know I am waking up, like I tell you, to find myself sleeping with Mahogany and Hymie, and as I lay there in the horse car slowly freezing to death, I get to thinking of 'Lasses in a drawing-room on the Florida Special, and I hope and trust that she and the Peke are sleeping nice and warm.

The train finally runs out of the blizzard and the weather heats up somewhat, so it is not so bad riding in the horse car, and Hymie and I pass the time away playing two-handed pinochle. Furthermore, I get pretty well acquainted with Mahogany, and I find he is personally not such a bad old pelter as many thousands of citizens think.

Finally we get to Miami, and at first it looks as if Hymie is going to have a tough time finding a place to keep Mahogany, as all the stable room at the Hialeah track is taken by cash customers, and Hymie certainly is not a cash customer and neither is Mahogany. Personally, I am not worried so much about stable room for Mahogany as I am about stable room for myself, because I am now down to a very few bobs and will need same to eat on.

Naturally, I figure Hymie Banjo Eyes will be joining his ever-loving wife 'Lasses, as I always suppose a husband and wife are an entry, but Hymie tells me 'Lasses is parked in the Roney Plaza over on Miami Beach, and that he is going to stay with Mahogany, because it will make her very nervous to have people around her, especially people who are training horses every day, and who may not smell so good.

Well, it looks as if we will wind up camping out with
Mahogany under a palm tree, although many of the palm
trees are already taken by other guys camping out with
horses, but finally Hymie finds a guy who has a garage
back of his house right near the race track, and having no
use for this garage since his car blows away in the hurri-
cane of 1926, the guy is willing to let Hymie keep Mahogany in the garage. Furthermore, he is willing to let
Hymie sleep in the garage with Mahogany, and pay him
now and then.

So Hymie borrows a little hay and grain, such as horses
love to eat, off a friend who has a big string at the track,
and moves into the garage with Mahogany, and about the
same time I run into a guy by the name of Pottsville Legs,
out of Pottsville, Pa., and he has a room in a joint down-
town, and I move in with him, and it is no worse than
sleeping with Hymie Banjo Eyes and Mahogany, at that.

I do not see Hymie for some time after this, but I hear
of him getting Mahogany ready for a race. He has the old
guy out galloping on the track every morning, and who is
galloping him but Hymie himself, because he cannot get
any stable boys to do the galloping for him, as they do not
wish to waste their time. However, Hymie rides himself
when he is a young squirt, so galloping Mahogany is not
such a tough job for him, except that it gives him a terrible
appetite, and it is very hard for him to find anything to
satisfy this appetite with, and there are rumors around
that Hymie is eating most of Mahogany's hay and grain.

In the meantime, I am going here and there doing the
best I can, and this is not so very good, at that, because
never is there such a terrible winter in Miami or so much

suffering among the horse players. In the afternoon I go
out to the race track, and in the evening I go to the dog
tracks, and later to the gambling joints trying to pick up
a few honest bobs, and wherever I go I seem to see Hymie's
ever-loving wife 'Lasses, and she is always dressed up more
than somewhat, and generally she is with Brick McCloskey,
for Brick shows up in Miami figuring to do a little business in bookmaking at the track.

When they turn off the books there and put in the mutuels, Brick still does a little booking to big betters who do
not wish to put their dough in the mutuels for fear of
ruining a price, for Brick is a very large operator at all
times. He is not only a large operator, but he is a big,
good-looking guy, and how 'Lasses can ever give him the
heave-o for such a looking guy as Hymie Banjo Eyes is
always a great mystery to me. But then this is the way
blondes are.

Of course Hymie probably does not know 'Lasses is
running around with Brick McCloskey, because Hymie
is too busy getting Mahogany ready for a race to make
such spots as 'Lasses and Brick are apt to be, and nobody
is going to bother to tell him, because so many ever-loving
wives are running around with guys who are not their
ever-loving husbands in Miami this winter that nobody
considers it any news.

Personally, I figure 'Lasses' running around with Brick
is a pretty fair break for Hymie, at that, as it takes plenty
of weight off him in the way of dinners, and maybe break-
fasts, for all I know, although it seems to me 'Lasses cannot love Hymie as much as Hymie thinks to be running
around with another guy. In fact, I am commencing to

figure 'Lasses does not care for Hymie Banjo Eyes whatever.

Well, one day I am looking over the entries, and I see where Hymie has old Mahogany in a claiming race at a mile and an eighth, and while it is a cheap race, there are some pretty fair hides in it. In fact, I can figure at least eight out of the nine that are entered to beat Mahogany by fourteen lengths.

Well, I go out to Hialeah very early, and I step around to the garage where Mahogany and Hymie are living, and Hymie is sitting out in front of the garage on a bucket looking very sad, and Mahogany has his beezer stuck out through the door of the garage, and he is looking even sadder than Hymie.

"Well," I say to Hymie Banjo Eyes, "I see the big horse goes today."

"Yes," Hymie says, "the big horse goes today if I can get ten bucks for the jockey fee, and if I can get a jock after I get the fee. It is a terrible situation," Hymie says. "Here I get Mahogany all readied up for the race of his life in a spot where he can win by as far as from here to Palm Beach and grab a purse worth six hundred fish, and me without as much as a sawbuck to hire one of these hop-toads that are putting themselves away as jocks around here."

"Well," I say, "why do you not speak to 'Lasses, your ever-loving wife, about this situation? I see 'Lasses playing the wheel out at Hollywood last night," I say, "and she has a stack of checks in front of her a greyhound cannot hurdle, and," I say, "it is not like 'Lasses to go away from there without a few bobs off such a start."

"Now there you go again," Hymie says, very impatient, indeed. "You are always making cracks about 'Lasses, and you know very well it will make the poor little doll very nervous if I speak to her about such matters as a sawbuck, because 'Lasses needs all the sawbucks she can get hold of to keep herself and Sooey-pow at the Roney Plaza. By the way," Hymie says, "how much scratch do you have on your body at this time?"

Well, I am never any hand for telling lies, especially to an old friend such as Hymie Banjo Eyes, so I admit I have a ten-dollar note, although naturally I do not mention another tenner which I also have in my pocket, as I know Hymie will wish both of them. He will wish one of my tenners to pay the jockey fee, and he will wish the other to bet on Mahogany, and I am certainly not going to let Hymie throw my dough away betting it on such an old crocodile as Mahogany, especially in a race which a horse by the name of Side Burns is a sure thing to win.

In fact, I am waiting patiently for several days for a chance to bet on Side Burns. So I hold out one sawbuck on Hymie, and then I go over to the track and forget all about him and Mahogany until the sixth race is coming up, and I see by the jockey board that Hymie has a jock by the name of Scroon riding Mahogany and while Mahogany is carrying only one hundred pounds, which is the light weight of the race, I will personally just as soon have Paul Whiteman up as Scroon. Personally I do not think Scroon can spell "horse," for he is nothing but a dizzy little guy who gets a mount about once every Pancake Tuesday. But of course Hymie is not a guy who can pick and choose his jocks, and the chances are he is pretty lucky to get anybody to ride Mahogany.

I see by the board where it tells you the approximate odds that Mahogany is 40 to 1, and naturally nobody is paying any attention to such a horse, because it will not be good sense to pay any attention to Mahogany in this race, what with it being his first start in months, and Mahogany not figuring with these horses, or with any horses, as far as this is concerned. In fact, many citizens think Hymie Banjo Eyes is either crazy, or is running Mahogany in this race for exercise, although nobody who knows Hymie will figure him to be spending dough on a horse just to exercise him.

The favorite in the race is this horse named Side Burns, and from the way they are playing him right from taw you will think he is Twenty Grand. He is even money on the board, and I hope and trust that he will finally pay as much as this, because at even money I consider him a very sound investment, indeed. In fact, I am willing to take four to five for my dough, and will consider it money well found, because I figure this will give me about eighteen bobs to bet on Tony Joe in the last race, and anybody will tell you that you can go to sleep on Tony Joe winning, unless something happens.

There is a little action on several other horses in the race, but of course there is none whatever for Mahogany and the last time I look he is up to fifty. So I buy my ticket on Side Burns, and go out to the paddock to take a peek at the horses, and I see Hymie Banjo Eyes in there saddling Mahogany with his jockey, this dizzy Scroon, standing alongside him in Hymie's colors of red, pink and yellow, and making wise-cracks to the guys in the next stall about Mahogany.

Hymie Banjo Eyes sees me and motions me to come into the paddock, so I go in and give Mahogany a pat on the snoot, and the old guy seems to remember me right away, because he rubs his beezer up and down my arm and lets out a little snicker. But it seems to me the old plug looks a bit peaked, and I can see his ribs very plain indeed, so I figure maybe there is some truth in the rumor about Hymie sharing Mahogany's hay and grain, after all.

Well, as I am standing there, Hymie gives this dizzy Scroon his riding instructions, and they are very short, for all Hymie says is as follows:

"Listen," Hymie says, "get off with this horse and hurry right home."

And Scroon looks a little dizzier than somewhat and nods his head, and then turns and tips a wink to Kurtsinger, who is riding the horse in the next stall.

Well, finally the post bugle goes, and Hymie walks back with me to the lawn as the horses are coming out on the track, and Hymie is speaking about nothing but Mahogany.

"It is just my luck," Hymie says, "not to have a bob or two to bet on him. He will win this race as far as you can shoot a rifle, and the reason he will win this far," Hymie says, "is because the track is just soft enough to feel nice and soothing to his sore feet. Furthermore," Hymie says, "after lugging my one hundred and forty pounds around every morning for two weeks, Mahogany will think it is

Christmas when he finds nothing but this Scroon's one hundred pounds on his back.

"In fact," Hymie says, "if I do not need the purse money, I will not let him run today, but will hide him for a bet. But," he says, "'Lasses must have five yards at once, and you know how nervous she will be if she does not get the five yards. So I am letting Mahogany run," Hymie says, "and it is a pity."

"Well," I says, "why do you not promote somebody to bet on him for you?"

"Why," Hymie says, "if I ask one guy I ask fifty. But they all think I am out of my mind to think Mahogany can beat such horses as Side Burns and the rest. Well," he says, "they will be sorry. By the way," he says, "do you have a bet down of any kind?"

Well, now, I do not wish to hurt Hymie's feelings by letting him know I bet on something else in the race, so I tell him I do not play this race at all, and he probably figures it is because I have nothing to bet with after giving him the sawbuck. But he keeps on talking as we walk over in front of the grand stand, and all he is talking about is what a tough break it is for him not to have any dough to bet on Mahogany. By this time the horses are at the post a little way up the track, and as we are standing there watching them, Hymie Banjo Eyes goes on talking, half to me and half to himself, but out loud.

"Yes," he says, "I am the unluckiest guy in all the world. Here I am," he says, "with a race that is a kick in the pants for my horse at fifty to one, and me without a quarter to bet. It is certainly a terrible thing to be poor," Hymie says.

"Why," he says, "I will bet my life on my horse in this race, I am so sure of winning. I will bet my clothes. I will bet all I ever hope to have. In fact," he says, "I will even bet my ever-loving wife, this is how sure I am."

Now of course this is only the way horse players rave when they are good and heated up about the chances of a horse, and I hear such conversations as this maybe a million times, and never pay any attention to it whatever, but as Hymie makes this crack about betting his ever-loving wife, a voice behind us says as follows:

"Against how much?"

Naturally, Hymie and I look around at once, and who does the voice belong to but Brick McCloskey. Of course I figure Brick is kidding Hymie Banjo Eyes, but Brick's voice is as cold as ice as he says to Hymie like this:

"Against how much will you bet your wife your horse wins this race?" he says. "I hear you saying you are sure this old buzzard meat you are running will win," Brick says, "so let me see how sure you are. Personally," Brick says, "I think they ought to prosecute you for running a broken-down hound like Mahogany on the ground of cruelty to animals, and furthermore," Brick says, "I think they ought to put you in an insane asylum if you really believe your old dog has a chance. But I will give you a bet," he says. "How much do you wish me to lay against your wife?"

Well, this is very harsh language indeed, and I can see that Brick is getting something off his chest he is packing there for some time. The chances are he is putting the blast on poor Hymie Banjo Eyes on account of Hymie grabbing 'Lasses from him, and of course Brick McCloskey never figures for a minute that Hymie will take his question seriously. But Hymie answers like this:

"You are a price maker," he says. "What do you lay?"

Now this is a most astonishing reply, indeed, when you figure that Hymie is asking what Brick will bet against Hymie's ever-loving wife 'Lasses, and I am very sorry to hear Hymie ask, especially as I happen to turn around and find that nobody but 'Lasses herself is listening in on the conversation, and the chances are her face will be very white, if it is not for her make-up, 'Lasses being a doll who goes in for make-up more than somewhat.

"Yes," Brick McCloskey says, "I am a price maker, all right, and I will lay you a price. I will lay you five C's against your wife that your plug does not win," he says.

Brick looks at 'Lasses as he says this, and 'Lasses looks at Brick, and personally I will probably take a pop at a guy who looks at my ever-loving wife in such a way, if I happen to have any ever-loving wife, and maybe I will take a pop at my ever-loving wife, too, if she looks back at a guy in such a way, but of course Hymie is not noticing such things as looks at this time, and in fact he does not see 'Lasses as yet. But he does not hesitate in answering Brick.

"You are a bet," says Hymie. "Five hundred bucks against my ever-loving wife 'Lasses. It is a chiseler's price such as you always lay," he says, "and the chances are I can do better if I have time to go shopping around, but as it is," he says, "it is like finding money and I will not let you get away. But be ready to pay cash right after the race, because I will not accept your paper."

Well, I hear of many a strange bet on horse races, but

never before do I hear of a guy betting his ever-loving wife, although to tell you the truth I never before hear of a guy getting the opportunity to bet his wife on a race. For all I know, if bookmakers take wives as a steady thing there will be much action in such matters at every track.

But I can see that both Brick McCloskey and Hymie Banjo Eyes are in dead earnest, and about this time 'Lasses tries to cop a quiet sneak, and Hymie sees her and speaks to her as follows:

"Hello, Baby," Hymie says, "I will have your five yards for you in a few minutes and five more to go with it, as I am just about to clip a sucker. Wait here with me, Baby," Hymie says.

"No," 'Lasses says; "I am too nervous to wait here. I am going down by the fence to root your horse in," she says, but as she goes away I see another look pass between her and Brick McCloskey.

Well, all of a sudden Cassidy gets the horses in a nice line and lets them go, and as they come busting down past the stand the first time who is right there on top but old Mahogany, with this dizzy Scroon kicking at his skinny sides and yelling in his ears. As they make the first turn, Scroon has Mahogany a length in front, and he moves him out another length as they hit the back side.

Now I always like to watch the races from a spot away up the lawn, as I do not care to have anybody much around me when the tough finishes come along in case I wish to bust out crying, so I leave Hymie Banjo Eyes and Brick McCloskey still glaring at each other and go to my usual place, and who is standing there, too, all by herself but

'Lasses. And about this time the horses are making the turn into the stretch and Mahogany is still on top, but something is coming very fast on the outside. It looks as if Mahogany is in a tough spot, because halfway down the stretch the outside horse nails him and looks him right in the eye, and who is it but the favorite, Side Burns.

They come on like a team, and I am personally giving Side Burns a great ride from where I am standing, when I hear a doll yelling out loud, and who is the doll but 'Lasses, and what is she yelling but the following:

"Come on with him, jock!"

Furthermore, as she yells, 'Lasses snaps her fingers like a crap shooter and runs a couple of yards one way and then turns and runs a couple of yards back the other way, so I can see that 'Lasses is indeed of a nervous temperament, just as Hymie Banjo Eyes is always telling me, although up to this time I figure her nerves are the old alzo.

"Come on!" 'Lasses yells again. "Let him roll!" she yells. "Ride him, boy!" she yells. "Come on with him, Frankie!"

Well, I wish to say that 'Lasses' voice may be all right if she is selling tomatoes from door to door, but I will not care to have her using it around me every day for any purpose whatever, because she yells so loud I have to move off a piece to keep my eardrums from being busted wide open. She is still yelling when the horses go past the finish line, the snozzles of old Mahogany and Side Burns so close together that nobody can hardly tell which is which.

In fact, there is quite a wait before the numbers go up, and I can see 'Lasses standing there with her program all wadded up in her fist as she watches the board, and I can

see she is under a very terrible nervous strain indeed, and
I am very sorry I go around thinking her nerves are the
old alzo. Pretty soon the guy hangs out No. 9, and No. 9
is nobody but old Mahogany, and at this I hear 'Lasses
screech, and all of a sudden she flops over in a faint, and
somebody carries her under the grand stand to revive her,
and I figure her nerves bog down entirely, and I am sorrier
than ever for thinking bad thoughts of her.

I am also very, very sorry I do not bet my sawbuck on
Mahogany, especially when the board shows he pays $102,
and I can see where Hymie Banjo Eyes is right about the
weight and all, but I am glad Hymie wins the purse and
also the five C's off of Brick McCloskey and that he saves
his ever-loving wife, because I figure Hymie may now pay
me back a few bobs.

I do not see Hymie or Brick or 'Lasses again until the
races are over, and then I hear of a big row going on under
the stand, and go to see what is doing, and who is having
the row but Hymie Banjo Eyes and Brick McCloskey. It
seems that Hymie hits Brick a clout on the beezer that
stretches Brick out, and it seems that Hymie hits Brick
this blow because as Brick is paying Hymie the five C's
he makes the following crack:

"I do not mind losing the dough to you, Banjo Eyes,"
Brick lays, "but I am sore at myself for overlaying the price.
It is the first time in all the years I am booking that I make
such an overlay. The right price against your wife," Brick
says, "is maybe two dollars and a half."

Well, as Brick goes down with a busted beezer from
Hymie's punch, and everybody is much excited, who steps

out of the crowd around them and throws her arms around
Hymie Banjo Eyes, but his ever-loving wife 'Lasses, and
as she kisses Hymie smack dab in the mush, 'Lasses says
as follows:

"My darling Hymie," she says, "I hear what this big
flannelmouth says about the price on me, and," she says,
"I am only sorry you do not cripple him for life. I know
now I love you, and only you, Hymie," she says, "and I
will never love anybody else. In fact," 'Lasses says, "I just
prove my love for you by almost wrecking my nerves in
rooting Mahogany home. I am still weak," she says, "but
I have strength enough left to go with you to the Sunset
Inn for a nice dinner, and you can give me my money
then. Furthermore," 'Lasses says, "now that we have a
few bobs, I think you better find another place for Mahogany to stay, as it does not look nice for my husband to
be living with a horse."

Well, I am going by the jockey house on my way home,
thinking how nice it is that Hymie Banjo Eyes will no
longer have to live with Mahogany, and what a fine thing
it is to have a loyal, ever-loving wife such as 'Lasses, who
risks her nerves rooting for her husband's horse, when I
run into this dizzy Scroon in his street clothes, and wishing to be friendly, I say to him like this:

"Hello, Frankie," I say. "You put up a nice ride today."

"Where do you get this 'Frankie'?" Scroon says. "My
name is Gus."

"Why," I say, commencing to think of this and that, "so
it is, but is there a jock called Frankie in the sixth race with
you this afternoon?"

"Sure," Scroon says, "Frankie Madeley. He rides Side Burns, the favorite; and I make a sucker of him in the stretch run."

But of course I never mention to Hymie Banjo Eyes that I figure his ever-loving wife roots herself into a dead faint for the horse that will give her to Brick McCloskey, because for all I know she may think Scroon's name is Frankie, at that.

THE BRAKEMAN'S DAUGHTER

It is coming on spring in Newark, New Jersey, and one nice afternoon I am standing on Broad Street with a guy from Cleveland, Ohio, by the name of The Humming Bird, speaking of this and that, and one thing and another, when along comes a very tasty-looking young doll.

In fact, she is a doll with black hair, and personally I claim there is nothing more restful to the eye than a doll with black hair, because it is even money, or anyway 9 to 10, that it is the natural color of the hair, as it seems that dolls will change the color of their hair to any color but black, and why this is nobody knows, except that it is just the way dolls are.

Well, besides black hair, this doll has a complexion like I do not know what, and little feet and ankles, and a way of walking that is very pleasant to behold. Personally, I always take a gander at a doll's feet and ankles before I start handicapping her, because the way I look at it, the feet and ankles are the big tell in the matter of class, although I wish to state that I see some dolls in my time who have large feet and big ankles, but who are by no means bad.

But this doll I am speaking of is one hundred per cent in every respect, and as she passes, The Humming Bird looks at her, and she looks at The Humming Bird, and it is just the same as if they hold a two hours' conversation on the telephone, for they are both young, and it is spring, and the way language can pass between young guys and young dolls in the spring without them saying a word is really most surprising, and in fact it is practically uncanny.

Well, I can see that The Humming Bird is somewhat confused for a minute, while the young doll seems to go right off into a trance, and she starts crossing the street against the lights, which is not only unlawful in Newark, New Jersey, but most indiscreet, and she is about to be run down and mashed like a turnip by one of Big False Face's beer trucks when The Humming Bird hops out into the street and yanks her out of danger, while the beer truck goes on down the street with the jockey looking back and yelling words you will scarcely believe are known to anybody in Newark, New Jersey.

Then The Humming Bird and the young doll stand on the sidewalk chewing the fat for a minute or two, and it is plain to be seen that the doll is very much obliged to The Humming Bird, and it is also plain to be seen that The Humming Bird will give anyway four bobs to have the jockey of the beer truck where he can talk to him quietly.

Finally the doll goes on across the street, but this time she keeps her head up and watches where she is going, and The Humming Bird comes back to me, and I ask him if he finds out who she is, and does he date her up, or what? But in answer to my questions, The Humming Bird states to me as follows:

"To tell the truth," The Humming Bird says, "I neglect these details, because," he says, "I am already dated up to go out with Big False Face tonight to call on a doll who is daffy to meet me. Otherwise," he says, "I will undoubtedly make arrangements to see more of this pancake I just save from rack and ruin.

"But," The Humming Bird says, "Big Falsy tells me I am going to meet the most wonderful doll in the world, and one that is very difficult to meet, so I cannot be picking up any excess at this time. In fact," he says, "Big Falsy tells me that every guy in this town will give his right leg for the privilege of meeting the doll in question, but she will have no part of them. But it seems that she sees me talking to Big Falsy on the street yesterday, and now nothing will do but she must meet up with me personally. Is it not remarkable," The Humming Bird says, "the way dolls go for me?"

Well, I says it is, for I can see that The Humming Bird is such a guy as thinks he has something on the dolls, and for all I know maybe he has, at that, for he has plenty of youth, and good looks, and good clothes, and a nice line of gab, and all these matters are given serious consideration by the dolls, especially the youth.

But I cannot figure any doll that Big False Face knows being such a doll as the one The Humming Bird just yanks out the way of the beer truck, and in fact I do not see how any doll whatever can have any truck with a guy as ugly as Big False Face. But then of course Big False Face is now an important guy in the business world, and has plenty of potatoes, and of course potatoes are also something that is taken into consideration by the dolls.

Big False Face is in the brewery business, and he controls a number of breweries in different spots on the Atlantic seaboard, and especially in New Jersey, and the reason The Humming Bird is in Newark, New Jersey, at this time, is because Big False Face gets a very huge idea in connection with these breweries.

It seems that they are breweries that Big False Face takes over during the past ten years when the country is trying to get along without beer, and the plants are laying idle, and Big False Face opens up these plants, and puts many guys to work, and turns out plenty of beer, and thus becomes quite a philanthropist in his way, especially to citizens who like their beer, although up to the time he gets going good as a brewer, Big False Face is considered a very humble character, indeed.

He comes from the lower East Side of New York, and he is called Big False Face from the time he is very young, because he has a very large and a very homely kisser, and on this kisser there is always a castor-oil smile that looks as if it is painted on. But this smile is strictly a throw-off, and Big False Face is often smiling when he is by no means amused at anything, though I must say for him that he is generally a very light-hearted guy.

In his early youth, it is Big False Face's custom to stand chatting with strangers to the city around the railroad stations and ferryboat landings, and smiling very genially at them, and in this way Big False Face learns much about other parts of the country. But it seems that while he is chatting with these strangers, friends of Big False Face search the strangers' pockets, sometimes removing articles from these pockets such as watches, and lucky pieces, and keepsakes of one kind and another, including money.

Of course it is all in fun, but it seems that some of the strangers become greatly annoyed when they find their pockets empty, and go out of their way to mention the matter to the gendarmes. Well, after the gendarmes hear some little mention from strangers about their pockets being searched while they are chatting with a guy with a large, smiling kisser, the gendarmes take to looking around for such a guy.

Naturally, they finally come upon Big False Face, for at the time I am speaking of, it is by no means common to find guys with smiles on their kissers on the lower East Side, and, especially, large smiles. So what happens but Big False Face is sent to college in his youth by the gendarmes, and the place where the college is located is Auburn, New York, where they teach him that it is very, very wrong to smile at strangers while their pockets are being searched.

After Big False Face is in college for several years, the warden sends for him one day and gives him a new suit of clothes, and a railroad ticket, and a few bobs, and plenty of sound advice, and tells him to go back home again, and afterwards Big False Face says he is only sorry he can never remember the advice, as he has no doubt it will be of great value to him in his subsequent career.

Well, later on Big False Face takes a post-graduate course at Ossining, and also at Dannemora, and by the time he is through with all this, he finds that conditions change throughout the country, and that his former occupation is old-fashioned, and by no means genteel, so Big False Face has to think up something else to do. And while he is thinking, he drives a taxicab and has his station in front of the Pekin restaurant on Broadway, which is a real hot spot at this time.

Then one night a sailor off a U. S. battleship hires Big False Face to take him riding in Central Park, and it seems that somewhere on this ride the sailor loses his leather containing a month's salary, and he hops out of the taxicab and starts complaining to a gendarme, making quite a mountain out of nothing but a molehill, for anybody knows that if the sailor does not lose his leather in the taxicab, he is bound to spend it at ten cents a clip dancing with the dolls in the Flowerland dance hall, or maybe taking boat rides on the lagoon in the park.

Well, Big False Face can see an argument coming up, and rather than argue, he retires from the taxicab business at once, leaving his taxicab right there in the park, and going over into New Jersey, and Big False Face always says that one of the regrets of his life is he never collects the taxi fare off the sailor.

In New Jersey, Big False Face secures a position with the late Crowbar Connolly, riding loads down out of Canada, and then he is with the late Hands McGovern, and the late Dark Tony de More, and also the late Lanky-lank Watson, and all this time Big False Face is advancing step by step in the business world, for he has a great personality, and is well liked by one and all.

Naturally, many citizens are jealous of Big False Face,

and sometimes when they are speaking of him they speak
of the days of his youth when he is on the whizz, as if
this is something against him, but I always say it is very
creditable of Big False Face to rise from such a humble
beginning to a position of affluence in the business world.

Personally, I consider Big False Face a remarkable character, especially when he takes over the idle breweries, because it is at a time when everybody is going around saying that if they can only have beer everything will be all
right. So Big False Face starts turning out beer that tastes
very good, indeed, and if everything is not all right, it is
by no means his fault.

You must remember that at the time he starts turning
out his beer, and for years afterwards, Big False Face is
being most illegal and quite against the law, and I claim
that the way he is able to hide several breweries, each cover-
ing maybe half a block of ground, from the gendarmes all
these years is practically magical, and proves that what I
say about Big False Face being a remarkable character is
very true.

Well, when Congress finally gets around to saying that
beer is all right again, Big False Face is a well-established,
going concern, and has a fair head-start on the old-fashioned
brewers who come back into the business again, but Big
False Face is smart enough to know that he will be able
to keep ahead of them only by great enterprise and industry, because it seems that certain parties are bound and
determined to make it tough on the brewers who supply
this nation with beer when beer is illegal, such as Big False
Face, forgetting all the hardships and dangers that these
brewers face through the years to give the American people

their beer, and all the bother they are put to in hiding breweries from the gendarmes.

In fact, these certain parties are making it so tough that Big False Face himself has to write twice before he can get permits for his breweries, and naturally this annoys Big False Face no little, as he hates to write letters.

Furthermore, he hears this condition prevails all over the country, so Big False Face gets to thinking things over, and he decides that the thing to do is to organize the independent brewers like himself into an association to protect their interests. So he calls a meeting in Newark, New Jersey, of all these brewers, and this is how it comes that The Humming Bird is present, for The Humming Bird represents certain interests around Cleveland, Ohio, and furthermore The Humming Bird is personally regarded as a very able young guy when it comes to breweries.

Well, the only reason I am in Newark, New Jersey, at this time is because a guy by the name of Abie Schumtzenheimer is a delegate representing a New York brewery, and this Abie is a friend of mine, and after the meeting lasts three days he sends for me to come over and play pinochle with him, because he cannot make heads or tails of what they are all talking about.

And anyway Abie does not care much, because the brewery he represents is going along for nearly twelve years, and is doing all the business it can handle, and any time it fails to do all the business it can handle, Abie will be around asking a lot of people why.

So Abie's brewery does not care if it enters any association or not, but of course Abie cannot disregard an invita-

tion from such a guy as Big False Face. So there he is,
and by and by there I am, and in this way I meet up with
The Humming Bird, and after watching the way he goes
darting around and about, especially if a doll happens to
pop up in his neighborhood, I can understand why they call
him The Humming Bird.

But, personally, I do not mind seeing a young guy dis-
playing an interest in dolls, and in fact if a young guy
does not display such an interest in dolls, I am apt to figure
there is something wrong with him. And anyway what is
the use of being young if a guy does not display an interest
in dolls?

Well, there are delegates to the meeting from as far west
as Chicago, and most of them seem to be greatly interested
in Big False Face's proposition, especially a delegate from
South Chicago who keeps trying to introduce a resolution
to sue the government for libel for speaking of brewers
who supply the nation with beer after prohibition sets in,
as racket guys and wildcatters.

The reason the meeting lasts so long is partly because
Big False Face keeps making motions for recesses so he
can do a little entertaining, for if there is one thing Big
False Face loves, it is to entertain, but another reason is
that not all the delegates are willing to join Big False Face's
association, especially certain delegates who are operating
in Pennsylvania.

These delegates say it is nothing but a scheme on the
part of Big False Face to nab the business on them, and in
fact it seems that there is much resentment among these
delegates against Big False Face, and especially on the part
of a guy by the name of Cheeks Sheracki, who comes from

Philadelphia, Pennsylvania, and I wish to state that if there is one guy in the United States I will not care to have around resenting me, it is Cheeks Sheracki, for nobody knows how many guys Cheeks cools off in his time, not even himself.

But Big False Face does not seem to notice anybody resenting him, and he is putting on entertainment for the delegates right and left, including a nice steak dinner on the evening of the day I am speaking of, and it is at this dinner I state to Big False Face that I hear he is taking The Humming Bird out in society.

"Yes," Big False Face says, "I am going to take The Humming Bird to call on the brakeman's daughter."

Well, when I hear this, I wish to say I am somewhat surprised, because the brakeman's daughter is nothing but a practical joke, and furthermore it is a practical joke that is only for rank suckers, and The Humming Bird does not look to be such a sucker to me.

In fact, when Big False Face speaks of the brakeman's daughter, I take a gander at The Humming Bird, figuring to see some expression on his kisser that will show he knows what the brakeman's daughter is, but instead The Humming Bird is only looking quite eager, and then I get to thinking about what he tells me in the afternoon about Big False Face taking him to see a doll who is daffy to meet him, and I can see that Big False Face is working on him with the brakeman's daughter for some time.

And I also get to thinking that a lot of smarter guys than The Humming Bird will ever be, no matter how smart he gets, fall for the brakeman's daughter joke, including Big False Face himself. In fact, Big False Face falls for it in the spring of 1928 at Hot Springs, Arkansas, and ever since it is his favorite joke, and it becomes part of his entertainment of all visitors to Newark, New Jersey, unless of course they happen to be visitors who are jerry to the brakeman's daughter. In fact, Big False Face builds up the brakeman's daughter into quite a well-known institution in Newark, New Jersey, and the way the brakeman's daughter joke goes is as follows:

The idea is Big False Face picks out some guy that he figures is a little doll-dizzy, and the way Big False Face can rap to a doll-dizzy guy is really quite remarkable. Then he starts telling this guy about the brakeman's daughter, who is the most beautiful doll that ever steps in shoe leather, to hear Big False Face tell it. In fact, I once hear Big False Face telling a sucker about how beautiful the brakeman's daughter is, and I find myself wishing to see her, although of course I know there is no such thing as the brakeman's daughter.

Furthermore, everybody around Big False Face starts putting in a boost for the brakeman's daughter, stating to the sucker that she is so lovely that guys are apt to go silly just looking at her. But it seems that the brakeman's daughter has a papa who is a brakeman on the Central, and who is the orneriest guy in the world when it comes to his daughter, and who will not let anybody get close enough to her to hand her a slice of fruit cake.

In fact, this brakeman is so ornery he will shoot you setting if he catches you fooling around his daughter, the way Big False Face and other citizens of Newark, New Jersey, state the situation to the sucker, and everybody is afraid of the brakeman, including guys who are not supposed to be afraid of anything in this world.

But it seems that Big False Face is acquainted with the brakeman's daughter, and knows the nights the brakeman has to be out on his run, and on these nights the brakeman's daughter is home alone, and on such a night Big False Face occasionally calls on her, and sometimes takes a friend. But Big False Face and everybody else says that it is a dangerous proposition, because if the brakeman ever happens to come home unexpectedly and find callers with his daughter, he is pretty sure to hurt somebody.

Well, the chances are the sucker wishes to call on the brakeman's daughter, no matter what, especially as Big False Face generally lets on that the brakeman's daughter sees the sucker somewhere and is very anxious to meet him, just as he lets on to The Humming Bird, so finally some night Big Falsy takes the sucker to the house where the brakeman's daughter lives, making their approach to the house very roundabout, and mysterious, and sneaky.

Then the minute Big Falsy knocks on the door, out pops a guy from somewhere roaring at them in a large voice, and Big False Face yells that it is the brakeman's daughter's papa himself, and starts running, telling the sucker to follow, although as a rule this is by no means necessary. And when the sucker starts running, he commences to hear shots, and naturally he figures that the old brakeman is popping at him with a Betsy, but what he really hears is incandescent light bulbs going off around him and sometimes they hit him if the bulb-thrower has good control.

Now, the house Big False Face generally uses is an old

empty residence pretty well out in a suburb of Newark, New Jersey, and it sits away off by itself in a big yard near a piece of woods, and when he starts running, Big False Face always runs into this woods, and naturally the sucker follows him. And pretty soon Big False Face loses the sucker in the woods, and doubles back and goes on down-town and leaves the sucker wandering around in the woods for maybe hours.

Then when the sucker finally makes his way back to his hotel, he always finds many citizens gathered to give him the ha-ha, and to make him buy refreshments for one and all, and the sucker tries to make out that he is greatly amused himself, although the chances are he is so hot you can fry an egg on any part of him.

The biggest laugh that Big False Face ever gets out of the brakeman's daughter joke is the time he leaves a guy from Brooklyn by the name of Rocco Scarpati in the woods one cold winter night, and Rocco never does find his way out, and freezes as stiff as a starched shirt. And of course Big False Face has quite a time explaining to Rocco's Brooklyn friends that Rocco is not cooled off by other means than freezing.

Well, now the way I tell it, you say to yourself how can anybody be sucker enough to fall for such a plant at this? But Big False Face's record with the brakeman's daughter joke in Newark, New Jersey, includes a congressman, a justice of the peace, three G-guys, eighteen newspaper scribes, five prize fighters, and a raft of guys from different parts of the country, who are such guys as the ordinary citizens will hesitate about making merry with.

In fact, I hear Big False Face is putting the feel on

Cheeks Sheracki with reference to the brakeman's daughter until he finds out Cheeks knows this joke as well as he does himself, and then Big False Face discovers The Humming Bird, and no one is talking stronger for the brakeman's daughter with The Humming Bird than Cheeks.

Well, anyway, along about nine o'clock on the night in question, Big False Face tells The Humming Bird that the brakeman is now well out on his run on the Central, so they get in Big False Face's car and start out, and I notice that as they get in the car, Big False Face gives The Humming Bird a quick fanning, as Big False Face does not care to take chances on a sucker having that certain business on him.

The Humming Bird is all sharpened up for this occasion, and furthermore he is quite excited, and one and all are telling him what a lucky guy he is to get to call on the brakeman's daughter, but anybody can see from the way The Humming Bird acts that he feels that it is really the brakeman's daughter who is having the luck.

It seems that Cheeks Sheracki and a couple of his guys from Philadelphia go out to the house in advance to heave the incandescent bulbs and do the yelling, and personally I sit up playing pinochle with Abie Schumtzenheimer waiting to hear what comes off, although Abie says it is all great foolishness, and by no means worthy of grown guys. But Abie admits he will be glad to see the brakeman's daughter himself if she is as beautiful as Big False Face claims.

Well, when they come within a couple of blocks of the empty house in the suburbs of Newark, New Jersey, Big False Face tells his driver, a guy by the name of Ears

Acosta, who afterwards informs me on several points in this transaction, to pull up and wait there, and then Big False Face and The Humming Bird get out of the car and Big False Face leads the way up the street and into the yard.

This yard is filled with big trees and shrubbery, but the moon is shining somewhat, and it is easy enough to make out objects around and about, but there are no lights in the house, and it is so quiet you can hear your watch tick in your pocket, if you happen to have a watch.

Well, Big False Face has The Humming Bird by the coat sleeve, and he tiptoes through the gate and up a pathway, and The Humming Bird tiptoes right with him, and every now and then Big False Face stops and listens, and the way Big False Face puts this on is really wonderful, because he does it so often he can get a little soul into his work.

Now, The Humming Bird has plenty of moxie from all I hear, but naturally seeing the way Big False Face is acting makes him feel a little nervous, because The Humming Bird knows that Big False Face is as game as they come and he figures that any situation that makes Big False Face act as careful as all this must be a very dangerous situation indeed.

When they finally get up close to the house, The Humming Bird sees there is a porch, and Big False Face tiptoes up on this porch, still leading The Humming Bird by the coat sleeve, and then Big False Face knocks softly on the door, and lets out a little low whistle, and just as The Humming Bird is commencing to notice that this place seems to be somewhat deserted, all of a sudden a guy comes busting around the corner of the house.

This guy is making a terrible racket, what with yelling and swearing, and among other things he yells as follows:

"Ah-ha!" the guy yells, "now I have you dead to rights!"

And with this, something goes pop, and then something goes pop-pop, and Big False Face says to The Humming Bird like this:

"My goodness," Big False Face says, "it is the brakeman! Run!" he says. "Run for your life!"

Then Big False Face turns and runs, and The Humming Bird is about to turn and run with him, because The Humming Bird figures if a guy like Big False Face can afford to run there can be no percentage in standing still himself, but before he can move the door of the house flies open and The Humming Bird feels himself being yanked inside the joint, and he puts up his dukes and gets ready to do the best he can until he is overpowered. Then he hears a doll's voice going like this:

"Sh-h-h-h!" the doll's voice goes. "Sh-h-h-h!"

So The Humming Bird sh-h-h-h's, and the racket goes on outside a while with a guy still yelling, and much pop-pop-popping away. Then the noise dies out, and all is still, and by the moonlight that is coming through a window on which there is no curtain, The Humming Bird can see a lot of furniture scattered around and about the room, but some of it is upside down, and none of it is arranged in any order.

Furthermore, The Humming Bird can now also see that the doll who pulls him into the house and gives him

the sh-h-h-h is nobody but the black-haired doll he hauls
out of the way of the beer truck in the afternoon, and
naturally The Humming Bird is somewhat surprised to
see her at this time.

Well, the black-haired doll smiles at The Humming
Bird, and finally he forgets his nervousness to some extent,
and in fact drops his dukes which he still has up ready to
sell his life dearly, and by and by the black-haired doll says
to him like this:

"I recognize you through the window in the moonlight,"
she says. "As I see you coming up on the porch, I also see
some parties lurking in the shrubbery, and," she says, "I
have a feeling they are seeking to do you harm, so I pull
you inside the house. I am glad to see you again," she says.

Well, Big False Face does not show up in his accustomed
haunts to laugh at the joke on The Humming Bird, but
Ears Acosta returns with disquieting news such as causes
many citizens to go looking for Big False Face, and they
find him face downward on the path just inside the gate-
way, and when they turn him over the old castor-oil smile
is still on his kisser, and even larger than ever, as if Big
False Face is greatly amused by some thought that hits
him all of a sudden.

And Big False Face is extremely dead when they find
him, as it seems that some of the incandescent bulbs that
go pop-popping around him are really sawed-off shotguns,
and it also seems that Cheeks Sheracki and his guys from
Philadelphia are such careless shots that they tear off half
the gate with their slugs, so it is pretty lucky for The
Humming Bird that he is not running with Big False

Face for this gate at the moment, or in fact anywhere near him.

And back in the house while they are lugging Big False Face away, The Humming Bird and the black-haired doll are sitting on an overturned sofa in the parlor with the moonlight streaming through the window on which there is no curtain and spilling all over them as The Humming Bird is telling her how much he loves her, and how he hopes and trusts she feels the same towards him, for they are young, and it is spring in Newark, New Jersey.

"Well," The Humming Bird says, "so you are the brakeman's daughter, are you? Well," he says, "I wish to state that they do not overboost you a nickel's worth when they tell me you are the most beautiful doll in all this world, and I am certainly tickled to find you."

"But how do you learn my new address so soon?" the black-haired doll says. "We just move in here this morning, although," she says, "I guess it is a good thing for you we do not have time to put up any window shades. And what do you mean," the black-haired doll says, "by calling me the brakeman's daughter? My papa is one of the oldest and best known conductors anywhere on the Erie," she says.

LITTLE MISS MARKER

ONE evening along toward seven o'clock, many citizens are standing out on Broadway in front of Mindy's restaurant, speaking of one thing and another, and particularly about the tough luck they have playing the races in the afternoon, when who comes up the street with a little doll hanging onto his right thumb but a guy by the name of Sorrowful.

This guy is called Sorrowful because this is the way he always is about no matter what, and especially about the way things are with him when anybody tries to put the bite on him. In fact, if anybody who tries to put the bite on Sorrowful can listen to him for two minutes about how things are with him and not bust into tears, they must be very hard-hearted, indeed.

Regret, the horse player, is telling me that he once tries to put the bite on Sorrowful for a sawbuck, and by the time Sorrowful gets through explaining how things are with him, Regret feels so sorry for him that he goes out and puts the bite on somebody else for the saw and gives it to Sorrowful, although it is well known to one and all that Sorrowful has plenty of potatoes hid away somewhere.

He is a tall, skinny guy with a long, sad, mean-looking kisser, and a mournful voice. He is maybe sixty years old, give or take a couple of years, and for as long as I can remember he is running a handbook over in Forty-ninth Street next door to a chop-suey joint. In fact, Sorrowful is one of the largest handbook makers in this town.

Any time you see him he is generally by himself, because being by himself is not apt to cost him anything, and it is therefore a most surprising scene when he comes along Broadway with a little doll.

And there is much speculation among the citizens as to how this comes about, for no one ever hears of Sorrowful having any family, or relations of any kind, or even any friends.

The little doll is a very little doll indeed, the top of her noggin only coming up to Sorrowful's knee, although of course Sorrowful has very high knees, at that. Moreover, she is a very pretty little doll, with big blue eyes and fat pink cheeks, and a lot of yellow curls hanging down her back, and she has fat little legs and quite a large smile, although Sorrowful is lugging her along the street so fast that half the time her feet are dragging the sidewalk and she has a license to be bawling instead of smiling.

Sorrowful is looking sadder than somewhat, which makes his face practically heart-rending as he pulls up in front of Mindy's and motions us to follow him in. Anybody can see that he is worried about something very serious, and many citizens are figuring that maybe he suddenly discovers all his potatoes are counterfeit, because nobody can think of anything that will worry Sorrowful except money.

Anyway, four or five of us gather around the table where Sorrowful sits down with the little doll beside him, and he states a most surprising situation to us.

It seems that early in the afternoon a young guy who is playing the races with Sorrowful for several days pops into his place of business next door to the chop-suey joint, leading the little doll, and this guy wishes to know how much time he has before post in the first race at Empire.

Well, he only has about twenty-five minutes, and he seems very down-hearted about this, because he explains to Sorrowful that he has a sure thing in this race, which he gets the night before off a guy who is a pal of a close friend of Jockey Workman's valet.

The young guy says he is figuring to bet himself about a deuce on this sure thing, but he does not have such a

sum as a deuce on him when he goes to bed, so he plans
to get up bright and early in the morning and hop down
to a spot on Fourteenth Street where he knows a guy who
will let him have the deuce.

But it seems that he oversleeps, and here it is almost post
time, and it is too late for him to get to Fourteenth Street
and back before the race is run off, and it is all quite a
sad story indeed, although of course it does not make much
impression on Sorrowful, as he is already sadder than
somewhat himself just from thinking that somebody may
beat him for a bet during the day, even though the races
do not start anywhere as yet.

Well, the young guy tells Sorrowful he is going to try
to get to Fourteenth Street and back in time to bet on the
sure thing, because he says it will be nothing short of a
crime if he has to miss such a wonderful opportunity.

"But," he says to Sorrowful, "to make sure I do not
miss, you take my marker for a deuce, and I will leave the
kid here with you as security until I get back."

Now, ordinarily, asking Sorrowful to take a marker will
be considered great foolishness, as it is well known to one
and all that Sorrowful will not take a marker from Andrew
Mellon. In fact, Sorrowful can almost break your heart
telling you about the poorhouses that are full of bookmakers who take markers in their time.

But it happens that business is just opening up for the
day, and Sorrowful is pretty busy, and besides the young
guy is a steady customer for several days, and has an honest
pan, and Sorrowful figures a guy is bound to take a little
doll out of hock for a deuce. Furthermore, while Sorrowful

does not know much about kids, he can see the little doll must be worth a deuce, at least, and maybe more.

So he nods his head, and the young guy puts the little doll on a chair and goes tearing out of the joint to get the dough, while Sorrowful marks down a deuce bet on Cold Cuts, which is the name of the sure thing. Then he forgets all about the proposition for a while, and all the time the little doll is sitting on the chair as quiet as a mouse, smiling at Sorrowful's customers, including the Chinks from the chop-suey joint who come in now and then to play the races.

Well, Cold Cuts blows, and in fact is not even fifth, and along late in the afternoon Sorrowful suddenly realizes that the young guy never shows up again, and that the little doll is still sitting in the chair, although she is now playing with a butcher knife which one of the Chinks from the chop-suey joint gives her to keep her amused.

Finally it comes on Sorrowful's closing time, and the little doll is still there, so he can think of nothing else to do in this situation, but to bring her around to Mindy's and get a little advice from different citizens, as he does not care to leave her in his place of business alone, as Sorrowful will not trust anybody in there alone, not even himself.

"Now," Sorrowful says, after giving us this long spiel, "what are we to do about this proposition?"

Well, of course, up to this minute none of the rest of us know we are being cut in on any proposition, and personally I do not care for any part of it, but Big Nig, the crap shooter, speaks up as follows:

"If this little doll is sitting in your joint all afternoon," Nig says, "the best thing to do right now is to throw a feed into her, as the chances are her stomach thinks her throat is cut."

Now this seems to be a fair sort of an idea, so Sorrowful orders up a couple of portions of ham hocks and sauerkraut, which is a very tasty dish in Mindy's at all times, and the little doll tears into it very enthusiastically, using both hands, although a fat old doll who is sitting at the next table speaks up and says this is terrible fodder to be tossing into a child at such an hour and where is her mamma?

"Well," Big Nig says to the old doll, "I hear of many people getting a bust in the snoot for not minding their own business in this town, but you give off an idea, at that. Listen," Big Nig says to the little doll, "where is your mamma?"

But the little doll does not seem to know, or maybe she does not wish to make this information public, because she only shakes her head and smiles at Big Nig, as her mouth is too full of ham hocks and sauerkraut for her to talk.

"What is your name?" Big Nig asks, and she says something that Big Nig claims sounds like Marky, although personally I think she is trying to say Martha. Anyway, it is from this that she gets the name we always call her afterward, which is Marky.

"It is a good monicker," Big Nig says. "It is short for marker, and she is certainly a marker unless Sorrowful is telling us a large lie. Why," Big Nig says, "this is a very cute little doll, at that, and pretty smart. How old are you, Marky?"

She only shakes her head again, so Regret, the horse player, who claims he can tell how old a horse is by its teeth, reaches over and sticks his finger in her mouth to get a peek at her crockery, but she seems to think Regret's finger is a hunk of ham hock and shuts down on it so hard Regret lets out an awful squawk. But he says that before she tries to cripple him for life he sees enough of her teeth to convince him she is maybe three, rising four, and this seems reasonable, at that. Anyway, she cannot be much older.

Well, about this time a guinea with a hand organ stops out in front of Mindy's and begins grinding out a tune while his ever-loving wife is passing a tambourine around among the citizens on the sidewalk and, on hearing this music, Marky slides off of her chair with her mouth still full of ham hock and sauerkraut, which she swallows so fast she almost chokes, and then she speaks as follows:

"Marky dance," she says.

Then she begins hopping and skipping around among the tables, holding her little short skirt up in her hands and showing a pair of white panties underneath. Pretty soon Mindy himself comes along and starts putting up a beef about making a dance hall of his joint, but a guy by the name of Sleep-out, who is watching Marky with much interest, offers to bounce a sugar bowl off of Mindy's sconce if he does not mind his own business.

So Mindy goes away, but he keeps muttering about the white panties being a most immodest spectacle, which of

course is great nonsense, as many dolls older than Marky
are known to do dances in Mindy's, especially on the late
watch, when they stop by for a snack on their way home
from the night clubs and the speaks, and I hear some of
them do not always wear white panties, either.

Personally, I like Marky's dancing very much, although
of course she is no Pavlowa, and finally she trips over her
own feet and falls on her snoot. But she gets up smiling
and climbs back on her chair and pretty soon she is sound
asleep with her head against Sorrowful.

Well, now there is much discussion about what Sorrowful ought to do with her. Some claim he ought to take her
to a police station, and others say the best thing to do is
to put an ad in the Lost and Found columns of the morning bladders, the same as people do when they find Angora
cats, and Pekes, and other animals which they do not
wish to keep, but none of these ideas seems to appeal to
Sorrowful.

Finally he says he will take her to his own home and let
her sleep there while he is deciding what is to be done
about her, so Sorrowful takes Marky in his arms and lugs
her over to a fleabag in West Forty-ninth Street where he
has a room for many years, and afterwards a bell hop tells
me Sorrowful sits up all night watching her while she is
sleeping.

Now what happens but Sorrowful takes on a great fond-
ness for the little doll, which is most surprising, as Sorrowful is never before fond of anybody or anything, and after
he has her overnight he cannot bear the idea of giving
her up.

Personally, I will just as soon have a three-year-old baby

wolf around me as a little doll such as this, but Sorrowful thinks she is the greatest thing that ever happens. He has a few inquiries made around and about to see if he can find out who she belongs to, and he is tickled silly when nothing comes of these inquiries, although nobody else figures anything will come of them anyway, as it is by no means uncommon in this town for little kids to be left sitting in chairs, or on doorsteps, to be chucked into orphan asylums by whoever finds them.

Anyway, Sorrowful says he is going to keep Marky, and his attitude causes great surprise, as keeping Marky is bound to be an expense, and it does not seem reasonable that Sorrowful will go to any expense for anything. When it commences to look as if he means what he says, many citizens naturally figure there must be an angle, and soon there are a great many rumors on the subject.

Of course one of these rumors is that the chances are Marky is Sorrowful's own offspring which is tossed back on him by the wronged mamma, but this rumor is started by a guy who does not know Sorrowful, and after he gets a gander at Sorrowful, the guy apologizes, saying he realizes that no wronged mamma will be daffy enough to permit herself to be wronged by Sorrowful. Personally, I always say that if Sorrowful wishes to keep Marky it is his own business, and most of the citizens around Mindy's agree with me.

But the trouble is Sorrowful at once cuts everybody else in on the management of Marky, and the way he talks to the citizens around Mindy's about her, you will think we are all personally responsible for her. As most of the citizens around Mindy's are bachelors, or are wishing they

are bachelors, it is most inconvenient to them to suddenly
find themselves with a family.

Some of us try to explain to Sorrowful that if he is going
to keep Marky it is up to him to handle all her play, but
right away Sorrowful starts talking so sad about all his pals
deserting him and Marky just when they need them most
that it softens all hearts, although up to this time we are
about as pally with Sorrowful as a burglar with a copper.
Finally every night in Mindy's is meeting night for a
committee to decide something or other about Marky.

The first thing we decide is that the fleabag where
Sorrowful lives is no place for Marky, so Sorrowful hires
a big apartment in one of the swellest joints on West Fifty-
ninth Street, overlooking Central Park, and spends plenty
of potatoes furnishing it, although up to this time Sorrowful never sets himself back more than about ten bobs per
week for a place to live and considers it extravagance, at
that. I hear it costs him five G's to fix up Marky's bedroom
alone, not counting the solid gold toilet set that he buys
for her.

Then he gets her an automobile and he has to hire a
guy to drive it for her, and finally when we explain to
Sorrowful that it does not look right for Marky to be
living with nobody but him and a chauffeur, Sorrowful
hires a French doll with bobbed hair and red cheeks by
the name of Mam'selle Fifi as a nurse for Marky, and this
seems to be quite a sensible move, as it insures Marky
plenty of company.

In fact, up to the time that Sorrowful hires Mam'selle
Fifi, many citizens are commencing to consider Marky
something of a nuisance and are playing the duck for her

and Sorrowful, but after Mam'selle Fifi comes along you can scarcely get in Sorrowful's joint on Fifty-ninth Street, or around his table in Mindy's when he brings Marky and Mam'selle Fifi in to eat. But one night Sorrowful goes home early and catches Sleep-out guzzling Mam'selle Fifi and Sorrowful makes Mam'selle Fifi take plenty of breeze, claiming she will set a bad example to Marky.

Then he gets an old tomato by the name of Mrs. Clancy to be Marky's nurse, and while there is no doubt Mrs. Clancy is a better nurse than Mam'selle Fifi and there is practically no danger of her setting Marky a bad example, the play at Sorrowful's joint is by no means as brisk as formerly.

You can see that from being closer than a dead heat with his potatoes, Sorrowful becomes as loose as ashes. He not only spends plenty on Marky, but he starts picking up checks in Mindy's and other spots, although up to this time picking up checks is something that is most repulsive to Sorrowful.

He gets so he will hold still for a bite, if the bite is not too savage and, what is more, a great change comes over his kisser. It is no longer so sad and mean-looking, and in fact it is almost a pleasant sight at times, especially as Sorrowful gets so he smiles now and then, and has a big hello for one and all, and everybody says the Mayor ought to give Marky a medal for bringing about such a wonderful change.

Now Sorrowful is so fond of Marky that he wants her with him all the time, and by and by there is much criticism of him for having her around his handbook joint among the Chinks and the horse players, and especially the horse

players, and for taking her around night clubs and keeping
her out at all hours, as some people do not consider this
a proper bringing-up for a little doll.

We hold a meeting in Mindy's on this proposition one
night, and we get Sorrowful to agree to keep Marky out
of his joint, but we know Marky is so fond of night clubs,
especially where there is music, that it seems a sin and a
shame to deprive her of this pleasure altogether, so we
finally compromise by letting Sorrowful take her out one
night a week to the Hot Box in Fifty-fourth Street, which
is only a few blocks from where Marky lives, and Sorrowful can get her home fairly early. In fact, after this Sorrowful seldom keeps her out any later than 2 A.M.

The reason Marky likes night clubs where there is music
is because she can do her dance there, as Marky is practically daffy on the subject of dancing, especially by herself, even though she never seems to be able to get over
winding up by falling on her snoot, which many citizens
consider a very artistic finish, at that.

The Choo-Choo Boys' band in the Hot Box always play
a special number for Marky in between the regular dances,
and she gets plenty of applause, especially from the Broadway citizens who know her, although Henri, the manager
of the Hot Box, once tells me he will just as soon Marky
does not do her dancing there, because one night several
of his best customers from Park Avenue, including two
millionaires and two old dolls, who do not understand
Marky's dancing, bust out laughing when she falls on her
snoot, and Big Nig puts the slug on the guys, and is trying
to put the slug on the old dolls, too, when he is finally
headed off.

Now one cold, snowy night, many citizens are sitting around the tables in the Hot Box, speaking of one thing and another and having a few drams, when Sorrowful drops in on his way home, for Sorrowful has now become a guy who is around and about, and in and out. He does not have Marky with him, as it is not her night out and she is home with Mrs. Clancy.

A few minutes after Sorrowful arrives, a party by the name of Milk Ear Willie from the West Side comes in, this Milk Ear Willie being a party who is once a prize fighter and who has a milk ear, which is the reason he is called Milk Ear Willie, and who is known to carry a John Roscoe in his pants pocket. Furthermore, it is well known that he knocks off several guys in his time, so he is considered rather a suspicious character.

It seems that the reason he comes into the Hot Box is to shoot Sorrowful full of little holes, because he has a dispute with Sorrowful about a parlay on the races the day before, and the chances are Sorrowful will now be very dead if it does not happen that, just as Milk Ear outs with the old equalizer and starts taking dead aim at Sorrowful from a table across the room, who pops into the joint but Marky.

She is in a long nightgown that keeps getting tangled up in her bare feet as she runs across the dance floor and jumps into Sorrowful's arms, so if Milk Ear Willie lets go at this time he is apt to put a slug in Marky, and this is by no means Willie's intention. So Willie puts his rod back in his kick, but he is greatly disgusted and stops as he is going out and makes a large complaint to Henri about allowing children in a night club.

Well, Sorrowful does not learn until afterward how

Marky saves his life, as he is too much horrified over her coming four or five blocks through the snow bare-footed to think of anything else, and everybody present is also horrified and wondering how Marky finds her way there. But Marky does not seem to have any good explanation for her conduct, except that she wakes up and discovers Mrs. Clancy asleep and gets to feeling lonesome for Sorrowful.

About this time, the Choo-Choo Boys start playing Marky's tune, and she slips out of Sorrowful's arms and runs out on the dance floor.

"Marky dance," she says.

Then she lifts her nightgown in her hands and starts hopping and skipping about the floor until Sorrowful collects her in his arms again, and wraps her in an over-coat and takes her home.

Now what happens, but the next day Marky is sick from being out in the snow bare-footed and with nothing on but her nightgown, and by night she is very sick indeed, and it seems that she has pneumonia, so Sorrowful takes her to the Clinic hospital, and hires two nurses and two croakers, and wishes to hire more, only they tell him these will do for the present.

The next day Marky is no better, and the next night she is worse, and the management of the Clinic is very much upset because it has no place to put the baskets of fruit and candy and floral horseshoes and crates of dolls and toys that keep arriving every few minutes. Furthermore, the management by no means approves of the citizens who are tiptoeing along the hall on the floor where Marky has her room, especially such as Big Nig, and Sleep-out, and Wop Joey, and the Pale Face Kid and Guinea Mike and many other prominent characters, especially as these characters keep trying to date up the nurses.

Of course I can see the management's point of view, but I wish to say that no visitor to the Clinic ever brings more joy and cheer to the patients than Sleep-out, as he goes calling in all the private rooms and wards to say a pleasant word or two to the inmates, and I never take any stock in the rumor that he is looking around to see if there is anything worth picking up. In fact, an old doll from Rockville Center, who is suffering with yellow jaundice, puts up an awful holler when Sleep-out is heaved from her room, because she says he is right in the middle of a story about a traveling salesman and she wishes to learn what happens.

There are so many prominent characters in and around the Clinic that the morning bladders finally get the idea that some well-known mob guy must be in the hospital full of slugs, and by and by the reporters come buzzing around to see what is what. Naturally they find out that all this interest is in nothing but a little doll, and while you will naturally think that such a little doll as Marky can scarcely be worth the attention of the reporters, it seems they get more heated up over her when they hear the story than if she is Jack Diamond.

In fact, the next day all the bladders have large stories about Marky, and also about Sorrowful and about how all these prominent characters of Broadway are hanging around the Clinic on her account. Moreover, one story tells about Sleep-out entertaining the other patients in the hospital, and it makes Sleep-out sound like a very large-hearted guy.

It is maybe three o'clock on the morning of the fourth day Marky is in the hospital that Sorrowful comes into Mindy's looking very sad, indeed. He orders a sturgeon sandwich on pumpernickel, and then he explains that Marky seems to be getting worse by the minute and that he does not think his doctors are doing her any good, and at this Big Nig, the crap shooter, speaks up and states as follows:

"Well," Big Nig says, "if we are only able to get Doc Beerfeldt, the great pneumonia specialist, the chances are he will cure Marky like breaking sticks. But of course," Nig says, "it is impossible to get Doc Beerfeldt unless you are somebody like John D. Rockefeller, or maybe the President."

Naturally, everybody knows that what Big Nig says is very true, for Doc Beerfeldt is the biggest croaker in this town, but no ordinary guy can get close enough to Doc Beerfeldt to hand him a ripe peach, let alone get him to go out on a case. He is an old guy, and he does not practice much any more, and then only among a few very rich and influential people. Furthermore, he has plenty of potatoes himself, so money does not interest him whatever, and anyway it is great foolishness to be talking of getting Doc Beerfeldt out at such an hour as this.

"Who do we know who knows Doc Beerfeldt?" Sorrowful says. "Who can we call up who may have influence enough with him to get him to just look at Marky? I will pay any price," he says. "Think of somebody," he says.

Well, while we are all trying to think, who comes in but Milk Ear Willie, and he comes in to toss a few slugs at Sorrowful, but before Milk Ear can start blasting Sleep-out sees him and jumps up and takes him off to a corner table, and starts whispering in Milk Ear's good ear.

As Sleep-out talks to him Milk Ear looks at Sorrowful in great surprise, and finally he begins nodding his head, and by and by he gets up and goes out of the joint in a hurry, while Sleep-out comes back to our table and says like this:

"Well," Sleep-out says, "let us stroll over to the Clinic. I just send Milk Ear Willie up to Doc Beerfeldt's house on Park Avenue to get the old Doc and bring him to the hospital. But, Sorrowful," Sleep-out says, "if he gets him, you must pay Willie the parlay you dispute with him, whatever it is. The chances are," Sleep-out says, "Willie is right. I remember once you out-argue me on a parlay when I know I am right."

Personally, I consider Sleep-out's talk about sending Milk Ear Willie after Doc Beerfeldt just so much nonsense, and so does everybody else, but we figure maybe Sleep-out is trying to raise Sorrowful's hopes, and anyway he keeps Milk Ear from tossing these slugs at Sorrowful, which everybody considers very thoughtful of Sleep-out, at least, especially as Sorrowful is under too great a strain to be dodging slugs just now.

About a dozen of us walk over to the Clinic, and most of us stand around the lobby on the ground floor, although Sorrowful goes up to Marky's floor to wait outside her door. He is waiting there from the time she is first taken to the hospital, never leaving except to go over to Mindy's once in a while to get something to eat, and occasionally they open the door a little to let him get a peek at Marky.

Well, it is maybe six o'clock when we hear a taxi stop

outside the hospital and pretty soon in comes Milk Ear Willie with another character from the West Side by the name of Fats Finstein, who is well known to one and all as a great friend of Willie's, and in between them they have a little old guy with a Vandyke beard, who does not seem to have on anything much but a silk dressing gown and who seems somewhat agitated, especially as Milk Ear Willie and Fats Finstein keep prodding him from behind.

Now it comes out that this little old guy is nobody but Doc Beerfeldt, the great pneumonia specialist, and personally I never see a madder guy, although I wish to say I never blame him much for being mad when I learn how Milk Ear Willie and Fats Finstein boff his butler over the noggin when he answers their ring, and how they walk right into old Doc Beerfeldt's bedroom and haul him out of the hay at the point of their Roscoes and make him go with them.

In fact, I consider such treatment most discourteous to a prominent croaker, and if I am Doc Beerfeldt I will start hollering copper as soon as I hit the hospital, and for all I know maybe Doc Beerfeldt has just such an idea, but as Milk Ear Willie and Fats Finstein haul him into the lobby who comes downstairs but Sorrowful. And the minute Sorrowful sees Doc Beerfeldt he rushes up to him and says like this:

"Oh, Doc," Sorrowful says, "do something for my little girl. She is dying, Doc," Sorrowful says. "Just a little bit of a girl, Doc. Her name is Marky. I am only a gambler, Doc, and I do not mean anything to you or to anybody else, but please save the little girl."

Well, old Doc Beerfeldt sticks out his Vandyke beard and looks at Sorrowful a minute, and he can see there are large tears in old Sorrowful's eyes, and for all I know maybe the doc knows it has been many and many a year since there are tears in these eyes, at that. Then the doc looks at Milk Ear Willie and Fats Finstein and the rest of us, and at the nurses and internes who are commencing to come running up from every which way. Finally he speaks as follows:

"What is this?" he says. "A child? A little child? Why," he says, "I am under the impression that these gorillas are kidnapping me to attend to some other sick or wounded gorilla. A child? This is quite different. Why do you not say so in the first place? Where is the child?" Doc Beerfeldt says, "and," he says, "somebody get me some pants."

We all follow him upstairs to the door of Marky's room and we wait outside when he goes in, and we wait there for hours, because it seems that even old Doc Beerfeldt cannot think of anything to do in this situation no matter how he tries. And along toward ten-thirty in the morning he opens the door very quietly and motions Sorrowful to come in, and then he motions all the rest of us to follow, shaking his head very sad.

There are so many of us that we fill the room around a little high narrow bed on which Marky is lying like a flower against a white wall, her yellow curls spread out over her pillow. Old Sorrowful drops on his knees beside the bed and his shoulders heave quite some as he kneels there, and I hear Sleep-out sniffing as if he has a cold in his head. Marky seems to be asleep when we go in, but while we are standing around the bed looking down at her, she opens her eyes and seems to see us and, what is more, she seems to know us, because she smiles at each guy in turn and then tries to hold out one of her little hands to Sorrowful.

Now very faint, like from far away, comes a sound of music through a half-open window in the room, from a jazz band that is rehearsing in a hall just up the street from the hospital, and Marky hears this music because she holds her head in such a way that anybody can see she is listening, and then she smiles again at us and whispers very plain, as follows:

"Marky dance."

And she tries to reach down as if to pick up her skirt as she always does when she dances, but her hands fall across her breast as soft and white and light as snowflakes, and Marky never again dances in this world.

Well, old Doc Beerfeldt and the nurses make us go outside at once, and while we are standing there in the hall outside the door, saying nothing whatever, a young guy and two dolls, one of them old, and the other not so old, come along the hall much excited. The young guy seems to know Sorrowful, who is sitting down again in his chair just outside the door, because he rushes up to Sorrowful and says to him like this:

"Where is she?" he says. "Where is my darling child? You remember me?" he says. "I leave my little girl with you one day while I go on an errand, and while I am on this errand everything goes blank, and I wind up back in my home in Indianapolis with my mother and sister here, and recall nothing about where I leave my child, or anything else."

"The poor boy has amnesia," the old doll says. "The

stories that he deliberately abandons his wife in Paris and his child in New York are untrue."

"Yes," the doll who is not old puts in. "If we do not see the stories in the newspapers about how you have the child in this hospital we may never learn where she is. But everything is all right now. Of course we never approve of Harold's marriage to a person of the stage, and we only recently learn of her death in Paris soon after their separation there and are very sorry. But everything is all right now. We will take full charge of the child."

Now while all this gab is going on, Sorrowful never glances at them. He is just sitting there looking at Marky's door. And now as he is looking at the door a very strange thing seems to happen to his kisser, for all of a sudden it becomes the sad, mean-looking kisser that it is in the days before he ever sees Marky, and furthermore it is never again anything else.

"We will be rich," the young guy says. "We just learn that my darling child will be sole heiress to her maternal grandpapa's fortune, and the old guy is only a hop ahead of the undertaker right now. I suppose," he says, "I owe you something?"

And then Sorrowful gets up off his chair, and looks at the young guy and at the two dolls, and speaks as follows:

"Yes," he says, "you owe me a two-dollar marker for the bet you blow on Cold Cuts, and," he says, "I will trouble you to send it to me at once, so I can wipe you off my books."

Now he walks down the hall and out of the hospital, never looking back again, and there is a very great silence behind him that is broken only by the sniffing of Sleep-out, and by some first-class sobbing from some of the rest of us, and I remember now that the guy who is doing the best job of sobbing of all is nobody but Milk Ear Willie.

DANCING DAN'S CHRISTMAS

Now one time it comes on Christmas, and in fact it is the evening before Christmas, and I am in Good Time Charley Bernstein's little speakeasy in West Forty-seventh Street, wishing Charley a Merry Christmas and having a few hot Tom and Jerrys with him.

This hot Tom and Jerry in an old-time drink that is once used by one and all in this country to celebrate Christmas with, and in fact it is once so popular that many people think Christmas is invented only to furnish an excuse for hot Tom and Jerry, although of course this is by no means true.

But anybody will tell you that there is nothing that brings out the true holiday spirit like hot Tom and Jerry, and I hear that since Tom and Jerry goes out of style in the United States, the holiday spirit is never quite the same.

The reason hot Tom and Jerry goes out of style is because it is necessary to use rum and one thing and another in making Tom and Jerry, and naturally when rum becomes illegal in this country Tom and Jerry is also against the law, because rum is something that is very hard to get around town these days.

For a while some people try making hot Tom and Jerry without putting rum in it, but somehow it never has the same old holiday spirit, so nearly everybody finally gives up in disgust, and this is not surprising, as making Tom and Jerry is by no means child's play. In fact, it takes quite an expert to make good Tom and Jerry, and in the days when it is not illegal a good hot Tom and Jerry maker commands good wages and many friends.

Now of course Good Time Charley and I are not using rum in the Tom and Jerry we are making, as we do not wish to do anything illegal. What we are using is rye whiskey that Good Time Charley gets on a doctor's prescription from a drug store, as we are personally drinking this hot Tom and Jerry and naturally we are not foolish enough to use any of Good Time Charley's own rye in it.

The prescription for the rye whskey comes from old Doc Moggs, who prescribes it for Good Time Charley's rheumatism in case Charley happens to get any rheumatism, as Doc Moggs says there is nothing better for rheumatism than rye whiskey, especially if it is made up in a hot Tom and Jerry. In fact, old Doc Moggs comes around and has a few seidels of hot Tom and Jerry with us for his own rheumatism.

He comes around during the afternoon, for Good Time Charley and I start making this Tom and Jerry early in the day, so as to be sure to have enough to last us over Christmas, and it is now along toward six o'clock, and our holiday spirit is practically one hundred per cent.

Well, as Good Time Charley and I are expressing our holiday sentiments to each other over our hot Tom and Jerry, and I am trying to think up the poem about the night before Christmas and all through the house, which I know will interest Charley no little, all of a sudden there

is a big knock at the front door, and when Charley opens
the door who comes in carrying a large package under one
arm but a guy by the name of Dancing Dan.

This Dancing Dan is a good-looking young guy, who
always seems well-dressed, and he is called by the name of
Dancing Dan because he is a great hand for dancing around
and about with dolls in night clubs, and other spots where
there is any dancing. In fact, Dan never seems to be doing
anything else, although I hear rumors that when he is
not dancing he is carrying on in a most illegal manner at
one thing and another. But of course you can always hear
rumors in this town about anybody, and personally I am
rather fond of Dancing Dan as he always seems to be
getting a great belt out of life.

Anybody in town will tell you that Dancing Dan is a
guy with no Barnaby whatever in him, and in fact he has
about as much gizzard as anybody around, although I
wish to say I always question his judgment in dancing so
much with Miss Muriel O'Neill, who works in the Half
Moon night club. And the reason I question his judgment
in this respect is because everybody knows that Miss Muriel
O'Neill is a doll who is very well thought of by Heine
Schmitz, and Heine Schmitz is not such a guy as will take
kindly to anybody dancing more than once and a half with
a doll that he thinks well of.

This Heine Schmitz is a very influential citizen of
Harlem, where he has large interests in beer, and other
business enterprises, and it is by no means violating any
confidence to tell you that Heine Schmitz will just as
soon blow your brains out as look at you. In fact, I hear
sooner. Anyway, he is not a guy to monkey with and

many citizens take the trouble to advise Dancing Dan
that he is not only away out of line in dancing with Miss
Muriel O'Neill, but that he is knocking his own price
down to where he is no price at all.

But Dancing Dan only laughs ha-ha, and goes on dancing
with Miss Muriel O'Neill any time he gets a chance, and
Good Time Charley says he does not blame him, at that,
as Miss Muriel O'Neill is so beautiful that he will be dancing with her himself no matter what, if he is five years
younger and can get a Roscoe out as fast as in the days
when he runs with Paddy the Link and other fast guys.

Well, anyway, as Dancing Dan comes in he weighs up
the joint in one quick peek, and then he tosses the package
he is carrying into a corner where it goes plunk, as if there
is something very heavy in it, and then he steps up to the
bar alongside of Charley and me and wishes to know
what we are drinking.

Naturally we start boosting hot Tom and Jerry to Dancing Dan, and he says he will take a crack at it with us,
and after one crack, Dancing Dan says he will have another crack, and Merry Christmas to us with it, and the
first thing anybody knows it is a couple of hours later and
we are still having cracks at the hot Tom and Jerry with
Dancing Dan, and Dan says he never drinks anything so
soothing in his life. In fact, Dancing Dan says he will
recommend Tom and Jerry to everybody he knows, only
he does not know anybody good enough for Tom and
Jerry, except maybe Miss Muriel O'Neill, and she does
not drink anything with drugstore rye in it.

Well, several times while we are drinking this Tom and
Jerry, customers come to the door of Good Time Charley's

little speakeasy and knock, but by now Charley is commencing to be afraid they will wish Tom and Jerry, too, and he does not feel we will have enough for ourselves, so he hangs out a sign which says "Closed on Account of Christmas," and the only one he will let in is a guy by the name of Ooky, who is nothing but an old rum-dum, and who is going around all week dressed like Santa Claus and carrying a sign advertising Moe Lewinsky's clothing joint around in Sixth Avenue.

This Ooky is still wearing his Santa Claus outfit when Charley lets him in, and the reason Charley permits such a character as Ooky in his joint is because Ooky does the porter work for Charley when he is not Santa Claus for Moe Lewinsky, such as sweeping out, and washing the glasses, and one thing and another.

Well, it is about nine-thirty when Ooky comes in, and his puppies are aching, and he is all petered out generally from walking up and down and here and there with his sign, for any time a guy is Santa Claus for Moe Lewinsky he must earn his dough. In fact, Ooky is so fatigued, and his puppies hurt him so much that Dancing Dan and Good Time Charley and I all feel very sorry for him, and invite him to have a few mugs of hot Tom and Jerry with us, and wish him plenty of Merry Christmas.

But old Ooky is not accustomed to Tom and Jerry and after about the fifth mug he folds up in a chair, and goes right to sleep on us. He is wearing a pretty good Santa Claus make-up, what with a nice red suit trimmed with white cotton, and a wig, and false nose, and long white whiskers, and a big sack stuffed with excelsior on his back and if I do not know Santa Claus is not apt to be

such a guy as will snore loud enough to rattle the windows,
I will think Ooky is Santa Claus sure enough.

Well, we forget Ooky and let him sleep, and go on with
our hot Tom and Jerry, and in the meantime we try to
think up a few songs appropriate to Christmas, and Dancing Dan finally renders My Dad's Dinner Pail in a nice
baritone and very loud, while I do first rate with Will You
Love Me in December As You Do in May? But personally
I always think Good Time Charley Bernstein is a little out
of line trying to sing a hymn in Jewish on such an occasion, and it causes words between us.

While we are singing many customers come to the door
and knock, and then they read Charley's sign, and this
seems to cause some unrest among them, and some of them
stand outside saying it is a great outrage, until Charley
sticks his noggin out the door and threatens to bust somebody's beezer if they do not go on about their business and
stop disturbing peaceful citizens.

Naturally the customers go away, as they do not wish
their beezers busted, and Dancing Dan and Charley and I
continue drinking our hot Tom and Jerry, and with each
Tom and Jerry we are wishing one another a very Merry
Christmas, and sometimes a very Happy New Year, although of course this does not go for Good Time Charley
as yet, because Charley has his New Year separate from
Dancing Dan and me.

By and by we take to waking Ooky up in his Santa
Claus outfit and offering him more hot Tom and Jerry,
and wishing him Merry Christmas, but Ooky only gets
sore and calls us names, so we can see he does not have
the right holiday spirit in him, and let him alone until

along about midnight when Dancing Dan wishes to see how he looks as Santa Claus.

So Good Time Charley and I help Dancing Dan pull off Ooky's outfit and put it on Dan, and this is easy as Ooky only has this Santa Claus outfit on over his ordinary clothes, and he does not even wake up when we are undressing him of the Santa Claus uniform.

Well, I wish to say I see many a Santa Claus in my time, but I never see a better looking Santa Claus than Dancing Dan, especially after he gets the wig and white whiskers fixed just right, and we put a sofa pillow that Good Time Charley happens to have around the joint for the cat to sleep on down his pants to give Dancing Dan a nice fat stomach such as Santa Claus is bound to have.

In fact, after Dancing Dan looks at himself in a mirror awhile he is greatly pleased with his appearance, while Good Time Charley is practically hysterical, although personally I am commencing to resent Charley's interest in Santa Claus, and Christmas generally, as he by no means has any claim on these matters. But then I remember Charley furnishes the hot Tom and Jerry, so I am more tolerant toward him.

"Well," Charley finally says, "it is a great pity we do not know where there are some stockings hung up somewhere, because then," he says, "you can go around and stuff things in these stockings, as I always hear this is the main idea of a Santa Claus. But," Charley says, "I do not suppose anybody in this section has any stockings hung up, or if they have," he says, "the chances are they are so full of holes they will not hold anything. Anyway," Charley says, "even if there are any stockings hung up we do not have anything to stuff in them, although personally," he says, "I will gladly donate a few pints of Scotch."

Well, I am pointing out that we have no reindeer and that a Santa Claus is bound to look like a terrible sap if he goes around without any reindeer, but Charley's remarks seem to give Dancing Dan an idea, for all of a sudden he speaks as follows:

"Why," Dancing Dan says, "I know where a stocking is hung up. It is hung up at Miss Muriel O'Neill's flat over here in West Forty-ninth Street. This stocking is hung up by nobody but a party by the name of Gammer O'Neill, who is Miss Muriel O'Neill's grandmamma," Dancing Dan says. "Gammer O'Neill is going on ninety-odd," he says, "and Miss Muriel O'Neill tells me she cannot hold out much longer, what with one thing and another, including being a little childish in spots.

"Now," Dancing Dan says, "I remember Miss Muriel O'Neill is telling me just the other night how Gammer O'Neill hangs up her stocking on Christmas Eve all her life, and," he says, "I judge from what Miss Muriel O'Neill says that the old doll always believes Santa Claus will come along some Christmas and fill the stocking full of beautiful gifts. But," Dancing Dan says, "Miss Muriel O'Neill tells me Santa Claus never does this, although Miss Muriel O'Neill personally always takes a few gifts home and pops them into the stocking to make Gammer O'Neill feel better.

"But, of course," Dancing Dan says, "these gifts are nothing much because Miss Muriel O'Neill is very poor, and proud, and also good, and will not take a dime off of anybody and I can lick the guy who says she will, although," Dancing Dan says, "between me, and Heine Schmitz, and a raft of other guys I can mention, Miss Muriel O'Neill can take plenty."

Well, I know that what Dancing Dan states about Miss Muriel O'Neill is quite true, and in fact it is a matter that is often discussed on Broadway, because Miss Muriel O'Neill cannot get more than twenty bobs per week working in the Half Moon, and it is well known to one and all that this is no kind of dough for a doll as beautiful as Miss Muriel O'Neill.

"Now," Dancing Dan goes on, "it seems that while Gammer O'Neill is very happy to get whatever she finds in her stocking on Christmas morning, she does not understand why Santa Claus is not more liberal, and," he says, "Miss Muriel O'Neill is saying to me that she only wishes she can give Gammer O'Neill one real big Christmas before the old doll puts her checks back in the rack.

"So," Dancing Dan states, "here is a job for us. Miss Muriel O'Neill and her grandmamma live all alone in this flat over in West Forty-ninth Street, and," he says, "at such an hour as this Miss Muriel O'Neill is bound to be working, and the chances are Gammer O'Neill is sound asleep, and we will just hop over there and Santa Claus will fill up her stocking with beautiful gifts."

Well, I say, I do not see where we are going to get any beautiful gifts at this time of night, what with all the stores being closed, unless we dash into an all-night drug store and buy a few bottles of perfume and a bum toilet set as guys always do when they forget about their ever-loving wives until after store hours on Christmas Eve, but Danc-

ing Dan says never mind about this, but let us have a few
more Tom and Jerrys first.

So we have a few more Tom and Jerrys, and then Dancing Dan picks up the package he heaves into the corner,
and dumps most of the excelsior out of Ooky's Santa Claus
sack, and puts the bundle in, and Good Time Charley
turns out all the lights but one, and leaves a bottle of Scotch
on the table in front of Ooky for a Christmas gift, and
away we go.

Personally, I regret very much leaving the hot Tom and
Jerry, but then I am also very enthusiastic about going
along to help Dancing Dan play Santa Claus, while Good
Time Charley is practically overjoyed, as it is the first time
in his life Charley is ever mixed up in so much holiday
spirit. In fact, nothing will do Charley but that we stop
in a couple of spots and have a few drinks to Santa Claus'
health, and these visits are a big success, although everybody is much surprised to see Charley and me with Santa
Claus, especially Charley, although nobody recognizes
Dancing Dan.

But of course there are no hot Tom and Jerrys in these
spots we visit, and we have to drink whatever is on hand,
and personally I will always believe that the noggin I have
on me afterwards comes of mixing the drinks we get in
these spots with my Tom and Jerry.

As we go up Broadway, headed for Forty-ninth Street,
Charley and I see many citizens we know and give them
a large hello, and wish them Merry Christmas, and some
of these citizens shake hands with Santa Claus, not knowing he is nobody but Dancing Dan, although later I under-

stand there is some gossip among these citizens because they claim a Santa Claus with such a breath on him as our Santa Claus has is a little out of line.

And once we are somewhat embarrassed when a lot of little kids going home with their parents from a late Christmas party somewhere gather about Santa Claus with shouts of childish glee, and some of them wish to climb up Santa Claus' legs. Naturally, Santa Claus gets a little peevish, and calls them a few names, and one of the parents comes up and wishes to know what is the idea of Santa Claus using such language, and Santa Claus takes a punch at the parent, all of which is no doubt most astonishing to the little kids who have an idea of Santa Claus as a very kindly old guy. But of course they do not know about Dancing Dan mixing the liquor we get in the spots we visit with his Tom and Jerry, or they will understand how even Santa Claus can lose his temper.

Well, finally we arrive in front of the place where Dancing Dan says Miss Muriel O'Neill and her grandmamma live, and it is nothing but a tenement house not far back of Madison Square Garden, and furthermore it is a walk-up, and at this time there are no lights burning in the joint except a gas jet in the main hall, and by the light of this jet we look at the names on the letter boxes, such as you always find in the hall of these joints, and we see that Miss Muriel O'Neill and her grandmamma live on the fifth floor.

This is the top floor, and personally I do not like the idea of walking up five flights of stairs, and I am willing to let Dancing Dan and Good Time Charley go, but Dancing Dan insists we must all go, and finally I agree because

Charley is commencing to argue that the right way for us
to do is to get on the roof and let Santa Claus go down a
·chimney, and is making so much noise I am afraid he will
wake somebody up.

So up the stairs we climb and finally we come to a door
on the top floor that has a little card in a slot that says
O'Neill, so we know we reach our destination. Dancing
Dan first tries the knob, and right away the door opens,
and we are in a little two- or three-room flat, with not
much furniture in it, and what furniture there is is very
poor. One single gas jet is burning near a bed in a room
just off the one the door opens into, and by this light we
see a very old doll is sleeping on the bed, so we judge this
is nobody but Gammer O'Neill.

On her face is a large smile, as if she is dreaming of
something very pleasant. On a chair at the head of the
bed is hung a long black stocking, and it seems to be such
a stocking as is often patched and mended, so I can see
that what Miss Muriel O'Neill tells Dancing Dan about
her grandmamma hanging up her stocking is really true,
although up to this time I have my doubts.

Well, I am willing to pack in after one gander at the
old doll, especially as Good Time Charley is commencing
to prowl around the flat to see if there is a chimney where
Santa Claus can come down, and is knocking things over,
but Dancing Dan stands looking down at Gammer O'Neill
for a long time.

Finally he unslings the sack on his back, and takes out
his package, and unties this package, and all of a sudden
out pops a raft of big diamond bracelets, and diamond
rings, and diamond brooches, and diamond necklaces, and

I do not know what else in the way of diamonds, and Dancing Dan and I begin stuffing these diamonds into the stocking and Good Time Charley pitches in and helps us.

There are enough diamonds to fill the stocking to the muzzle, and it is no small stocking, at that, and I judge that Gammer O'Neill has a pretty fair set of bunting sticks when she is young. In fact, there are so many diamonds that we have enough left over to make a nice little pile on the chair after we fill the stocking plumb up, leaving a nice diamond-studded vanity case sticking out the top where we figure it will hit Gammer O'Neill's eye when she wakes up.

And it is not until I get out in the fresh air again that all of a sudden I remember seeing large headlines in the afternoon papers about a five-hundred-G's stick-up in the afternoon of one of the biggest diamond merchants in Maiden Lane while he is sitting in his office, and I also recall once hearing rumors that Dancing Dan is one of the best lone-hand git-'em-up guys in the world.

Naturally, I commence to wonder if I am in the proper company when I am with Dancing Dan, even if he is Santa Claus. So I leave him on the next corner arguing with Good Time Charley about whether they ought to go and find some more presents somewhere, and look for other stockings to stuff, and I hasten on home, and go to bed.

The next day I find I have such a noggin that I do not care to stir around, and in fact I do not stir around much for a couple of weeks.

Then one night I drop around to Good Time Charley's little speakeasy, and ask Charley what is doing.

"Well," Charley says, "many things are doing, and personally," he says, "I'm greatly surprised I do not see you at Gammer O'Neill's wake. You know Gammer O'Neill leaves this wicked old world a couple of days after Christmas," Good Time Charley says, "and," he says, "Miss Muriel O'Neill states that Doc Moggs claims it is at least a day after she is entitled to go, but she is sustained," Charley says, "by great happiness in finding her stocking filled with beautiful gifts on Christmas morning.

"According to Miss Muriel O'Neill," Charley says, "Gammer O'Neill dies practically convinced that there is a Santa Claus, although of course," he says, "Miss Muriel O'Neill does not tell her the real owner of the gifts, an all-right guy by the name of Shapiro leaves the gifts with her after Miss Muriel O'Neill notifies him of the finding of same.

"It seems," Charley says, "this Shapiro is a tender-hearted guy, who is willing to help keep Gammer O'Neill with us a little longer when Doc Moggs says leaving the gifts with her will do it.

"So," Charley says, "everything is quite all right, as the coppers cannot figure anything except that maybe the rascal who takes the gifts from Shapiro gets conscience stricken, and leaves them the first place he can, and Miss Muriel O'Neill receives a ten-G's reward for finding the gifts and returning them. And," Charley says, "I hear Dancing Dan is in San Francisco and is figuring on reforming and becoming a dancing teacher, so he can marry

Miss Muriel O'Neill, and of course," he says, "we all hope and trust she never learns any details of Dancing Dan's career."

Well, it is Christmas Eve a year later that I run into a guy by the name of Shotgun Sam, who is mobbed up with Heine Schmitz in Harlem, and who is a very, very obnoxious character indeed.

"Well, well, well," Shotgun says, "the last time I see you is another Christmas Eve like this, and you are coming out of Good Time Charley's joint, and," he says, "you certainly have your pots on."

"Well, Shotgun," I say, "I am sorry you get such a wrong impression of me, but the truth is," I say, "on the occasion you speak of, I am suffering from a dizzy feeling in my head."

"It is all right with me," Shotgun says. "I have a tip this guy Dancing Dan is in Good Time Charley's the night I see you, and Mockie Morgan, and Gunner Jack and me are casing the joint, because," he says, "Heine Schmitz is all sored up at Dan over some doll, although of course," Shotgun says, "it is all right now, as Heine has another doll.

"Anyway," he says, "we never get to see Dancing Dan. We watch the joint from six-thirty in the evening until daylight Christmas morning, and nobody goes in all night but old Ooky the Santa Claus guy in his Santa Claus make-up, and," Shotgun says, "nobody comes out except you and Good Time Charley and Ooky.

"Well," Shotgun says, "it is a great break for Dancing Dan he never goes in or comes out of Good Time Charley's, at that, because," he says, "we are waiting for him on the second-floor front of the building across the way with some nice little sawed-offs, and are under orders from Heine not to miss."

"Well, Shotgun," I say, "Merry Christmas."

"Well, all right," Shotgun says, "Merry Christmas."

PRINCESS O'HARA

Now of course Princess O'Hara is by no means a regular princess, and in fact she is nothing but a little red-headed doll, with plenty of freckles, from over in Tenth Avenue, and her right name is Maggie, and the only reason she is called Princess O'Hara is as follows:

She is the daughter of King O'Hara, who is hacking along Broadway with one of these old-time victorias for a matter of maybe twenty-five years, and every time King O'Hara gets his pots on, which is practically every night, rain or shine, he is always bragging that he has the royal blood of Ireland in his veins, so somebody starts calling him King, and this is his monicker as long as I can remember, although probably what King O'Hara really has in his veins is about ninety-eight per cent alcohol.

Well, anyway, one night about seven or eight years back, King O'Hara shows up on his stand in front of Mindy's restaurant on Broadway with a spindly-legged little doll about ten years of age on the seat beside him, and he says that this little doll is nobody but his daughter, and he is taking care of her because his old lady is not feeling so good, and right away Last Card Louie, the gambler, reaches up and dukes the little doll and says to her like this:

"If you are the daughter of the King, you must be the princess," Last Card Louie says. "How are you, Princess?"

So from this time on, she is Princess O'Hara, and afterwards for several years she often rides around in the early evening with the King, and sometimes when the King has his pots on more than somewhat, she personally drives Goldberg, which is the King's horse, although Goldberg does not really need much driving as he knows his way along Broadway better than anybody. In fact, this Goldberg is a most sagacious old pelter, indeed, and he is called Goldberg by the King in honor of a Jewish friend by the name of Goldberg, who keeps a delicatessen store in Tenth Avenue.

At this time, Princess O'Hara is as homely as a mud fence, and maybe homelier, what with the freckles, and the skinny gambs, and a few buck teeth, and she does not weigh more than sixty pounds, sopping wet, and her red hair is down her back in pigtails, and she giggles if anybody speaks to her, so finally nobody speaks to her much, but old King O'Hara seems to think well of her, at that.

Then by and by she does not seem to be around with the King any more, and when somebody happens to ask about her, the King says his old lady claims the Princess is getting too grown-up to be shagging around Broadway, and that she is now going to public school. So after not seeing her for some years, everybody forgets that King O'Hara has a daughter, and in fact nobody cares a cuss.

Now King O'Hara is a little shriveled-up old guy with

a very red beezer, and he is a most familiar spectacle to one and all on Broadway as he drives about with a stove-pipe hat tipped so far over to one side of his noggin that it looks as if it is always about to fall off, and in fact the King himself is always tipped so far over to one side that it seems to be a sure thing that he is going to fall off.

The way the King keeps himself on the seat of his victoria is really most surprising, and one time Last Card Louie wins a nice bet off a gambler from St. Louis by the name of Olive Street Oscar, who takes 8 to 5 off of Louie that the King cannot drive them through Central Park without doing a Brodie off the seat. But of course Louie is betting with the best of it, which is the way he always dearly loves to bet, because he often rides through Central Park with King O'Hara, and he knows the King never falls off, no matter how far over he tips.

Personally, I never ride with the King very much, as his victoria is so old I am always afraid the bottom will fall out from under me, and that I will run myself to death trying to keep up, because the King is generally so busy singing Irish-come-all-yeez up on his seat that he is not apt to pay much attention to what his passengers are doing.

There are quite a number of these old victorias left in this town, a victoria being a low-neck, four-wheeled carriage with seats for four or five people, and they are very popular in the summer-time with guys and dolls who wish to ride around and about in Central Park taking the air, and especially with guys and dolls who may wish to do a little offhand guzzling while taking the air.

Personally, I consider a taxicab much more convenient and less expensive than an old-fashioned victoria if you

wish to get to some place, but of course guys and dolls
engaged in a little offhand guzzling never wish to get any
place in particular, or at least not soon. So these victorias,
which generally stand around the entrances to the Park,
do a fair business in the summertime, because it seems
that no matter what conditions are, there are always guys
and dolls who wish to do a little offhand guzzling.

But King O'Hara stands in front of Mindy's because he
has many regular customers among the citizens of Broadway, who do not go in for guzzling so very much, unless
a case of guzzling comes up, but who love to ride around
in the Park on hot nights just to cool themselves out, although at the time I am now speaking of, things are so
tough with one and all along Broadway that King O'Hara
has to depend more on strangers for his trade.

Well, what happens one night, but King O'Hara is seen
approaching Mindy's, tipping so far over to one side of
his seat that Olive Street Oscar, looking to catch even on
the bet he loses before, is offering to take 6 to 5 off of Last
Card Louie that this time the King goes plumb off, and
Louie is about to give it to him, when the old King tumbles
smack-dab into the street, as dead as last Tuesday, which
shows you how lucky Last Card Louie is, because nobody
ever figures such a thing to happen to the King, and even
Goldberg, the horse, stops and stands looking at him very
much surprised, with one hind hoof in the King's stove-
pipe hat. The doctors state that King O'Hara's heart just
naturally hauls off and quits working on him, and afterwards Regret, the horse player, says the chances are the
King probably suddenly remembers refusing a drink somewhere.

A few nights later, many citzens are out in front of Mindy's, and Big Nig, the crap shooter, is saying that things do not look the same around there since King O'Hara puts his checks back in the rack, when all of a sudden up comes a victoria that anybody can see is the King's old rattletrap, especially as it is being pulled by Goldberg.

And who is on the driver's seat, with King O'Hara's bunged-up old stovepipe hat sitting jack-deuce on her noggin but a red-headed doll of maybe eighteen or nineteen with freckles all over her pan, and while it is years since I see her, I can tell at once that she is nobody but Princess O'Hara, even though it seems she changes quite some.

In fact, she is now about as pretty a little doll as any-body will wish to see, even with the freckles, because the buck teeth seem to have disappeared, and the gambs are now filled out very nicely, and so has the rest of her. Furthermore, she has a couple of blue eyes that are most delightful to behold, and a smile like six bits, and all in all, she is a pleasing scene.

Well, naturally, her appearance in this manner causes some comment, and in fact some citizens are disposed to criticize her as being unladylike, until Big Nig, the crap shooter, goes around among them very quietly stating that he will knock their ears down if he hears any more cracks from them, because it seems that Big Nig learns that when old King O'Hara dies, all he leaves in this world besides his widow and six kids is Goldberg, the horse, and the victoria, and Princess O'Hara is the eldest of these kids, and the only one old enough to work, and she can think of nothing better to do than to take up her papa's business where he leaves off.

After one peek at Princess O'Hara, Regret, the horse
player, climbs right into the victoria, and tells her to ride
him around the Park a couple of times, although it is well
known to one and all that it costs two bobs per hour to ride
in anybody's victoria, and the only dough Regret has in a
month is a pound note that he just borrows off of Last Card
Louie for eating money. But from this time on, the chances
are Regret will be Princess O'Hara's best customer if he
can borrow any more pound notes, but the competition gets
too keen for him, especially from Last Card Louie, who
is by this time quite a prominent character along Broadway,
and in the money, although personally I always say you
can have him, as Last Card Louie is such a guy as will
stoop to very sharp practice, and in fact he often does not
wait to stoop.

He is called Last Card Louie because in his youth he is a
great hand for riding the tubs back and forth between here
and Europe and playing stud poker with other passengers,
and the way he always gets much strength from the last
card is considered quite abnormal, especially if Last Card
Louie is dealing. But of course Last Card Louie no longer
rides the tubs as this occupation is now very old-fashioned,
and anyway Louie has more profitable interests that require
his attention, such as a crap game, and one thing and another.

There is no doubt but what Last Card Louie takes quite
a fancy to Princess O'Hara, but naturally he cannot spend
all his time riding around in a victoria, so other citizens get
a chance to patronize her now and then, and in fact I once
take a ride with Princess O'Hara myself, and it is a

very pleasant experience, indeed, as she likes to sing while she is driving, just as old King O'Hara does in his time.

But what Princess O'Hara sings is not Irish-come-all-yeez but Kathleen Mavourneen, and My Wild Irish Rose, and Asthore, and other such ditties, and she has a loud contralto voice, and when she lets it out while driving through Central Park in the early hours of the morning, the birds in the trees wake up and go tweet-tweet, and the coppers on duty for blocks around stand still with smiles on their kissers, and the citizens who live in the apartment houses along Central Park West and Central Park South come to their windows to listen.

Then one night in October, Princess O'Hara does not show up in front of Mindy's, and there is much speculation among one and all about this absence, and some alarm, when Big Nig, the crap shooter, comes around and says that what happens is that old Goldberg, the horse, is down with colic, or some such, so there is Princess O'Hara without a horse.

Well, this news is received with great sadness by one and all, and there is some talk of taking up a collection to buy Princess O'Hara another horse, but nobody goes very far with this idea because things are so tough with everybody, and while Big Nig mentions that maybe Last Card Louie will be glad to do something large in this matter, nobody cares for this idea, either, as many citizens are displeased with the way Last Card Louie is pitching to Princess O'Hara, because it is well known that Last Card Louie is nothing but a wolf when it comes to young dolls, and

anyway about now Regret, the horse player, speaks up as
follows:

"Why," Regret says, "it is great foolishness to talk of
wasting money buying a horse, even if we have any money
to waste, when the barns up at Empire City are packed at
this time with crocodiles of all kinds. Let us send a committee up to the track," Regret says, "and borrow a nice
horse for Princess O'Hara to use until Goldberg is back
on his feet again."

"But," I say to Regret, "suppose nobody wishes to lend us
a horse?"

"Why," Regret says, "I do not mean to ask anybody to
lend us a horse. I mean let us borrow one without asking
anybody. Most of these horse owners are so very touchy that
if we go around asking them to lend us a horse to pull a
hack, they may figure we are insulting their horses, so let
us just get the horse and say nothing whatever."

Well, I state that this sounds to me like stealing, and
stealing is something that is by no means upright and
honest, and Regret has to admit that it really is similar to
stealing, but he says what of it, and as I do not know what
of it, I discontinue the argument. Furthermore, Regret says
it is clearly understood that we will return any horse we
borrow when Goldberg is hale and hearty again, so I can
see that after all there is nothing felonious in the idea, or
anyway, not much.

But after much discussion, it comes out that nobody along
Broadway seems to know anything about stealing a horse.
There are citizens who know all about stealing diamond
necklaces, or hot stoves, but when it comes to horses, everybody confesses themselves at a loss. It is really amazing

the amount of ignorance there is on Broadway about stealing horses.

Then finally Regret has a bright idea. It seems that a
rodeo is going on at Madison Square Garden at this time,
a rodeo being a sort of wild west show with bucking
bronchos, and cowboys, and all this and that, and Regret
seems to remember reading when he is a young squirt that
stealing horses is a very popular pastime out in the wild
west.

So one evening Regret goes around to the Garden and
gets to talking to a cowboy in leather pants with hair on
them, and he asks this cowboy, whose name seems to be
Laramie Pink, if there are any expert horse stealers con-
nected with the rodeo. Moreover, Regret explains to Laramie Pink just why he wants a good horse stealer, and Pink
becomes greatly interested and wishes to know if the loan
of a nice bucking broncho, or a first-class cow pony will
be of any assistance, and when Regret says he is afraid
not, Laramie Pink says like this:

"Well," he says, "of course horse stealing is considered a
most antique custom out where I come from, and in fact
it is no longer practiced in the best circles, but," he says,
"come to think of it, there is a guy with this outfit by the
name of Frying Pan Joe, who is too old to do anything
now except mind the cattle, but who is said to be an ex-
cellent horse stealer out in Colorado in his day. Maybe Frying Pan Joe will be interested in your proposition," Laramie
Pink says.

So he hunts up Frying Pan Joe, and Frying Pan Joe
turns out to be a little old pappy guy with a chin whisker,
and a sad expression, and a wide-brimmed cowboy hat, and

when they explain to him that they wish him to steal a horse, Frying Pan Joe seems greatly touched, and his eyes fill up with tears, and he speaks as follows:

"Why," Frying Pan Joe says, "your idea brings back many memories to me. It is a matter of over twenty-five years since I steal a horse, and the last time I do this it gets me three years in the calabozo. Why," he says, "this is really a most unexpected order, and it finds me all out of practice, and with no opportunity to get myself in shape. But," he says, "I will put forth my best efforts on this job for ten dollars, as long as I do not personally have to locate the horse I am to steal. I am not acquainted with the ranges hereabouts, and will not know where to go to find a horse."

So Regret, the horse player, and Big Nig, the crap shooter, and Frying Pan Joe go up to Empire this very same night, and it turns out that stealing a horse is so simple that Regret is sorry he does not make the tenner himself, for all Frying Pan Joe does is to go to the barns where the horses live at Empire, and walk along until he comes to a line of stalls that do not seem to have any watchers around in the shape of stable hands at the moment. Then Frying Pan Joe just steps into a stall and comes out leading a horse, and if anybody sees him, they are bound to figure he has a right to do this, because of course not even Sherlock Holmes is apt to think of anybody stealing a horse around this town.

Well, when Regret gets a good peek at the horse, he sees right away it is not just a horse that Frying Pan Joe steals. It is Gallant Godfrey, one of the greatest handicap horses in this country, and the winner of some of the biggest stakes

of the year, and Gallant Godfrey is worth twenty-five G's if
he is worth a dime, and when Regret speaks of this, Frying
Pan Joe says it is undoubtedly the most valuable single
piece of horseflesh he ever steals, although he claims that
once when he is stealing horses along the Animas River in
Colorado, he steals two hundred horses in one batch that
will probably total up more.

They take Gallant Godfrey over to Eleventh Avenue,
where Princess O'Hara keeps Goldberg in a little stable
that is nothing but a shack, and they leave Gallant Godfrey
there alongside old Goldberg, who is groaning and carrying on in a most distressing manner, and then Regret and
Big Nig shake hands with Frying Pan Joe and wish him
goodby.

So there is Princess O'Hara with Gallant Godfrey hitched
up to her victoria the next night, and the chances are it is
a good thing for her that Gallant Godfrey is a nice tame old
dromedary, and does not mind pulling a victoria at all, and
in fact he seems to enjoy it, although he likes to go along
at a gallop instead of a slow trot, such as the old skates
that pull these victorias usually employ.

And while Princess O'Hara understands that this is a
borrowed horse, and is to be returned when Goldberg is
well, nobody tells her just what kind of a horse it is, and
when she gets Goldberg's harness on Gallant Godfrey, his
appearance changes so that not even the official starter is apt
to recognize him if they come face to face.

Well, I hear afterwards that there is great consternation
around Empire when it comes out that Gallant Godfrey is
missing, but they keep it quiet as they figure he just wan-
ders away, and as he is engaged in certain large stakes later

on, they do not wish it made public that he is absent from
his stall. So they have guys looking for him high and
low, but of course nobody thinks to look for a high-class
race horse pulling a victoria.

When Princess O'Hara drives the new horse up in front
of Mindy's, many citizens are anxious to take the first ride
with her, but before anybody has time to think, who steps
up but Ambrose Hammer, the newspaper scribe who has
a foreign-looking young guy with him, and Ambrose states
as follows:

"Get in, Georges," Ambrose says. "We will take a spin
through the Park and wind up at the Casino."

So away they go, and from this moment begins one of
the greatest romances ever heard of on Broadway, for it
seems that the foreign-looking young guy that Ambrose
Hammer calls Georges takes a wonderful liking to Princess
O'Hara right from taw, and the following night I learn
from Officer Corbett, the motorcycle cop who is on duty
in Central Park, that they pass him with Ambrose Hammer
in the back seat of the victoria, but with Georges riding on
the driver's seat with Princess O'Hara.

And moreover, Officer Corbett states that Georges is
wearing King O'Hara's old stovepipe hat, while Princess
O'Hara is singing Kathleen Mavourneen in her loud contralto in such a way as nobody ever hears her sing before.

In fact, this is the way they are riding along a little later
in the week, and when it is coming on four bells in the
morning. But this time, Princess O'Hara is driving north
on the street that is called Central Park West because it
borders the Park on the west, and the reason she is taking
this street is because she comes up Broadway through

Columbus Circle into Central Park West, figuring to cross
over to Fifth Avenue by way of the transverse at 66th
Street, a transverse being nothing but a roadway cut
through the Park from Central Park West to the Avenue.

There are several of these transverses, and why they do
not call them roads, or streets, instead of transverses, I do
not know, except maybe it is because transverse sounds
more fancy. These transverses are really like tunnels without any roofs, especially the one at 66th Street, which is
maybe a quarter of a mile long and plenty wide enough for
automobiles to pass each other going in different directions,
but once a car is in the transverse there is no way it can
get out except at one end or the other. There is no such
thing as turning off to one side anywhere between Central
Park West and the Avenue, because the 66th Street transverse is a deep cut with high sides, or walls.

Well, just as Princess O'Hara starts to turn Gallant Godfrey into the transverse, with the foreign-looking young
guy beside her on the driver's seat, and Ambrose Hammer
back in the cushions, and half asleep, and by no means interested in the conversation that is going on in front of
him, a big beer truck comes rolling along Central Park
West, going very slow.

And of course there is nothing unusual in the spectacle
of a beer truck at this time, as beer is now very legal, but
just as this beer truck rolls alongside Princess O'Hara's
victoria, a little car with two guys in it pops out of nowhere,
and pulls up to the truck, and one of the guys requests the
jockey of the beer truck to stop.

Of course Princess O'Hara and her passengers do not
know at the time that this is one of the very first cases of

histing a truckload of legal beer that comes off in this country, and that they are really seeing history made, although it all comes out later. It also comes out later that one of the parties committing this historical deed is nobody but a guy by the name of Fats O'Rourke, who is considered one of the leading characters over on the west side, and the reason he is histing this truckload of beer is by no means a plot against the brewing industry, but because it is worth several C's, and Fats O'Rourke can use several C's very nicely at the moment.

It comes out that the guy with him is a guy by the name of Joe the Blow Fly, but he is really only a fink in every respect, a fink being such a guy as is extra nothing, and many citizens are somewhat surprised when they learn that Fats O'Rourke is going around with finks.

Well, if the jockey of the beer truck does as he is requested without any shilly-shallying, all that will happen is he will lose his beer. But instead of stopping the truck, the jockey tries to keep right on going, and then all of a sudden Fats O'Rourke becomes very impatient and outs with the old thing, and gives it to the jockey, as follows: Bang, bang.

By the time Fats O'Rourke lets go, The Fly is up on the seat of the truck and grabs the wheel just as the jockey turns it loose and falls back on the seat, and Fats O'Rourke follows The Fly up there, and then Fats O'Rourke seems to see Princess O'Hara and her customers for the first time, and he also realizes that these parties witness what comes off with the jockey, although otherwise Central Park West is quite deserted, and if anybody in the apartment houses along there hears the shots the chances are they figure it must be nothing but an automobile backfiring.

And in fact The Fly has the beer truck backfiring quite some at this moment as Fats O'Rourke sees Princess O'Hara and her customers, and only somebody who happens to observe the flashes from Fats O'Rourke's duke, or who hears the same buzzes that Princess O'Hara, and the foreign-looking young guy, and Ambrose Hammer hear, can tell that Fats is emptying that old thing at the victoria.

The chances are Fats O'Rourke will not mind anybody witnessing him histing a legal beer truck, and in fact he is apt to welcome their testimony in later years when somebody starts disputing his claim to being the first guy to hist such a truck, but naturally Fats does not wish to have spectators spying on him when he is giving it to somebody, as very often spectators are apt to go around gossiping about these matters, and cause dissension.

So he takes four cracks at Princess O'Hara and her customers, and it is a good thing for them that Fats O'Rourke is never much of a shot. Furthermore, it is a good thing for them that he is now out of ammunition, because of course Fats O'Rourke never figures that it is going to take more than a few shots to hist a legal beer truck, and afterwards there is little criticism of Fats' judgment, as everybody realizes that it is a most unprecedented situation.

Well, by now, Princess O'Hara is swinging Gallant Godfrey into the transverse, because she comes to the conclusion that it is no time to be loitering in this neighborhood, and she is no sooner inside the walls of the transverse than she knows this is the very worst place she can go, as she hears a rumble behind her, and when she peeks back over her shoulder she sees the beer truck coming lickity-split, and what is more, it is coming right at the victoria.

Now Princess O'Hara is no chump, and she can see that the truck is not coming right at the victoria by accident, when there is plenty of room for it to pass, so she figures that the best thing to do is not to let the truck catch up with the victoria if she can help it, and this is very sound reasoning, indeed, because Joe the Blow Fly afterwards says that what Fats O'Rourke requests him to do is to sideswipe the victoria with the truck and squash it against the side of the transverse, Fats O'Rourke's idea being to keep Princess O'Hara and her customers from speaking of the transaction with the jockey of the truck.

Well, Princess O'Hara stands up in her seat, and tells Gallant Godfrey to giddap, and Gallant Godfrey is giddapping very nicely, indeed, when she looks back and sees the truck right at the rear wheel of the victoria, and coming like a bat out of what-is-this. So she grabs up her whip and gives Gallant Godfrey a good smack across the vestibule, and it seems that if there is one thing Gallant Godfrey hates and despises it is a whip. He makes a lunge that pulls the victoria clear of the truck, just as The Fly drives it up alongside the victoria and is bearing over for the squash, with Fats O'Rourke yelling directions at him, and from this lunge, Gallant Godfrey settles down to running.

While this is going on, the foreign-looking young guy is standing up on the driver's seat of the victoria beside Princess O'Hara, whooping and laughing, as he probably figures it is just a nice, friendly little race. But Princess O'Hara is not laughing, and neither is Ambrose Hammer.

Now inside the next hundred yards, Joe the Blow Fly gets the truck up alongside again and this time it looks as if they are gone goslings when Princess O'Hara gives Gallant Godfrey another smack with the whip, and the chances are Gallant Godfrey comes to the conclusion that Westrope is working on him in a stretch run, as he turns on such a burst of speed that he almost runs right out of his collar and leaves the truck behind by anyway a length and a half.

And it seems that just as Gallant Godfrey turns on, Fats O'Rourke personally reaches over and gives the steering wheel of the beer truck a good twist, figuring that the squashing is now a cinch, and the next thing anybody knows the truck goes smack-dab into the wall with a loud kuh-boom, and turns over all mussed up, with beer kegs bouncing around very briskly, and some of them popping open and letting the legal beer leak out.

In the meantime, Gallant Godfrey goes tearing out of the transverse into Fifth Avenue and across Fifth Avenue so fast that the wheels of Princess O'Hara's victoria are scarcely touching the ground, and a copper who sees him go past afterwards states that what Gallant Godfrey is really doing is flying, but personally I always consider this an exaggeration.

Anyway, Gallant Godfrey goes two blocks beyond Fifth Avenue before Princess O'Hara can get him to whoa-up, and there is still plenty of run in him, although by this time Princess O'Hara is plumb worn out, and Ambrose Hammer is greatly fatigued, and only the foreign-looking young guy seems to find any enjoyment in the experience, although he is not so jolly when he learns that the coppers take two dead guys out of the truck, along with Joe the Blow Fly, who lives just long enough to relate the story.

Fats O'Rourke is smothered to death under a stack of kegs of legal beer, which many citizens consider a most gruesome finish, indeed, but what kills the jockey of the truck is the bullet in his heart, so the smash-up of the truck does not make any difference to him one way or the other, although of course if he lives, the chances are his employers will take him to task for losing the beer.

I learn most of the details of the race through the transverse from Ambrose Hammer, and I also learn from Ambrose that Princess O'Hara and the foreign-looking young guy are suffering from the worst case of love that Ambrose ever witnesses, and Ambrose Hammer witnesses some tough cases of love in his day. Furthermore, Ambrose says they are not only in love but are planning to get themselves married up as quickly as possible.

"Well," I say, "I hope and trust this young guy is all right, because Princess O'Hara deserves the best. In fact," I say, "a Prince is none too good for her."

"Well," Ambrose says, "a Prince is exactly what she is getting. I do not suppose you can borrow much on it in a hock shop in these times, but the title of Prince Georges Latour is highly respected over in France, although," he says, "I understand the proud old family does not have as many potatoes as formerly. But he is a nice young guy, at that, and anyway, what is money compared to love?"

Nàturally, I do not know the answer to this, and neither does Ambrose Hammer, but the very same day I run into Princess O'Hara and the foreign-looking young guy on

Broadway, and I can see the old love light shining so brightly in their eyes that I get to thinking that maybe money does not mean so much alongside of love, at that, although personally, I will take a chance on the money.

I stop and say hello to Princess O'Hara, and ask her how things are going with her, and she says they are going first class.

"In fact," she says, "it is a beautiful world in every respect. Georges and I are going to be married in a few days now, and are going to Paris, France, to live. At first I fear we will have a long wait, because of course I cannot leave my mamma and the rest of the children unprovided for. But," Princess O'Hara says, "what happens but Regret sells my horse to Last Card Louie for a thousand dollars, so everything is all right.

"Of course," Princess O'Hara says, "buying my horse is nothing but an act of great kindness on the part of Last Card Louie as my horse is by no means worth a thousand dollars, but I suppose Louie does it out of his old friendship for my papa. I must confess," she says, "that I have a wrong impression of Louie, because the last time I see him I slap his face thinking he is trying to get fresh with me. Now I realize it is probably only his paternal interest in me, and I am very sorry."

Well, I know Last Card Louie is such a guy as will give you a glass of milk for a nice cow, and I am greatly alarmed by Princess O'Hara's statement about the sale, for I figure Regret must sell Gallant Godfrey, not remembering that he is only a borrowed horse and must be returned in good order, so I look Regret up at once and mention my fears, but he laughs and speaks to me as follows:

"Do not worry," he says. "What happens is that Last Card Louie comes around last night and hands me a G note and says to me like this: 'Buy Princess O'Hara's horse off of her for me, and you can keep all under this G that you get it for.'

"Well," Regret says, "of course I know that old Last Card is thinking of Gallant Godfrey, and forgets that the only horse that Princess O'Hara really owns is Goldberg, and the reason he is thinking of Gallant Godfrey is because he learns last night about us borrowing the horse for her. But as long as Last Card Louie refers just to her horse, and does not mention any names, I do not see that it is up to me to go into any details with him. So I get him a bill of sale for Princess O'Hara's horse, and I am waiting ever since to hear what he says when he goes to collect the horse and finds it is nothing but old Goldberg."

"Well," I say to Regret, "it all sounds most confusing to me, because what good is Gallant Godfrey to Last Card Louie when he is only a borrowed horse, and is apt to be recognized anywhere except when he is hitched to a victoria? And I am sure Last Card Louie is not going into the victoria business."

"Oh," Regret says, "this is easy. Last Card Louie undoubtedly sees the same ad in the paper that the rest of us see, offering a reward of ten G's for the return of Gallant Godfrey and no questions asked, but of course Last Card Louie has no way of knowing that Big Nig is taking Gallant Godfrey home long before Louie comes around and buys Princess O'Hara's horse."

Well, this is about all there is to tell, except that a couple of weeks later I hear that Ambrose Hammer is in the Clinic

Hospital very ill, and I drop around to see him because I am very fond of Ambrose Hammer no matter if he is a newspaper scribe.

He is sitting up in bed in a nice private room, and he has on blue silk pajamas with his monogram embroidered over his heart, and there is a large vase of roses on the table beside him, and a nice-looking nurse holding his hand, and I can see that Ambrose Hammer is not doing bad, although he smiles very feebly at me when I come in.

Naturally I ask Ambrose Hammer what ails him, and after he takes a sip of water out of a glass that the nice-looking nurse holds up to his lips, Ambrose sighs, and in a very weak voice he states as follows:

"Well," Ambrose says, "one night I get to thinking about what will happen to us in the transverse if we have old Goldberg hitched to Princess O'Hara's victoria instead of one of the fastest race horses in the world, and I am so overcome by the thought that I have what my doctor claims is a nervous breakdown. I feel terrible," Ambrose says.